CW00373175

AUTHOR'S NOTE

It's usual, in a book of this sort, to state categorically that none of the characters or places have the slightest resemblance to real life. This is so. All these people are imaginary. St. Frideswide's College never existed; neither did the Lakeside Hotel.

There is one exception. I pay tribute to the memory of 'Harry' who was one of the nicest men who have ever lived and whose kindness and philanthropy will be gratefully remembered by all who met him.

▶ campus confessions

PETER GILBERT

a novel

PROWLER BOOKS

Campus Confessions by Peter Gilbert

Copyright © 1999 Peter Gilbert
3 Broadbent Close London N6 5GG. All rights reserved.

No part of this book may be reproduced, stored in retrieval system, or transmitted in any form, by any means, including mechanicals, electronic, photocopying, recording or otherwise, without prior written permission of the publishers.

First printing April 1999. Printed in Finland by Werner Soderstrom Oy.
Cover photography © 1999 Prowler Press

web-site: prowler.co.uk
• ISBN 1-902644-11-5

British Library Cataloguing in Publication Data.
A catalogue record for this book is available from the British Library.

contents

CHAPTER ONE

"It can't be an invitation. We would have got one if it was," said Ben dreamily. "You have a curious mind," replied Adam. "Now lean back and shut up about the bloody letter."

Adam sat at the end of the long sofa. Ben lay on the sofa with his head in Adam's lap. It was the position they usually adopted after a day's studying.

"But why should an agricultural college be writing to Mark? He doesn't even know which end of a carrot goes into the ground." Ben persisted. "Mmm! That feels nice!" he added. Adam's fingers were stroking the rapidly developing bulge in his jeans.

Adam glanced at the clock on the mantelpiece. "I wonder..." he said.

"You wonder what?" asked Ben eagerly. "I've been racking my brains ever since the postman brought it.

Adam laughed. "Sod the letter!" he said. "I was wondering if there would be time for you-know-what before Mark gets back."

"I should think so. He doesn't usually get home before seven on a Tuesday. He has a late lecture. Anyway, what does it matter if he does come in? He's not likely to barge in."

"I just thought it would be fun to do it down here," said Adam. "We haven't christened the sofa yet."

"We'd have to be careful about stains on the upholstery," said Ben. "Charles and Simon would go mad if we spoiled it." The idea was attractive, he thought. It would save staggering upstairs with a raging hard-on.

"My spunk, old dear, will go straight into your nice, tight, fat ass. We'll put a towel under you."

"Means going upstairs to get one."

"I'll use my football towel. It's in my bag."

Adam stood up, drew the curtains tightly together and began to undress. At twenty-three, thought Ben, Adam was better looking than when they first met.

His fair hair was longer, though still immaculately clean and tidy. His body had filled out too. The moment Adam's shirt was off, Ben feasted his eyes on his friend's enormous pectoral muscles and strong arms. When Adam slid down his torn jeans, Ben gazed longingly at his long legs. They were hairy now, not downy as they had been. More interesting still was what lay under Adam's boxer shorts. Ben knew it well but still got a thrill when it was uncovered. Adam didn't waste any time and Ben gasped, as he always did, as the huge, rigid cock leapt upwards, its circumcised purple head gleaming with health and eagerness.

"Let me suck it," Ben pleaded.

"When I've undressed you. Stand up!"

Conscious of the protuberance in his jeans, Ben did as he was told.

"Quite keen this evening, aren't you?" Adam murmured as he began slowly to remove Ben's clothes. "I like it when you're eager. I'm going to fuck you really hard. I want to feel this great fat ass of yours squirming." As he spoke he fondled Ben's buns through his shorts. It was not a fat ass. Nobody could possibly describe Ben as being fat but Adam had coined the nickname 'Pudge' for Ben several years previously and it had stuck. Not that Ben minded. He didn't mind anything that Adam did. Adam was... well, Adam was Adam. He was good looking, intelligent and, apart from the precious times when they had sex, Adam was the most caring, helpful person Ben had ever known. It was only at times like this, he thought, feeling his shorts being dragged down, that the other Adam came to the fore.

"Oh yes! Just look at you! Dying to get my cock right up you!" said Adam, seizing Ben's penis and squeezing it hard. "Well, you can start by sucking it." He pushed Ben back onto the couch. "Go on then," he said. "Get a good mouthful of it. Make it nice and wet and slippery so that it slides into you."

Ben didn't need to be told. Eagerly, he placed his lips against its tip and let them slide over the plum - like head. It tasted superb as it always did after Adam had played football. He let his tongue slide up and down the shaft and then, slowly took the whole mighty organ into his mouth. Praying desperately that he wouldn't gag, he let it touch the back of his throat and moved his moistened lips from side to side over the shaft. His mouth filled with saliva. He reached between Adam's legs and put his hand under his friend's loose - hanging scrotum. It felt cool and slightly damp.

"You're doing well. Keep going," Adam commanded. Ben had to let some of it out of his mouth in order to swallow but soon took most of its length again. Adam stood motionless with his feet apart and his hands clasped behind his back. If the curtains hadn't been closed, one of the many passers by would have assumed that this strangely naked young man was studying the picture above the couch.

"Enough!" he said, suddenly. Reluctantly, Ben let it slide out of his mouth. A long stream of saliva dripped from it. He caught it just in time. Adam walked over to the corner where he had left his sports bag and drew out a rather muddy towel. He slung it onto the couch.

"Lie down!" he said, as if he was talking to a disobedient dog. Ben did so, lying face downwards with his face in a cushion.

"Not much room to spread my legs," he said in a muffled voice.

"All the better. I like you tight." Adam's cool hands parted his ass - cheeks. He felt something cold against his anus and gasped as a gout of lubricant squirted into him. Adam hadn't gone upstairs. He must have bought it on the way home. Ben grinned into the cushion but it didn't do to grin when Adam was aroused. He moaned. "That's cold!" he complained.

"You'll be warm enough in a minute," Adam chuckled. "You'll be as hot as a barbecued pig when my skewer's in you."

There was a sound of tearing paper and Ben grinned again. That clinched the matter. Adam kept them in the drawer of the bedside table. He must have stopped on the way home and stocked up. He felt Adam's breath on the back of his neck and winced as Adam climbed onto the sofa. He was no light-weight. Ben shouted out in genuine pain when Adam knelt on his calf muscles. A powerful slap on his behind ensued, but Adam shifted his position and sank down on top of him. Ben felt his friend's breath on the back of his neck. Adam began to nibble him, grasping his shoulders as he did so. Most important, he could feel Adam's giant, damp member sliding up and down his furrow, seeking an entrance. With difficulty, he managed to part his legs slightly. It moved a little deeper, slid forward slightly and, as if guided by Ben's gasps, poised itself right on the target.

"Aaaagh!" he shouted - as loudly as he could. It wasn't in the least painful. It was the nicest feeling in the world but Adam wasn't to know that. Ben knew what was expected of him.

"Hurting is it?" Adam panted. "Good! I like hurting you."

Ben let it slide right into him. That was a glorious feeling. Adam, who had achieved straight 'A's in the last exams. The man who played football for the university, swam for the county; the best medical student the University had ever seen, was his! That was Adam inside him. In a few minutes, Adam's seed would pump into him. He wriggled with pleasure at the thought.

"Good! Squirm away. Squirm like a worm on a hook. Christ! You're going to... get it... today!" and that was Adam, using those magnificent muscles of his to push deeper and deeper into him. He didn't deserve it. He was just Ben. Plodding old Ben. Ben the English Literature student. All he cared about was being Ben, Adam's friend.

"Oh! Ah! Oh! Ah!" Adam panted.

"Christ! Shit! Ouch! Aaah!" cried Ben. He shuddered as it rubbed against his prostate. He was being fucked by a master. That was all he cared about. A thought flashed through his mind. In a few days' time it would be Simon or Charles. He was so mystified by Mark's letter that he had forgotten to tell Adam about the letter from Charles. It could wait.

"Oh! Oh! Oh!" he groaned.

"Oh! Ah! Aaaah!" The slap of loins against buttocks became a slurping sound. Adam had come. It felt warm and damp and nice. Ben kept writhing around, feeling the roughness of the towel against his cock. Just thinking about Adam was enough. He felt Adam's cock subsiding inside him. It was funny really. There were hundreds of girls in the university who would give a lot just to see that cock and he, Ben, had it inside him and its owner lying sweating and panting on his back. He gave one more desperate wriggle and lay still, feeling his spunk jetting out onto the towel.

"Christ! You were good!" said Adam.

"So were you." Cold air rushed into Ben's anus as Adam slid out of him. Would Adam do it? Yes, he was sliding back onto Ben's legs.

"Ouch!" Ben yelled. "I wish you wouldn't do that!"

"Nice fat asses need to be slapped," said Adam. He stood up and stretched his arms above his head.

Ben turned over and slid his legs off the couch. He pulled the sodden towel from under him. "I'll have a shower and then get a meal ready," he said.

"No. I'll do that. Have your shower and take it easy. Egg and chips suit you?"

"Perfectly." Ben looked at the clock. "Might as well cook for Mark too," he said. "He should be back soon."

Adam took the towel from him. "And then he'll read his letter and tell you what it's about," he said, laughing.

"Well... I confess that I am a bit curious," said Ben. He picked up the letter for the sixth time.

"Go and have your shower," said Adam. "If you stand there much longer there'll be spunk stains on the carpet."

"Sure you don't want any help?"

"Of course I'm sure. Even I can do three egg and chips."

"Shall I lay the table?"

"No, leave it to me."

Ben left the room, meditating as he always did on such occasions, upon the extraordinary personality of the one person in the world who he loved so much.

He was drying himself in the bathroom when he heard the front door open and close. Mark's voice said "That smells good!" Adam said something. Ben couldn't hear what it was. He dressed as quickly as he could and ran downstairs.

Mark was sitting on the couch. He was a tall, powerfully built young man. Neither Ben nor Adam considered him to be particularly handsome but there was something about Mark which caused female (and some male) hearts to flutter.

"I wondered where you were," said Mark.

"Upstairs taking a shower," said Ben. "Have you seen your letter?"

"No."

Ben took it from the mantelpiece and handed it down. "What on earth is an agricultural college writing to you about?" he asked.

"It's private," said Mark as he tore the envelope open.

"It's a long letter," said Ben. It seemed to consist of at least six typed pages. Mark didn't answer but sat there reading.

Adam came in with a tray. "Grub's up!" he announced.

"Mark's reading his letter," said Ben. Adam put the tray onto the table and grinned. "Amazing intuition!" he said. "A letter arrives addressed to Mark. Mark is seen reading some papers. A torn envelope is on the floor at his feet. Inference; Mark is reading the letter. You ought to be studying philosophy; not literature."

"You're not thinking of changing, are you, Mark?" Ben asked. "I'd have thought there were more chances in computers than in agriculture."

Mark said nothing but continued to read.

"Would I be right in assuming that this letter is something to do with those late night calls you get on your mobile?" Ben asked.

"What late night calls?"

"Oh come off it! The walls of this place aren't so thick. We've both heard it go off, haven't we Adam? What time was it? Something after midnight, that's for sure."

"I was concentrating on something else at the time," said Adam. Ben caught the warning look in his eye.

Mark put the pages he had read upside down on the table. "If you must know, the answer is yes. His name is Howard Ainsworth and I met him in the vac. Now can I read the bloody thing without this inquisition?"

"Good for you," said Adam. "Tell us all about him - when you've finished reading the letter of course."

"It's a long one," said Ben. There were three typed sheets on the table and Mark held at least another three.

Mark frowned and read on. "Nobody told me that Charles and Simon are coming up next weekend," he said.

"Nor me," Adam replied.

"Well, Howard says they are and Charles is bringing him too."

"My fault," said Ben. "The letter came this morning. I meant to tell you when you got home. He didn't mention Howard though."

"That's a bloody nuisance," said Adam. "I've got a big match on Saturday."

Ben leaned back in his chair. "Dear boy," he began in a very good imitation of Charles' aristocratic drawl, "When one considers that you are comfortably accommodated in a house rather than some crummy student hostel; you receive a generous allowance and one provides you with a car, your reluctance to show your appreciation seems ill mannered to say the least."

"Oh I don't mind the showing appreciation bit. I suppose I can get away for the match. They're hardly likely to want us on Saturday afternoon."

"And you will come back smelling disgracefully of drink," Ben replied, maintaining the imitation. "One will be disinclined to screw a sweaty drunken oaf. That means Mark will have to oblige on Saturday night."

"Of course he won't. I'll get back sober and clean. Anyway, I guess Mark will be occupied with Howard," said Adam. "Your meal's getting cold, Mark. Read the letter later."

"Don't feel like eating, thanks," said Mark. He put down the last few pages of the letter.

"Don't be daft. You have to eat."

"I said I don't feel like it! Are you deaf?" He swept up the pages of his letter and left the room, slamming the door behind him.

"Well, well. What was that all about?" asked Ben. "He usually enjoys my imitation. Did I hit a raw nerve or something?"

"Something, certainly," Adam replied. "He's a moody devil at the best of times. Can you eat a bit more? Good old Pudge. Take the lot. Put a bit more fat on your ass. I might want to screw you again later."

"Always ready to oblige, that's me," said Ben, pulling Mark's plate towards him, "but don't you think we ought to ease up? We ought not to disappoint our sponsors."

"Oh, I'll be all right. I'll be as randy as a March hare. I'll do the washing up. Why don't you select a nice video? That will cheer Mark up and put us in the mood."

The front door slammed and they heard the sound of the car being started. "Well! He might have asked us if we needed the car," said Ben. "It belongs to the three of us. Where on earth can he be going?"

"I suspect some huge crisis in his computer club. A coup or a revolution of some kind," said Adam. He gathered up the plates and took them into the kitchen. Ben went to the bookshelf, parted the row of medical textbooks and produced a cassette. 'TEAM BUDDIES' - just the thing. He straightened the books and, as he did so, caught a glimpse of a piece of paper under the table. He retrieved it. It was the last page of Howard's letter.

'...and that's about as far as I've got but the last two look as if they might be on the point of offering to admit me. I won't take no for an answer! As you suggested I rang your friend Charles. He and someone called Simon are coming up to see you next weekend (4,5,6 July) and I'm coming too. I can't wait to see you again. I can't wait to feel you again. How is that telegraph pole of yours? See you at the Lakeside Hotel. Lots of you know what. Howard.:'

The letter ended with a neatly typed row of x's. Ben put it on the mantelpiece and went to help Adam, who had nearly finished.

"Find one?" said Adam.

"Yes. I also found a page of Howard's letter."

"Which, knowing you, you have read."

"Uh huh! What do you think this means: 'The last two look as if they might be on the point of offering to admit me'?"

"Could be anything. Some clubs possibly. Must be something to do with farming or something like that."

"I don't think so. I'll tell you something else."

"Mmm. What?"

"This Howard person loves our Mark very much. Very, very much," said Ben.

"Good for Mark. It's about time he found somebody. It's not good to bottle up your instincts like he does. We shan't be seeing much of him at the Lakeside."

"I think he ought to at least show willing. After all, the three of us share the house and the car. I know Simon's keen on him."

"Ben old dear. You do talk crap sometimes. You know as well as I do that neither Charles nor Simon would dream of even hinting. Mark will have Howard. There is no way that either of them would even suggest such a thing."

"I guess you're right. Not that I mind. Who do you want to be with?"

"Er... Simon I think."

"Lucky old Simon."   Ben switched into his Lord Charles voice again. "Incidentally, dear boy," he said. "One didn't mean what one said about your drinking habits and sweaty body in there. In fact, or en effet as one's friends would say, one finds you... fucking gorgeous!" he added in his own voice, and kissed the back of Adam's neck.

CHAPTER TWO

Mark leaned back in the armchair and smiled. He felt radiantly happy as he always did when he was with Howard. Howard sat on the floor, at his feet. If an eighteen and a half year old agriculture student could purr, Howard would have certainly been purring. He lay back against Mark's legs. His long, fair hair flopped down over his forehead. Mark reached down and absent-mindedly tickled the back of his neck. A whole weekend with Howard! His heart began to beat faster.

As for Howard, everything was a revelation. He'd been nervous of phoning Lord Charles but the man had soon put him at ease. He'd been frightened, during the long journey up to the hotel that the man might make some sort of advances but he hadn't. No hand on his knee. No nasty little innuendoes. Just a pleasant journey in a luxurious car with an extremely entertaining man.

The Lakeside Hotel had seen better days. So, for that matter, had many of its long term guests. For the most part they were elderly men who styled themselves Captain this or Major that and subsisted on the cheapest items on the menu. The lake which gave it its name was green and fetid, and defied every effort of the proprietors to stock it with trout. The 'extensive gardens' were overgrown and the buildings were in urgent need of attention.

But, as Charles often pointed out, it had advantages. It was near enough to the university city where the lads were studying to make it convenient, but far enough to make sure they were not seen there by their fellow students. The owner was one of Charles' friends and sympathetic to the cause. No eyebrows were raised at the various comings and goings in the night.

The early part of the evening had been reserved, as always, for business. Ben accounted for their household expenditure; Adam and Ben were responsible for the house and the furniture and Mark for the car. Cheques had been written to top up depleted bank accounts. Everybody felt comfortably full and it was, as Charles said, time to relax and think of more pleasant matters than roof insulation, new piston rings and supermarket bills.

Charles - Lord Charles Beresford to give him his full name and title - was thirty eight. Brother to the Earl of Beresford and therefore a member of one of the richest families in the land, he was extremely tall, a factor which added to his aristocratic air. When Charles spoke to anyone, he found it necessary to stoop condescendingly to hear what they were saying. He was dark and undoubtedly handsome though his companion, Simon Spencer, was probably the better looking of the two. Simon was one of those people who look well dressed in the roughest of clothes. Old ladies bought copies of his books just for the photographs on the cover flaps.

Simon Spencer? Yes, I do mean *the* Simon Spencer, the author of over fifty novels, almost all of which have been made into box office successes. Simon lived in Hardwick St. Mary where he had first met Adam and then Ben. When they went off to university, Simon's life and literary output declined badly in quality. A chance meeting with Mark changed that. Naturally enough he had introduced all three to his friend Lord Charles and the two men had offered to sponsor them through university; an arrangement which the three young men accepted with various degrees of eagerness.

Simon and Charles sat at one end of the room with Adam and Ben. From where he sat, at the other end of the room, Mark could see Charles' hand running up and down Ben's thigh. Not that it was anything to do with him. He found Adam and Ben's readiness to please Simon and Charles difficult to understand but as all three of them benefited, he never said anything. The days when he had been Simon's boyfriend were long over.
"Adam's got to play football tomorrow," said Ben.
"Yes, I'm sorry about that," said Adam. "They do the fixture list months in advance."
"No problem," said Simon. "Presumably you'll be back in the evening?"
"Oh yes."
"He'll probably be as drunk as a lord!" said Ben.
"A slur upon my fellow peers which I shall ignore," said Charles. "There was one ancestor however. Beresford of the Bottle they called him..."
Mark twined his fingers in Howard's hair. "Let's go up," he whispered. "This story takes hours."

Howard, who had been wondering whether he should wait for Mark or suggest it himself, stood up so rapidly that Mark's arm was flung aside. They excused themselves to knowing smiles and went upstairs. Howard unlocked the bedroom door and closed it behind them.

"I thought they would never make a move," said Mark.

Howard grinned. "Do you know something?" he said.

"What?" For a moment Mark wondered if this was to be the moment. The thing had to be thrashed out that weekend.

"I love you. I love you. I love you to bits!" said Howard hugging him and nibbling his ears.

"Not half as much as I love you. You going to get ready?"

"Can you wait?"

"Only just. Don't be long." Howard vanished into the bathroom and Mark got undressed. Howard was a strange lad. He always insisted on going into the bathroom before having sex. On the last occasion they'd spent a weekend together he had left the bathroom door open and had given a running commentary starting with the process of undressing ("Ah well, off with my shoes. Ah well, off with my socks. Ah well, off with my jeans..") and ending with an estimate of its size at that moment ("It must be five inches at least and it's getting longer every minute!")

On that evening the ritual was performed in silence though it amused Mark to think that Howard was probably miming the words in the mirror. He felt down to his cock. It was already standing up in anticipation. It had twitched into life the moment Howard got out of Charles' car and had been taking an interest ever since. He lay back and thought how lucky he was to have met someone quite so beautiful who loved him so much. What had Howard said? "I love you to bits." Did he? Mark reached over to the chair on which his jacket hung and reached into the inside pocket for the letter. He lay there reading it. He would have to speak to Howard about it. When? That was the problem.

The bathroom door lock clicked. He put the letter under the bed. Howard appeared. He had wrapped a towel round his middle like a sarong. He looked down at Mark and giggled. "Great heavens!" he exclaimed theatrically, "A space rocket or do you use it to transmit television pictures?"

"It's for exploring inner space," said Mark. "Come here, gorgeous."

Howard threw himself onto the bed. Mark felt the boy's arms go round him and squeeze him. He felt Howard's breath on his face. It smelt of toothpaste.

("I won't be long. I've just got to clean my teeth.") He put his hands on Howard's head and kissed him gently on the lips. Howard's tongue poked out from between his teeth and played over Mark's lips, moistening them. The clinch suddenly became tighter. Their mouths met. Tongues touched and explored. Howard's mouth tasted delightfully of mint and antiseptic. Mark wished he had cleaned his teeth too. He stroked the boy's back. Howard's skin was as smooth as silk. He felt the shoulder blades gliding underneath it as Howard began to do the same to him. Their legs touched, parted and then touched again.

Mark reached down to the towel. He could feel Howard's cock straining against the material.
"What the hell have you done here?" he whispered as his hands fumbled with the towel. "It's like Fort Knox."
"Just wait till you come to the gold," said Howard. "It's waiting for you."

Patience was never one of Mark's strong points. In the end he stuck his fingers between Howard's skin and the towel and wrenched. There was a slight tearing noise and a yell from Howard. "Be careful!" he said. "That was a handful of pubes. They took long enough to grow. I can't afford to lose any."

Mark laughed. "Looks to me as if you've got enough left," he said.

All of Howard was perfect but the region Mark had just exposed was so beautiful that he couldn't take his eyes off it. Howard's great, stubby cock with its pursed foreskin was as hard as ivory and almost parallel with his flat stomach. It seemed to grow as he watched it, moving very slowly like the minute hand of a clock, following the fine line of hair which linked the boy's navel with his bush. The hair there was darker than that under his arms and much darker than his blond head. His balls hung low, pink and puckered.
"You're beautiful!" Mark whispered, touching Howard's cock reverently.
"You're not so bad yourself," said Howard. Mark felt a hand clasp his cock.
"Lie back," Howard commanded. Mark would have preferred to spend a little more time admiring and exploring but, he thought, they had all night and all the following night. Now was the time to let Howard do what he wanted.

He felt Howard's lips on the tip of his cock and Howard's fingers sliding gently up and down the shaft. He closed his eyes. Howard's mouth enveloped him. He felt the boy's teeth against it and his tongue licking it lasciviously.

"That feels good!" he gasped. He reached down and tickled Howard's ears. The boy's head was rising and falling. His mouth made rhythmic slurping noises. Mark fell into a reverie about Howard's beauty. They had first met during the previous summer vacation. Simon and Mark had driven down to Combleton to visit Charles and happened to pass the agricultural college. A small knot of students was standing in the grounds listening attentively to a lecturer who, from his gesticulating arms, seemed to be demonstrating bird scaring.

"Extraordinary," Simon said. "Some people don't seem able to communicate without waving their arms about. I must put him into a book."

At that moment, one of the students turned to look at them. He waved. Mark waved back. His knees suddenly felt weak. He'd found the most beautiful boy in the world. His anorak was dirty. His jeans were torn. There was mud on his forehead but none of those things mattered. He was... well... unique and exquisite! He waited until the lecturer had finished and the students dispersed. Simon must have realised, he thought. Simon suddenly remembered that the car needed topping up.

Howard walked over to him. "Hi!" he said.
"Oh! Hi!"

Simon's car vanished round a corner.
"Smart car," said Howard.
"Yeah."
"Your dad?"
"No. Just a friend."
"Close friend or just friend?"
"Both I guess."
"Lucky you. Live round here?"
"No. Miles away."
"Pity."
"What's that supposed to mean?"
"I wouldn't mind seeing some more of you - if you know what I mean."
"We could go for a drink this evening."
"What about the close friend with the Porsche?"
"He won't mind. He's staying with Lord Beresford. They're old friends."
"In Mill Cottage? "
"That's him."

"I like young friends myself. How old are you?"

"Twenty two," said Mark.

"I'm eighteen. Eighteen and a bit actually. Howard Ainsworth."

"Mark Lee," said Mark, extending a hand. Howard took it and grasped it for some minutes. "Let's see much more of each other," he whispered.

They did. The sight of Howard stretched out, naked on his bed in his college room that night stayed with Mark for weeks.

"God! You're beautiful!" he had gasped then and he said it every time.

Howard stopped and knelt between his feet. He grinned at Mark. "What now?" he said.

"Anything you like. I don't mind."

"Would you let me fuck you?"

"If you want."

This was a total surprise. Howard had tried it once before. Mark had said that he could if he wished and they had tried it. Poor Howard. It had gone down the moment the tip touched Mark's asshole. What had initially felt like an steel rod turned into something that felt like a bit of wet clay. Mark wondered if he was being sensible in agreeing. Howard had been so upset at his failure on that occasion. It would be dreadful if he failed again.

"Sure you want to?" he asked.

"I wouldn't suggest it if I didn't. It's time your ass had something in it and I've got just the thing."

There was no denying that. The thought alone made Mark's ass itch. It had been a long, long time. He tried to remember exactly when. Three years ago? Simon? That was probably about right unless one counted the evening when Adam came home drunk but that hadn't worked properly either. It had been much better with Simon.

Howard got the tube and the condom out of the drawer. Mark lifted his legs and placed them on the boy's shoulders.

"Probably better this way," he said. "It's been a long time."

He felt Howard's cold greasy finger press against him. "That's it," he said. He closed his eyes and concentrated on relaxing. The finger pushed. He let himself go slack in the way Simon had taught him years ago and which he, in turn, had taught Howard. He lay on the bed with the palms of his hands uppermost... and Howard's finger went in. He gasped. It slid into him, feeling agreeably smooth and cool. He'd forgotten what it felt like to have a finger in there exploring.

Howard shuffled up the bed. Mark lifted his legs from Howard's shoulders. The finger was removed. He felt it pushing against him. It certainly wasn't soft this time! Another push - and it went in. He yelped as it forced the muscle ring open. After that it was a glorious feeling. With difficulty, he focused his vision on Howard. He was perspiring and his hair had fallen down in front of his eyes again. But he was grinning, an almost devilish grin, as his cock drove deeper and deeper. Mark let his legs rest on the boy's warm, damp shoulders again and abandoned himself to a pleasure he hadn't experienced for years. He was aware of Howard's loins slapping against him and the feel of Howard's balls on his skin. He arched upwards and groaned as it touched his button. That was it. Could he hold that position? Yes, he could. It was uncomfortable but he could - and did. Convulsive shudders ran through his body. He knew what was going to happen. There was no time to warn Howard. The first jet landed on his chest. He didn't know where the rest went. He only knew that there was a lot of it. Howard didn't seem to notice. He was panting like an athlete. His hair hung down lank. His tongue hung out of his mouth and sweat dropped from him onto Mark's belly.

He gave one almighty thrust. Mark cried out. He couldn't help it. Then there was that warm feeling inside him. It was over. He lifted his legs again. "Phew! That was great!" said Howard. He fell forwards onto Mark who caught him and held him tight.
"Certainly was," he whispered. "It's a long time since I was screwed so well as that."
"When was the last time?"
"I was wondering about that. It would have been Simon. About three years ago."

Howard puckered his nose. "I wouldn't fancy doing it with him," he said. "He's too old."
"Simon's okay. Not as good as you though." He patted Howard's butt affectionately. "We'd better clean up," he said.
"Not much point. We're going to do it again," said Howard.
"And again and again and again but it feels as if I've got a gate-post in my ass.

I'd better use the toilet."
"Don't be long."
"I won't."

    It was when he was washing his hands that he remembered the letter. He opened the bathroom door.
"Howard," he said.
"Mmm?" said a sleepy voice from the bedroom.
"Your letter. Will you promise me something?"
"What?"
"Will you stop this business in the library office."
"Why? They don't mind."
"No. You explained that but I think you ought to stop."
"Why?"

    Mark put the towel on the rail and went into the bedroom again. Howard was still lying on the bed.
"Well," said Mark. "In the first place it's immoral. In the second it's risky and in the third you're my friend. I mean... well... you and I are a couple now."
"Of course we are. But it's good fun. I like doing it."
"No need to get uptight about it," said Mark. "I just don't want you to do it. You can't love them. Not the way I love you."
"Of course not. Like I said, it's fun."
"But immoral..."
"Ha! In this very hotel at this very moment, your two friends are having their asses screwed by Charles and Simon. You can't tell me that Adam or Ben love either of them."
"I think they're very fond of them. We all are."
"Balls! They do it for money. I saw the cheques being written out, remember."

    Mark flushed. "Now that," he said, "is a wicked thing to say. You know damn well it's not true. We are all very fond of Charles and Simon. They have been very good to us. All Adam and Ben are doing is trying to repay some of their kindness."
"Don't shout at me."
"I'm not shouting!"
"Yes you are. As for the risk business, there isn't any. They're over eighteen. They do it voluntarily and nobody's likely to find out.
"That's as maybe. I still don't want you to carry on. You're worth more than

that. Tossing students off in the library. It's childish."

"What the fuck is it to do with you? It's my life! I'll bet you had it off with umpteen people before we met!" Howard's face was crimson.

"There weren't any others. Honestly. Only Simon."

"I'm not sure that I believe you."

"Well, there weren't. Now, will you promise me you'll stop it?"

"In a word, no. In two words, fuck off! In four words, mind your own business. Do I make myself clear?"

"But Howard..."

"Oh for Christ's sake! I've had enough. Good night. And stay on your side of the bed. I'm moving out of this room tomorrow morning."

Mark could have kicked himself. He should have known better. Both he and Howard were quick tempered. It would have been much better to broach the subject in broad daylight. He lay for hours, thinking and wondering how to remedy the situation. Howard appeared to be asleep. He was snoring slightly. Mark put out a reassuring and friendly hand.

Howard woke up with a start. "Fuck off. Keep your hands to yourself!" he said. Another failure.

Hour followed hour. He heard the church clocks striking. Eleven, twelve, one, two, three...

He was unaware of the sunrise; unaware of Howard getting up. When Howard went downstairs he was still fast asleep.

The restaurant wasn't open for breakfast. Howard went out into the gardens and sat on a log to think. He was still furious. He hadn't realised how possessive Mark could be. Hypocritical too. He'd looked forward to this weekend for a long time and Mark had ruined it. He felt like crying. "Sod him!" he said.

CHAPTER THREE

Adam took off his shoes and lay back on the bed and contemplated his room-mate. Simon looked pretty good when he was dressed. He looked even better when he was naked. His torso wasn't particularly hairy but what hair there was formed a 'Y' shape from his nipples leading down to his navel. Below that it started again, growing more and more dense until it merged into a mass of dark hair. He stood with his legs lightly apart. They were very hairy and, together with the pattern of his body hair seemed designed to draw attention to his cock which hung slightly outwards like the trunk of an elephant at that moment but which was swelling and stiffening visibly.

"What time have you got to leave here tomorrow for this match?" Simon asked.

"Oh, not till just before lunch-time."

"Just as well. Gives me lots of time. You'll play better than ever tomorrow and I'll have you tomorrow night as well if it's okay by you."

"Sure. No change over this weekend then?"

"No. Charles seems happy with Ben and vice versa."

"And Mark is happy with Howard," said Adam as Simon stepped forward, grinned, and bent over him to undo his jeans. The two of them had a lot in common, Adam thought. Undressing Ben was a turn on for him and Simon always insisted on undressing him, albeit he was considerably more patient and tidier than Adam. The jeans slid down his legs.

"Superb!" said Simon. He folded the jeans and put them on the armchair in the corner. Then he peeled off Adam's socks. The shirt was the next to go. Adam sat up. Simon unbuttoned the cuffs and then, starting at the top, he undid the other buttons and the shirt, neatly folded for the first time since it came back from the laundry, joined the other clothes.

"There!" said Simon and he sat on the edge of the bed. Adam felt a hand on his thigh.

"Do you know something?" said Simon.

"What?"

"You're beautiful."

"I'll bet you say that to all the boys."

"No. Just you." The hand moved upwards slightly.

"What about Mark? You were dotty about him once."

"Not dotty. I was very fond of Mark. I still am but you're something else. You're just magnificent."

The hand moved even further up. Adam raised a knee. The hand slid under his boxers and felt oddly cool. A finger touched his balls lightly. He turned his head. Simon's cock was fully erect. It seemed impossible that something that size would shortly be inside him but he knew it would. He closed his eyes.

"What do you think Mark's doing at the moment?" he asked.

"Bugger Mark."

"You have. Several times. Was he good?"

Simon's fingers were playing in his bush: a nice, comforting feeling.

"I don't ask you about Ben. Why do you ask me about Mark?"

"I don't know. Interest I guess. I tried once but I was pissed. It didn't work."

The fingers slid up under the elastic waist band. The shorts were pulled away. Adam lifted his behind slightly. Cool air wafted across his groin. Simon's fingers curled round hard flesh. That was an even nicer feeling. Adam wanted to prolong it.

"The one I fancy is Howard. What do you reckon about him?" he asked.

"A nice enough lad. I'm glad Mark's found him. A bit on the young side for me though. Give me a twenty-three year old footballer any day. Especially one with a cock as beautiful as this."

A series of delightful images formed in Adam's mind; sometimes they merged. At others they were like instant snaps. It happened often enough, usually at Medical School. There they had to be instantly repressed but lying on a bed in the Lakeside Hotel was different. He could enjoy them and feast on them. Simon let go of his cock and began softly to stroke his thighs. It was as if Simon could read his mind. The images became clearer. There was no need for sublimation.

"He's got a lovely little ass," he murmured.

"Who has?"

"Howard. What couldn't I do with that."

"Aren't you happy with Ben?"

"Oh sure. Ben's great but Howard... Even thinking about him turns me on."

"So I see."

"Lovely white flesh," said Adam - words that he wouldn't have dreamed of using anywhere else. "Tight as a lock I'll bet."

"Hardly," Simon replied. "At this very moment..."

The remark suffused Adam with rage. He didn't understand why. He gave himself no time to think. The mental picture of Mark shafting Howard was enough in itself. All the other images were erased at once to be replaced by one. He'd seen Mark's behind often enough but never rising and falling as it was in his imagination. He'd never heard Howard cry out. He'd heard him speaking enough times to imagine how his voice would sound as Mark's seven inches drove into him.

"Bite him," he murmured.

"Eh?" Simon asked. The hand was back on Adam's thigh.

"Bite him," Adam repeated. "Get your teeth into his buns. Give him a few tooth marks."

Simon stopped and stared down at him. "I had no idea..." he said. "What do you want to do that for?"

That question opened the flood-gates. Even with Ben, Adam had never felt really free. Ben didn't mind the occasional slap on his broad buttocks but as for the other the other things Adam would have liked to do - no way!

He felt the blood rush to his face and, so that Simon wouldn't see, he turned over. His cock was so hard that it felt as if he was lying on a piece of a broom-stick. Simon caressed the backs of his legs.

"Eighteen and a half," he murmured. "Nearly nineteen. Just right. He'd be a lovely fuck."

Simon laughed. "I think it more than possible that he'd reject your advances," he said. "He's got Mark."

"I wouldn't give him the chance to say no. I'd tie him up. Yes... that's what I'd do. Tie him to the bed. Not too tightly. I want him to wriggle a bit when I do it."

"Do what?" Simon was using both hands now, sliding them up and down the insides of Adam's thighs.

Adam opened his mouth to speak but at first he couldn't bring himself to say it. He made another effort.

"Whip him," he said and, as the words escaped from his mouth, he felt the first drop of moisture exude from his swollen cock.

"Tell me more," said Simon. He didn't sound in the least shocked or even surprised and Adam relaxed with relief.

"I've never done it. Have you?" he asked.

"No. It's not unusual I believe. I can think of much nicer ways to enjoy a man than hitting him. A question of putting in rather than laying on."

"Ah, but he'd know who was boss wouldn't he? I'd put a few welts in that round, white little bum of his and while he was still wriggling with pain I'd go into him. Just imagine that!"

"Every man to his own," said Simon, "and Howard is very much Mark's own so keep your fantasy in your imagination. I wouldn't want anything to happen that might cause friction."

"I guess you're right," said Adam. "I'm ready when you are."

Simon laughed again. "Ever the romantic, aren't you?" he said. "'I'm ready when you are', indeed. What was that line you gave me for 'Love Nest in the Elders' years ago?"

This time it was Adam's turn to laugh. "Oh that! 'Wrap me in your heavenly arms '. Something like that."

"That's it. Now turn over and let's put it into practice."

Simon's arms were anything but heavenly but they were strong. There were times, during the next few moments when Adam thought his ribs might break. Simon hugged him, kissed him and then let his hands drift downwards until his fingers were kneading Adam's buttocks, pulling them apart and then letting them relax again. Slowly, all thoughts of Howard and of Howard and Mark together vanished.

Simon's cock slipped between his legs. It felt warm, slightly damp and very big.

"Better get the stuff. I'll come in a minute," Adam whispered.

"Not tonight."

"Why not?"

"Not if you're playing a match. That can wait till tomorrow."

Simon slid his hands out from under Adam who, panting, lifted himself slightly in time to see Simon's close cropped blond head descend to his middle.

After that, one sensation followed another in quick succession. Simon's tongue lapped at his balls. He heaved his body upwards. It moved further back and stroked the smooth surface of his perineum. In the past that had always been a sure way of knowing what Simon wanted. Not that night however. It touched his outer sphincter and then retreated. He next felt it lapping up his steel-hard cock. Then, slowly and apparently savouring every centimetre, Simon's lips slid down the shaft until they were buried in hair and the top of Adam's cock was pressing against something wet and hard. Simon's hands slid up and down the outside of his thighs. For a second or two Adam wondered what Howard's cock was like. He'd never thought about it before. The image of Howard sitting on the floor between Mark's legs a hour or so ago was still vivid. Long legs, a tight little bottom only slightly compressed against the unyielding floor. That lovely smile. Mark must have whispered something amusing. It wasn't amusement Howard needed. Howard needed discipline. He'd make Mark watch. That would be good. Howard would be writhing on the bed. The ropes and bedposts would certainly groan at the strain. Howard was a powerfully built lad. His superbly round bottom, already bearing the marks of the first few lashes, would squirm. People not into the great secret had no idea of the enjoyment one could get from whipping a boy. There was no better way of making a boy amenable to what would come later. No better way of making him come really well - spurting - not just running out. That was what people of Howard's age were meant to do - spurt and gush and gasp.

All of which Adam did. There was no time to give Simon a warning. It just exploded out of Adam, one jet following another. The room seemed to revolve, stop and then turn in the opposite direction before everything went misty and he lay back panting like a long distance runner. He heard Simon gulp.
"Been saving it for me then?" the man said at last. Adam didn't reply. He couldn't.
"Going to have another?" Adam asked some hours later when they were under the sheets and hugging each other happily.
"Not tonight. You've got the game to think about."
"Football or another sort?"
"Football. The other sort can wait till tomorrow."

Charles' cock felt soft; a big and very appetising sausage. Charles put out a hand and touched Ben's.
"Good?" the man asked.
"Very good," Ben replied. "Did I do it again?"
"I didn't notice. One doesn't when one is deep in an ass as nice as yours."

"You noticed last time. I wouldn't have known if you hadn't told me."

Being fucked by Charles was an experience like no other. It felt pretty good when Adam did it but, with Adam, it was over in a matter of minutes and Ben stayed clear-headed. Charles' technique was quite different. Charles took his time. He stroked and caressed what he always referred to as the 'crown jewels' until the 'sceptre' was as hard as ebony and the 'orbs' ached and their owner lay panting with a heart beating at what felt like twice the normal rate.

Then, just as Ben felt he couldn't possibly hold out for much longer, he'd have to turn over and kneel on the bed. That gave Charles an opportunity to do what he called 'appreciation'. It was then that Ben's excitement waned slightly from anxiety. He'd lost count of the number of times Charles had fucked him but it happened every time. Ben had once seen a hospital programme on television in which a patient's heart had stopped beating and he was resuscitated by an electric shock. The spasm made him appear to leap up from the trolley on which he lay. It was just like that with Charles. Ben was always clear-headed as the first few inches drove into him. He could hear and he could certainly feel. Charles' cock felt like a hammer-handle being forced into him. He had to bite his lip to prevent himself from calling out.

"Oh that's so good. Oh yes. Yes. Yes!" said Charles and then it happened. It happened very time. The shock wasn't painful but Ben was just aware that he'd shouted out and jerked as every muscle in his body went taut. After that, everything was a confused blur. He wasn't even aware of his own ejaculation until it was all over and the towel which Charles had put on the bed was soaked and the last long string of semen dripped on to it and snapped. Consciousness returned. Charles' cock was twitching deep inside him making strange squelching noises. He became aware that he was dribbling and tried to swallow. Charles' hands slid up and down over his ribs.

As usual, they had showered together. As usual Charles had dried him and, as usual, they went to bed and lay there fondling each other and talking through the early hours.

"How do the three of you get on actually," Charles asked.

"Pretty well, considering."

"Considering what? Open your legs a bit. That's better."

"Well there's Adam and me. Mark's a bit on his own but he doesn't seem to mind that."

"No big rows?"

"Not really."

Charles tickled under Ben's balls. "Simon said it would never work out," he said. "Two's company and that sort of thing. I'm rather hoping that I can persuade Howard and his parents to change universities next year. It would be so much better for Mark. Howard too. You and Adam. Mark and Howard."

Suddenly, everything clicked together in Ben's mind. "I think it's possible that Howard is already thinking on the same lines," he said. "He can't possibly enjoy being at that dump he's in."

"What makes you think that?"

"He had a letter from Howard a few days ago. I didn't read all of it but Howard said something about two offers to admit him. University places I guess."

"Oh, I'd better find out. Perhaps one's attempts are being pre-empted," said Charles. His finger was stroking Ben's anus now and having a definite but slow effect.

"He is exceptionally bright by all accounts. According to Mark he gets straight A's for every assignment. Don't stop. I like that."

"I'd better have words as soon as possible then," said Charles. "It would be a disaster if he were to change universities and not join Mark. Mark is besotted with the boy and Howard is mad about Mark. He couldn't be thinking of going elsewhere. I really worry about Mark sometimes. I have a strange feeling that he's going to need a lot of help shortly."

"I can only tell you what I read," said Ben. "If he ever does need help, I'd be there and I know Adam would do anything he could to help him. "Anyway, let's talk about something else. Tell me about that ancestor of yours again."

"Beresford the Bottle or the other one?"

"The other one. The seventeenth century one."

"Aha! One begins to see what you have in mind."

"Not yet. Tell me about him first. All about him."

"Well, his name was William and he was the fifteenth earl. There's a picture of him on the castle staircase."

"Has he got thick lips?"

"He has actually, yes."

"I guessed as much. Is he good looking?"

"Insofar as a person in his thirties can be good looking, yes. Not a patch on you though. You're beautiful."

"Adam reckons I'm fat."

"Rubbish. You're just right." Charles ran a hand over Ben's right buttock.

"And the page boys?" Ben asked. "Tell me about the page boys."

"I've told you as much as I know."

"Tell me again."

"Well, he only employed boys at the castle. He put it out that he was afraid of being assassinated and that the gang after him might infiltrate the assassin into the castle as a servant. Hence it was only boys. Boy cooks in the kitchen. Boys in the pantry. Boy gardeners. The odd thing is that nobody seems to have clicked. Apparently he sucked one of them off every evening at dinner."

"Sounds great to me," said Ben, sleepily.

"He claimed that drinking their semen kept him healthy. Maybe he was right. He lived to a good old age."

"Sounds like a good life to me," said Ben.

"For whom? My revered ancestor or the boys?"

"Both I guess. He would have looked after them."

"I think he did. His letters seem to show affection for them."

———

"You just stay still and don't move or you'll disturb the place settings, though I'll wager there'll be several plates on the floor when his grace has finished with you," said the steward.

Ben had some idea of the duties expected of a stable boy at Beresford Castle. Village gossip was a well-informed source of such information but he'd never expected to see the inside of the dining hall - especially from such a strange viewpoint. He stared fixedly at the cupids who flew round the clouds painted on the ceiling. The top of his head was touching the elaborate silver centre-piece and his legs dangled over the edge of the table with his feet on either side of the high-backed chair. The sound of a door being slammed echoed along the corridors.

"That's him coming now," said the steward. "Mind you keep still."

Ben concentrated hard on the cupids. If he had access to his fingers he would have been able to count them. He got as far as five and then gave up to ponder whether such beings really existed. He had never seen one.

The steward opened the door. A cold draught wafted over Ben's naked thighs.

"Aha! The new stable lad eh?" Ben was suddenly alarmed. One stood up and bowed to earls. Everybody knew that. Even when the carriage swept along the road, people stopped what they were doing and bowed low. To be lying naked on a table was more than a serious breach of etiquette. It was a crime. But the steward had told him to lie still. The best thing to do, he thought, would be to close his eyes and pretend to be asleep.

"Yes, my lord."

"Splendid! Splendid! One hopes he's been thoroughly washed, eh? What?"

"Most thoroughly your lordship. I attended to him personally."

He had. Ben had never had a bath before and had been frightened to sit in warm water at first. For two hours the steward had scrubbed and washed every part of him.

"Good one, eh Master Harris?" one of the other boys had said when Ben stood up in the tub to have what, up to then, he'd thought of as his 'private parts' washed.

"Pretty good. His lordship will enjoy his dinner tonight. You'll have to watch out young William. Young Ben here might take your place."

"I doubt it. His lordship's interest in me is more fundamental. I rode inside the carriage with him when we came back from London."

"I know and I won't ask what you got up to on the journey."

The boy laughed. "Very little in the carriage. It was in London that his lordship got up. So did that playwright Master Shakespeare."

"Yes? Well you just take my advice and keep it for his lordship. His last favourite was sent packing for letting other people into his lordship's property. Those London ways don't go down well here. Now hand me a dry cloth. Then you'd better go and have a rest in case his lordship wants you tonight."

Ben felt the chair being pulled back. "He appears to be asleep," said the earl. Ben felt something silky brush against the inside of his leg and then the chair was replaced. He felt the earl's breath on his thighs.

"How old is he?"

"Difficult to say, your lordship. Older than the last boy certainly."

"So one hopes. That one should never have been dragged from his mother's breast. One needs more than a minim of watery seed to keep fit. This one has hair - and in all the right places."

A hand landed on Ben's thigh. He opened his eyes. Looking downwards as far as he could without moving his head, he saw the rings on the earl's fingers glittering in the candle light.

"A veritable love nest," commented the earl as his fingers moved up and began

to twine in Ben's newly washed private hair. "And graced with a fine sceptre and jewels fit for His Majesty. I shall drink well of his youthful seed."
"Oh... your lordship..." Ben murmured as the earl lowered his head over it.

It didn't take long. Longer, certainly, than when Ben was lying in bed at home in the cottage but not too long. His cock was rammed hard against the earl's throat. At one time it felt as though the earl had actually swallowed the first inch or so of his cock. A platter or something similarly big clattered down on to the floor. He wanted to say that he was sorry but he couldn't find the right words. Something else fell. He heard the steward laughing. If only he could keep still, he thought - but it was no good. At home his brothers used to laugh about the way Ben made the bed creak.

He felt himself charging up - just like a musket. The strange full feeling in his loins as if powder, a wad and a ball had been pushed into him. He was primed. The earl's hands ran up and down his thighs. He lifted his rear from the table, reached out desperately to hold on to something but couldn't.
"Shall I hold him still, my lord?" said the steward. Naturally enough, the earl didn't answer.
"I... I ... Ah! Aaaah!" Just like a bullet, it shot out of him. In fact it was like several bullets being fired one after the other. For a second he thought what a wonderful invention such a gun would be, but then, remembering where he was, he lay subservient and still. The earl wiped his lips with a silk kerchief.
"Very good! Very good indeed. You have excelled yourself, Harris."
"Thank you my lord."
"I met that new playwright Master Shakespeare when I was in London."
"I heard something of the sort, my lord."
"I invited him to spend a few days here. We shall have to find a boy for him. Who do you suggest?"
"That rather depends on Master Shakespeare's preferences, my lord."
"Did not young William say anything about his journey to London?"
"Not a word. None of the boys ever say anything. They are all totally loyal to your lordship."
"Mmm, 'tis as well. Master Shakespeare enjoys dipping his quill into the ink well if you take my meaning."
"Enter back stage, you mean?"

The earl laughed. "Exactly," he said.
"This one has a friend. Adam is his name. A comely lad of about twenty-three

and well muscled. I could procure him."

"Do so. Why, the lad might one day be famous though I doubt the fact. I saw one of his plays once. A foolish impertinence about a fairy king and queen and a man they changed into an ass. Writing such rubbish won't make him famous. I can't even recall the name of the piece. "

"A Midsummer Night's Dream, my lord," said Ben.

———

"A Midsummer Night's Dream, my lord."

"Don't you ever stop thinking about English Literature?" said Charles. "Why the sudden formality, anyway?"

Ben shook his head. "I think I must have been dreaming," he said.

"You went quiet for a moment or two. I thought you were thinking. Anyway, this is no dream and it isn't midsummer."

Ben reached over and touched Charles' cock. It was beginning to wake up again.

"As you like it," he murmured. Charles turned to face him and then, holding Ben's face between the palms of his hands, he kissed him.

"Ready for another session?" he breathed. He put his arms right round Ben and hugged him tightly.

"Sure. Go slowly though. Let's not have love's labour lost."

Charles grinned. "Or make much ado about nothing," he said.

CHAPTER FOUR

Adam went off to his football match. Charles took Ben and Howard into town. Simon said he had some work to do and it was Mark's turn to walk alone in the gardens and try to sort things out. He couldn't and so knocked on Simon's door.

"Come in, Mark."

Simon was sitting at a writing desk tapping away at his lap-top.

"Am I interrupting?" Mark asked.

"No, I was expecting you." He closed the lap-top and put it to one side. "So... What's up?" he asked.

"Nothing."

Simon smiled. "You haven't changed, have you?" he said.

"Meaning?"

"I've known you too long, dear old Mark. Whenever you have a crisis you keep it bottled up. It's not a sensible thing to do. Come and sit down and tell me all about it."

"It's nothing really. It's just that I'm worried about Howard." He told Simon the whole story. "I've got the letter upstairs," he said. "Maybe you should read it for yourself."

"Certainly not. How old are these boys?"

"Oh they're old enough if you know what I mean."

"Mmm. He's being a bit silly, especially in a place like St. Frideswide's. The Catholic Church isn't exactly renowned for keeping up with the times. From all I've heard of the place, he'd get thrown out pretty promptly if they found out what was happening in their hallowed halls."

"Could you talk to him?"

"It wouldn't do an atom of good. If he won't listen to you, he certainly won't listen to me. He thinks the world of you."

"He did."

"He still does, Mark. Honestly."

"So what can I do?"

"Nothing. I think it might be an idea for one of us to tell Charles in confidence. He can't say anything but he lives near the college and is well in with the staff there. If Howard's behaviour does become public, he's well placed to help."

"Did I do the wrong thing to tell him off, Simon?"

"Probably. The trouble with you two is that you are so similar. Both of you fly off the handle at a moment's notice. You heard about Charles' plan?"

"Yes. It'd be great if he can do it. I was going to talk to Howard about it last night but I didn't get a chance."

"Leave it to Charles, Mark. Don't get involved. He needs to see Howard's parents and they may take a lot of convincing that agricultural engineering is best studied in a modern environment. My only worry is the insurance."

"Insurance? What do you mean?"

"You'll be slinging crockery at each other. I'll need to take out an extra insurance. But seriously, Mark. That's not all that's bothering you is it?"

Mark sat on the bed. "Oh God, Si!" he said. "I don't know how to say this..." Simon sat next to him and put an arm round his waist. "Try," he said.

"It's me. I mean, I shouted at Howard because he's having it off with other people. I'm not one to talk, am I? Look at you and me for instance. There's hardly a day goes by without me seeing some student I'd like to have it off with. I mean... deep down I'm the same. I feel such a bloody hypocrite. Am I? I mean... I know I'm possessive and I know I get jealous and I can't help that but I never thought I was a hypocrite. Not till today."

"You're not!" Simon hugged him. "The difference is perfectly simple. When you met Howard, you fell in love with him. Right?"

Mark nodded.

"And has Howard said that he loves these lads at the college?"

"No."

"So there you have it. There's love and there's sex. That's one of those facts of life that everybody knows but never really understands till they come up against a crisis like the one you are facing. Howard is very young. He'll realise the difference sooner or later. Sooner, I hope, for both your sakes. Your job at the moment is to guide him and that is best done quietly - not by having a row with him."

"When I used to help you and we... well, you know. Did you love me?" asked Mark.

"I was dotty about you. I couldn't sleep because I was thinking about you. I couldn't write because I found myself wondering what you were doing."

"That's just like I am about Howard," said Mark. "That's why I was late with my last assignment."

"Exactly. And now you're all boiled up because Howard has gone into town with Charles and Ben."

"I suppose I am."

"I know damned well you are. Well, don't be. Take my word for it. Howard loves you just as much as you love him. This is a temporary crisis."

"I hope you're right," said Mark.

"I know I am. Now then, let's play their own game."

"How do you mean?" Surely, he thought, Simon wouldn't want sex with him after a night with Adam.

"You can take me out for a drive. I need a break."

"Where to?"

"Somewhere nice and quiet."

"Your car or mine?"

"Take mine. I know you like driving it."

'Like' was not an adequate word. Simon changed his Porsche every year. That year's model was particularly good; fast and responsive and it held the road beautifully. They were soon speeding along country roads. Simon sat back, apparently unconcerned about the speed or the fact that one so young was in control of several thousand pounds worth of sophisticated machinery.

They found a small country pub. The landlord must have seen who was driving the car. Mark was treated with elaborate courtesy and, for once, not asked for proof of his age. Simon was ignored. They talked about many things; about Simon's latest book and the promotional trip to the United States he was to make at the end of the year; about Mark's studies and the eccentricities of his various lecturers but not once about Howard. It was just what Mark needed. By the time they were driving back to the Lakeside he felt better.

That night was different. With Simon's help, he forestalled Howard and moved into another room. He lay there in the darkness thinking. Simon was such a nice stable sort of person, he thought. Why couldn't Howard be like that? He smiled as he recalled the day he and Simon had first met.

He was sitting in the bus station in the nearest big town waiting for the bus back to Hardwick St. Mary. They only ran every two hours and he had a long wait in front of him. Suddenly the Porsche drew up in the place marked BUSES ONLY. He had seen the car in Hardwick. It was easily recognisable. Apart from the colour; a vivid red, it was the newest and most expensive car for miles around.

"Waiting for the Hardwick bus?" The driver was a young man and smartly dressed.

"Er. Yes. I am actually."

"Jump in."

"Thanks very much," he said and, with some difficulty, climbed into the car.

"I live opposite The Grange." said the man and Mark suddenly realised who he was. Rumours had been flying round for months. First as to the identity of the new owner. Mrs. Ticely in the Post Office said that The Grange had been bought by a film star. Mr. Laver in the bakery, who was well placed to know, said that the new owners were an 'international conglomeration' who were going to turn the place into offices. On the day when the removal vans arrived it was remarkable how many of the inhabitants of Hardwick St. Mary suddenly realised that they were short of bread. Mr. Laver did a double bake that day and the day after.

"Simon Spencer. That's who it is. Just imagine! Simon Spencer living here! We are going up in the world," said Mark's mother.

"Who the hell is Simon Spencer?" asked Mark. He felt particularly miserable on that day. The letter from the university still lay in a crumpled ball on the floor of the bedroom where he had thrown it. In view of the fact that he was only just eighteen and his A level grades were only just good enough, 'the Dean and faculty felt that he might benefit from a year away from studying'. A place was guaranteed for the next academic year. It was just that there were so many people wanting to read Computer Science...

"That's the trouble with you. You don't read half enough. He's ever so famous. Thrillers and war stories mostly but they say he's behind the 'From the man's point of view' column in 'Wives' Weekly'. If you'd read more books, you might have got a place at university. It's important that is. Reading makes for a mature personality. That's what it said in..."

Mark hadn't stopped to hear where his mother had read that particular gem of wisdom but had stormed out of the house.

It wasn't long before rumours were going the rounds again. Mr. Spencer was divorced and had a wife and two children in London. Mr. Spencer had lost his wife in a terrible car crash some years before. Mrs. Ticely remembered reading about it. Mr. Spencer had been engaged but his fiancee died of cancer a few days before the wedding.

A few days later his mother returned excitedly from the bakery. Mr. Spencer had actually gone into the bakery on the previous day and had actually bought a loaf of bread and a cake. Mr. Laver had taken the opportunity to ask and Mr. Spencer had said that he wasn't married; never been married or engaged.

"Perhaps he's gay," said Mark.

"Don't be so stupid. That's a wicked thing to say. A famous writer like him couldn't possibly be one of those."

"That's what they said about Oscar Wilde," said Mark but, deep down, he believed her. People like him were few on the ground. He'd only ever known one other boy and their occasional sessions in Tony Bletchford's attic were unsatisfactory to say the least.

"Driver calling passenger. Driver calling passenger..."

"Oh. Sorry. I was thinking about something." Mark felt his face redden with embarrassment.

"I asked what your name was."

"Mark Lee... sir."

"Mark Leeser or Mark Lee?"

"Mark Lee."

"Forget the other bit for God's sake. I'm Simon."

"I know. Simon Spencer. You're a writer."

Simon laughed. "Amazing!" he said. "I've been in this village for just nine days. They warned me this would happen in a small community. I'd better drop you off round the corner from the bakery. If any of the locals see you in the car with me they'll assume you've been raped at least."

Mark laughed. "Nobody really believes that," he said. "They just make up stories round here."

Simon didn't answer. They reached the bakery. Simon slowed down.

"Got time for a cup of tea and a natter?" he asked.

"Well, yes. Are you sure?"

"Of course I'm sure. Come on in. The place is still a bit of a mess but I am getting there slowly."

Inside the house, he was offered a comfortable chair, given a cup of tea and a large piece of cake. A book shelf along one wall was full of Simon Spencer books. Simon said he had written forty - three books so far and was working on another one.

"How many words in a book? On average, I mean?" Mark asked.

"Between seventy and eighty thousand."

Mark whistled. "I find it difficult to write a thousand," he said.

"That's because I enjoy it. To you it's just a school subject."

"I saw the film of 'Renegade Regiment'," said Mark. He had never actually read any Simon Spencer books. Reading was not one of his favourite occupations. "That was terrific!"

"Yes, they made a good job of that one. 'The Law of the Jungle' was a disaster. Did you see that one?"

"No."

"The jungle looked like a civic park. They could have made a much better job if they'd shot it in the garden here. That's a job I have to get round to before it becomes a complete wilderness."

"Perhaps I could help you," said Mark. "I've got nothing else to do."

"I wouldn't ask my worst enemy to tackle that. Have you seen it?"

Mark shook his head.

"Come with me." He followed the man out through the kitchen to the back garden. It really was a mess. You could see where the lawn had been. The grass was about two feet high. Occasional dots of colour marked a flower desperately trying to bloom over it. A great clump of dense greenery seemed once to have been some sort of fruit bush and what had once been a vegetable garden was entirely covered with a big - leafed plant which resembled no vegetable Mark had seen.

"It could be done," he said.

"Are you sure you want to? What about school?"

"I've left." He gulped slightly and then explained the position.

"How old are you then?" Simon asked.

"Eighteen."

"With great respect, you don't look eighteen."

"I know. That's why I have to carry my driving licence around all the time."

"And you've got a whole year with nothing to do?"

"Right. I'd like to go abroad but I haven't got the money. I'd like to get a job but the chances round here are nil."

"You've just got one. If you want it, that is," said Simon.
"What?"
"Gardener and personal assistant here. I'd pay of course."

Mark could hardly believe his good fortune. "Sure," he said. "When do I start?"

———

Mark found that he quite enjoyed gardening. Hacking away at the undergrowth was an excellent way to work off bad temper or impatience. When the patch of tall grass had been cut, trimmed and made into a small lawn he felt a glow of achievement. When Simon came out in the afternoons to sit there and work, Mark felt really thrilled. The summer that year was unusually warm and he worked wearing just his football shorts. There were times when he would suddenly turn round and find Simon staring at him but he paid no attention and carried on.

The relationship became closer as the weeks progressed. Mark took the cordless telephone into the garden with him to field calls when Simon was inside working or had gone out. Simon had obviously told several of his friends about Mark. Callers would say 'Is that Mark?' or 'Mark, can you ask Simon to call me?' One even went so far as to call him 'Simon's wonder-boy'. Sometimes, when Simon had a problem with a book, they would sit in the garden and thrash the problem out together. Simon was the sort of person one could talk to.

They talked in the garden. They talked in the lounge and in Simon's study. Once or twice, especially when Simon was stuck for ideas, he would come into the bathroom whilst Mark was taking a shower and perch on the stool. Mark thought nothing of it.

Then came the afternoon when a Mr. Lowenstein called. Simon had gone into town. Mr. Lowenstein was calling from the States and wanted Simon to know that the contract was on the way. Mark put down the phone and continued to hack away at a particularly thick branch. He heard the car pull up and the garage door opening. He put down the axe and went into the house. "A Mr. Lowenstein called," he said. "He wanted to tell you the contract is on the way. Hey! What are you doing?" Simon was hugging him. He even felt a kiss on his forehead. "Let me go!" he said, but Simon didn't and a very strange feeling came over Mark. He felt warm, but he shivered. He felt uncomfortable but instinctively hugged Simon back.

Later that evening, Mark got the whole story. Simon had tried to explain several times during the afternoon but they were both too preoccupied. They sat in the dining room of the George. One of Simon's stories; a story for which Mark had supplied one of the characters and some of the plot, was to be made into a million dollar film.
"Congratulations again," said Mark as the waiter refilled his glass.
"I'm sorry about this afternoon," said Simon. "No hard feelings?"

Mark's laughter exploded to such an extent that spots of wine spattered over the table-cloth. "Certainly not now," he said. "Anyway, hard feelings are nice feelings!"

At first he had only been aware of Simon's hands running up and down his back. Then, for no apparent reason, his cock had began to rise in his shorts. For a moment, that was embarrassing and then he realised that Simon's was doing the same thing. He could feel it, hard and throbbing and pressing against him, through Simon's pants. Simon kissed him again and Mark, who had never kissed a man before, reciprocated. He didn't know why. That was when his shorts fell down. He hadn't been aware of any force which made them do so. One moment they were firmly in place and in the next, they were round his ankles.
"You wonderful, gorgeous boy!" Simon whispered.
"You wonderful super successful writer," Mark replied. What happened after that was a blurred mixture of delightful feelings. He remembered Simon getting undressed. He remembered being laid on the sofa and gasping as Simon played with his cock and licked it. The sofa had almost fallen over when Simon lay on him. He felt the man's enormous cock pressing up between his legs. It was at that point that nervousness gave way to excitement. He just let himself go and when proper consciousness returned they were both on the sofa, wrapped in each other's arms and joined together by a warm stickiness, as if somebody had coated them both with paste.
"Can I ask you something, Si?" he asked later when he was lying in the bath and Simon was under the shower.
"Go ahead."
"Are you gay?"

"I'd have thought that was obvious."
"I thought so. I am too."
"So?"
"It's just that I've never told anybody before."
"No reason why you should. I get very pissed off by the gay banner waving brigade. We just live our lives and enjoy ourselves. Anyway, hurry up. The table's reserved for eight o'clock."

That year had been the best year of his life, he reflected. They had argued sometimes but making up afterwards compensated for those. They asked each other hundreds of personal questions and it wasn't long before Simon knew more about Mark than anyone else in the world and that was a nice feeling. There was no need to put on an act with Simon. He could be completely honest. Often, on their shopping expeditions into town, Mark would spot some young man and get Simon to slow down so that they could both admire him.

There was the day when he went home with a pre-publication date copy of 'And a Body to Boot ' and showed his mother the dedication - 'To Mark Lee in gratitude.' and the signature beneath it.

Yes... It had been a wonderful year. He fell asleep.

CHAPTER FIVE

"Closing time!" Howard tried to make his voice sound as authoritative as possible. Most of the students in the library began to pack away their things and return the books they had been using to the shelves. One or two asked for a few minutes longer.

"It's eight o'clock," said Howard. "Think yourself lucky the library's still open in the evenings. You'll have to come back tomorrow."

Grumbling, they put away their pens and shuffled out. Howard locked the main door behind them and walked back down the length of the library, replacing a few books on the shelves as he did so. He reached the office, went in and closed the door behind him. He looked at his watch and smiled. Some of the best were on display at that time in the evening. He turned off the light and took up his position at the window. It was time to do a little window shopping - and to hell with Mark and his possessiveness!

The window at ground level in the next building opened horizontally outwards. Despite the rain, it had been opened and steam billowed out. It had been raining almost continuously for three days. He looked at his watch again. Ten past eight. The steam thinned. The first one to come near the window was very unprepossessing but then, suddenly, they appeared. Jonathan was first, then Stuart. Howard smiled. Of the two of them, Stuart had the biggest and nicest cock but there was something about Jonathan which he found irresistible. Whether it was his downy upper lip or that drawling American accent, Howard did not know. The dense dark patches under Jon's arms and at the top of his legs were clearly visible. Stuart, on the other hand, was much shorter and fair haired. One couldn't really like Stuart. Stuart's father was the owner of the huge 'Cut-Price' supermarket chain and Stuart made sure that everyone knew. There was hardly a student at 'St. Fred's' who didn't have a 'Cut-Price' pen or a 'Cut-Price' key ring. He was selfish and self centred but whereas Jonathan had gently to be persuaded, Stuart was hungry for it. So, for that matter, was Howard. He smiled again to himself. The steam vanished. The gold chain Stuart always wore glinted under the bright lights.

Cautiously, Howard opened the window to get a better view and cursed the rain. The flash of gold again. Stuart. Howard wondered what they were talking about and leaned further out of the window. Were they talking about what happened in the library office? Probably not. They were friends but that didn't mean that they told each other everything. It was an intriguing thought though. They were a pretty close couple and though, individually, they denied it, it was possible that they were having it off with each other somewhere and, if they were, they'd talk - about him.

"Howard's cock is huge, isn't it?" That would be Stuart.

"Sure is! And I never saw a guy shoot as much spunk as Howard. I got some of it on my face. He said I did real good too. He sure likes the taste of real American spunk."

"British too. I can't wait for the next time."

"Nor me. Do you reckon he wants to fuck us?"

"You bet he does. He's just waiting for a chance. I saw what he did when you left the office the other day. That was no friendly pat on the behind. That was 'I can't wait to stick it up an all-American ass.' I wish I could be there to watch."

Howard closed the window again and shook the rain-drops out of his hair. It was an idea. A threesome. It hadn't occurred to him before.

He was still furious with Mark. Howard had known for years that Mark was unreasonably possessive but he hadn't expected the flare-up at the Lakeside Hotel. That Mark, of all people, should object puzzled him. Oh well, he thought, Mark could get stuffed. Mark wasn't the only person in the world. There were others. Admittedly, he didn't feel for them as he had for Mark but perhaps he would as they grew older. Life at St. Fred's wasn't as bad after all.

St. Frideswide's Roman Catholic College of Agriculture and Horticulture had been founded in the nineteenth century with the sole object of training farmers and market gardeners for famine-stricken Ireland. Built on a 'no expense spared' basis, it occupied a range of extraordinary Victorian buildings just outside Combleton village. The chapel, as big as a cathedral, loomed over the entire college. Howard hadn't wanted to go there but he really didn't have a lot of choice. In the first place his uncle was a bishop who was obsessed by the lack of moral values and discipline in ordinary universities and, it had to be admitted, a degree in Agricultural Engineering gained at St. Frideswide's was regarded highly.

He hated the place at first. The immensity of all the buildings made him feel claustrophobic. He found it difficult to keep up with his studies and he hated the geography of the place. One of the degree students bought a pedometer and found that he was having to walk over five miles a day just going from one building to another. If you used the library regularly, as Howard did, another two miles had to be added to the total. The only people in the college who were lucky were the so-called 'second muggers'. When the Irish found that they could grow potatoes without the well meaning help of St. Fred's alumni, the authorities had turned the Beaumont building next to the library into a cramming establishment for boys who hadn't made the required grades to enter university or their chosen career. They studied in the Beaumont building. They had their own canteen in the Beaumont building. The library was only about twenty feet from their front door and, worse, they lived in the Beaumont building. There was no doubt in Howard's mind that the Beaumont building housed the best looking students in the college.

There was nothing in the many rules of the college about degree students and cramming students not being permitted to mix. In fact the priests tried desperately to bring the two communities together but failed. Thus, in his first two terms, Howard studied hard but his social life was almost non-existent. An occasional beer down in the town with his fellow students when the conversation invariably turned to St. Frideswide's, the latest tractor or 'the girl back home' was as far as it went. He was bored and very frustrated.

Then, just before his first summer vacation, two things happened in quick succession. Father Harris, the elderly tutor librarian had some sort of stroke and could only work for a few hours a day. Someone was needed to take charge of the library. Nobody fancied the job but Howard could see certain advantages that the others missed. True, it meant being there till eight o'clock at night but one could work up there as well as stamp books and, at the end of the enormously long library with its rafters and pictures of past rectors, there was a comfortable office with no less than two locks on the door. Further, the office window looked down on to the shower room of the Beaumont block and, because the ventilation in there was non existent, second muggers usually opened a window when they took a shower. It was ideal for what Howard called 'window shopping'. He often sat up there until late at night, with the lights turned off, watching the muggers peel off their towels or dressing gowns, enabling him to admire the delightful curves of their behinds and their heavy hung cocks dangling from luxuriant hairy groins. If only, he thought many times, there was some way to get at them.

And then he met Mark and, through Mark, Simon and Charles - and life changed. He was almost sorry to be going home for the vacation.

It happened on a Thursday afternoon. He knew that because they were being lectured by Mr. Rawlins. Mr. Rawlins always chose to lecture outside. It would have been relatively easy to bring most farm machinery in under cover but Mr. Rawlins always wanted to demonstrate them. In the middle of a long aside about the dangers of chain-saws on trees with knotty wood, Howard was suddenly aware of a red Porsche drawing up in the road. When the passenger climbed out, he couldn't believe his eyes. He'd never set eyes on a more beautiful human being. The young man was not particularly tall and, although he looked very young he had an air of maturity and authority. He was the sort of young man who could walk in anywhere and not be challenged. Howard waved and, to his delight, the young man waved back.

And then it was as if the gods had arranged everything. The young man was gay. Howard didn't have to ask. Neither did Mark. For some reason neither of them understood, they knew about each other at the moment of the first handshake. Almost feverish with excitement, Howard smuggled Mark back to his room. He couldn't remember much about that first session; just arms clinging, legs thrashing wildly and loud panting noises. He couldn't even remember who had come first. All he knew was that when it was all over, they both lay side by side on his little steel bed running their hands over each other's sticky, warm bodies, occasionally lifting a head to plant a kiss.

On the following day he was invited to Mill Cottage to meet Lord Charles Beresford and none other than Simon Spencer the author. That Mark should be friendly with an extremely rich peer and a world famous author worried Howard at first. It need not have done. He took to both men very quickly. Anxiety that they might make demands on him vanished. He liked Lord Charles' cottage very much. He liked the man even more. He had a dry, languid sense of humour which appealed to Howard. He wasn't too sure about Simon to start with. Simon kept touching Mark and he didn't like that. But somebody must have said something during the course of the afternoon because when they all went out to dinner at the George - Charles' favourite eating place, the touching had stopped and it was Simon who insisted that he and Mark should sit together.

It had been Charles who suggested that they spend the first two weeks of the summer vacation together. Howard telephoned his parents and told them that he would spend the first two weeks staying with a friend in Combleton to study. He didn't do a lot of studying but he learned a lot. Up to that time, Howard's sex life had been fraught with fear. Fear that someone might disturb them; fear that it might hurt and fear that someone might find out about his secret. In bed in Charles' spare room with Mark, all his anxieties flew away. He could relax. He discovered that, providing you weren't frightened, it didn't hurt at all. Equally important was that Charles knew about them and all three could laugh over breakfast at the events of the previous night.

Charles never disturbed them. He never raised an aristocratic eyebrow when they went to bed at eight o'clock and breakfast was only served when they felt like it. Charles, Howard thought, was quite the nicest man he'd ever met. It had been Charles who drove into town to get a stock of the things they would certainly need.
"Just do me one favour," he had said when Howard had got over his embarrassment at being confronted with a plastic bag of condoms and cream. "Always, always, always do it the safe way. One's interest in you both is purely avuncular but I've seen enough misery in the world to want you two to live to a ripe old age - preferably still together."

They didn't go out much but one day Howard showed his new friend over the college. There were still quite a lot of the priests there so he couldn't show him everything but, as he still held the keys, he showed Mark the library and the view from the window.
"That's as far as it goes," he said. "Just a view from the window. There are some delights down there too."
"They use the library?" said Mark, leaning out of the window.
"Oh yes, often. All the A level texts and past papers are in here."
"So why don't you ask some of them to help? It's ridiculous to expect one student to run a place of this size single handed and cope with a degree course at the same time."

The tutor librarian thought it an excellent plan when Howard told him about it at the beginning of the following term. Howard began to spend longer and longer at his window. It didn't take him long to discover that there were two boys who always showered together - which might or might not be a promising sign. They invariably went into the showers just after eight o'clock in the evening. One was very tall and dark. The other was shorter, had blond hair and wore a gold chain round his neck.

His apparently accidental meeting with Jonathan Calder, the dark one was carefully planned. Jon was hoeing between the rows of lettuces. He straightened up as Howard strolled by.

"Pretty boring job eh?" said Howard. There were times when he felt really sorry for the second muggers. There was nothing in the college brochure about having to help with the gardening and everybody knew the college was making a mint out of selling vegetables. They could easily afford to employ labour.

"Sod all else to do," said the young man.

"You American?" asked Howard, though there was no mistaking that accent.

"Sure am."

"What the hell is an American doing in this place?" Jonathan put down the hoe and came over. His father, he said, was in the United States Army and in Britain for some years. For some reason which Howard didn't understand, Jon's father thought it would be better for his son to go to a British university and had set his heart (though not Jon's) on Oxford or Cambridge for which places quite a lot of cramming would be required.

"What else do you find to do, apart from hoeing gardens?" Howard asked.

"Bodybuilding. This place hasn't got the right equipment though. Gardening's the next best thing. Hoeing's good for the back muscles."

"I'd have thought you already have a pretty good body," said Howard. The words 'extremely good' and 'dazzlingly beautiful' ran through his mind as he spoke.

"Not good enough," said Jon.

"If you find time hangs a bit heavy, why don't you join the library committee?" Howard asked.

"Oh yeah. I heard about that. What do you have to do?"

"Not a lot. It's good fun. There's an office and a coffee machine."

"Could I bring a buddy with me?"

"Sure." Who?"

"Stuart Lynch."

"The one with the fair hair?" He very nearly added 'and a gold chain' which would have been a disaster.

"That's him."

It was arranged that Jonathan and Stuart would come up to the library on the following evening. Howard tried hard not to get too excited and it was quite a shock when they turned up. They stamped books and tidied the shelves. Finally, eight o'clock came round. They closed the outer doors and drew the bolts across.
"Coffee?" Howard asked.
"Sure," said Jonathan. Howard unlocked the office door and the three of them went in.
"Where are the reserve books then?" Stuart asked.
"How do you mean?"
"The books the priests don't want us to read."
"Oh those. In the cupboard behind you."

Everybody at St. Fred's seemed to have some idea about the 'reserve stock cupboard'. Some said it contained pornographic books confiscated over the years. The truth was that they were mostly reference books and, in the main, extremely dull. 'A New Approach to Sexual Education for Boys' had some good bits. 'Adolescent Development, Volume 1 - Male' had some quite pretty photographs. Best of all was 'The Male Nude in Photographs'.

Howard took out his keys again and unlocked the cupboard. "Absolutely nothing about girls, I'm afraid," he lied. "This one's quite good." He took out the book and handed it to Stuart.

Surprise number one was that Stuart accepted it and opened it. Howard had expected a dramatic rejection.

And then came surprise number two. "He's got a nice cock," said Stuart. "Look, Jon."

As calmly as possible, Howard made three mugs of coffee and handed them round. Jon and Stuart continued to flick through the pages of 'The Male Nude'.

It was arranged that they should work together on Mondays and separately on other days. Jon didn't think much of that idea. Jon turned out to be the most easily led nineteen-year-old Howard had ever met. Whatever Stuart suggested was all right by Jon.

"Do you two do everything together?" Howard asked one evening and they had looked at each other and laughed. A good sign.

Stuart's only interests in life seemed to money and the influence money could exert. Howard got sick and tired of listening to his accounts of his father's rich friends but gratefully accepted the 'Cut - Price' key ring, pens and overnight bag.

Stuart was the first one. Howard hadn't planned it. It just seemed to happen. Stuart's cock really was longer than the one in the book. Howard was only too happy to pay the ten pounds he'd bet. Charles, after all, had said that if he ever found himself short of money, he shouldn't hesitate to ask.

After that, Stuart was easy. It wasn't long before Howard returned happily to his room having had a teak-hard cock in his mouth.

Jon was difficult. Much more difficult. The key to success with Jon was to talk about bodybuilding. Howard found it difficult to understand why anyone with a body like Jon's should spend such a large proportion of his monthly allowance on bodybuilding magazines and diet supplements but was glad to part with another ten pounds. Jon's balls really were the biggest he'd ever seen and the most tactile he'd ever felt.

Was it going to be possible to get them both in the office at once with enough time to get them both really worked up? What he had in mind would take much longer than the usual sessions. He sat in the big, leather librarian's chair and put his legs up on the desk. Two of them at once! It was a thought. He hadn't screwed either of them yet. Jon had a really nice ass, he thought. Stuart too. One of them watching... Who would that be? Stuart probably. He was the younger of the two. Jon spread-eagled over the work table... or maybe Stuart would be better...

The sound of a key turning in the main door echoed through the library, followed by footsteps. Howard just had time to tuck it back into his trousers and put his feet back on the floor. The office door opened. It was the tutor librarian.

"I thought you'd gone home, Father," said Howard looking up from the book he had grabbed off the shelf.

"There was a staff meeting," said the man. "Shouldn't you be back in your house, Howard?"

"I thought I'd catch up with a bit of cataloguing," said Howard.

"Commendable, but don't let the library rule your life, will you?"

"Oh that's all right. I enjoy it."

"You're a good man, Howard. I've got some bad news for you though."

Howard's heart sank. Was it all going to come to an end? Was this some diabolical plan? Separate him from Mark and then take his boys away?

"Oh yes?"

"The rector wants to hold a governors' reception in the library on Saturday night."

"In the library?"

"Yes. The big reception room is being got ready for an exam."

"It wouldn't make a lot of difference, Father. We could close early on Saturday evening," he said.

"I think we shall have to close on Friday night. This place will have to be cleaned and tidied up. The caterers want to set up at three o'clock and we shall have to close for the whole of Sunday. The caterers won't collect their stuff until Monday."

Damn! Howard thought rapidly. "What we could do, Father," he said, "is do the clearing up for them. It would only be a question of putting things in boxes I suppose. Then they can come in on Monday and pick them up. That way we can be open for business as usual on Monday morning."

"It is an idea," the man mused. "But you couldn't do it all yourself and I always visit my mother on Sundays."

"I could get the two who help me to come in. They'd be glad of something to do."

"Do you think so? It would be the answer to the problem certainly."

"If you could do a note excusing us from chapel, Father. Then we can start early in the morning."

"It would be very irregular. You know what the rector is like over chapel attendance. It is very important."

"Perhaps we could go another time to make up for it," said Howard. There was as much chance of that happening as there was of his being made Pope, he thought.

"Yes. That would be all right." The librarian put a sheet of paper in the typewriter and laboriously typed the necessary note.

On Friday afternoon, Howard went on a shopping trip into town. He wished he had paid more attention to the brand names when Charles had tipped the contents of that embarrassing bag onto the table. However, he managed to get all that he considered necessary. He returned to school in time for his Friday library duty and secreted everything behind some books on a shelf in the office. Then he went off in search of Stuart and Jonathan. He found them in the Beaumont television room. They were reluctant to leave their favourite program and even more reluctant when they heard the official version of what he had in mind. It was only when he got round to the possibility of 'a bit of fun' that their complaints ceased.

"Nobody else at all?" asked Stuart.

"Absolutely nobody. The T L is going to visit his mother and the rector will make the library off limits all day. We can lock the outer door and the office door and stay as long as we like."

"We'll have to clear up first though, won't we?" said Jon, as always with duty uppermost in his mind.

"That shouldn't take long. Just a few plates and glasses to put away. And they're bound to leave loads of untouched food. They always do on these occasions. Booze too I guess," said Howard with a view to adding a little extra enticement.

"I can't. I have to go to chapel," said Jon.

"You don't. All three of us are excused," said Howard, handing over the paper.

———

It rained heavily all that night. He lay awake listening to it rattling against the window. He could hardly sleep for excitement and the noise of the departing governors only served to quicken his excitement. He found it amusing to think that the portraits on the library walls which had looked down upon the sober suits of the governors would soon overlook nakedness. In many ways it was a pity that they wouldn't be able to watch the unveiling ceremony but that was scheduled for the total security of the inner sanctum. He reached down under the bed-clothes. It was silly really but the only way to get some sleep.

Eight thirty the next morning found him waiting anxiously on the library steps. A vast, shallow lake covered the lawn. It crossed his mind to wonder how the governors had got in and out of the building without getting their expensively shod feet wet.

Eight forty - five, and the first of the chapel goers filed into the chapel across the road. Eight fifty - five, and the bell began its clanging chorus. Nine o'clock, and a few last minute worshippers dashed through the rain and vanished into the chapel's dark and cavernous interior. Nine zero one and the rector skirted the puddles with his umbrella held aloft. He looked over to Howard. Howard waved. The rector frowned. He remembered something about three students being excused from chapel attendance and made a mental note to address this lack of respect to Our Lord in his sermon.

Nine zero two. Howard was about to go up and start work when he spotted them racing over from the Beaumont building. Taking the long way round to avoid the deep water, they joined him, breathless, on the steps.
"Thought you'd forgotten," he said.
"Father Ramburton tried to kick up a fuss over that note," said Jon.
"He can't do anything about it."
"He knows that now. I told him to call the rector. Shall we go in? You Brits might like this weather but I don't."

Howard locked the main door from the inside. Security hatch one sealed. They climbed the stairs. He unlocked the door to the library.
"Good God!" he said.
"If we left it like this, we'd sure be in trouble," observed Jon.

Wine glasses had been overturned, causing great red and purple stains on the once - white table-cloths. There were plates everywhere. Plates on the tables; plates on the shelves; even on the books. An entire cold turkey together with several pies and bowls of salad lay on the buffet table amid the general debris of wine glasses, plates and cups.
"Ugh!" said Howard. "Okay, let's sling this lot away."
"We don't have to wash up, do we?" Stuart asked.
"Like hell. Just put everything into the baskets. Hang on."

Carefully, he locked the door. Security hatch two sealed.
"Can we have the leftovers, Howard?" Stuart called.
"Sure. They'll only get thrown out tomorrow."

He was aware, as he piled plates and stacked them away, of their frequent forays to the buffet table. By the time he had cleared six or seven tables and wiped them down, they were giggling.

A glass crashed onto the floor. "Be careful," he said. "They belong to the caterers."

"Sorry," Stuart's voice came from behind a book-stack. He continued to work. Another crash. This time it was louder. A plate probably. "Watch out!" he said. There was no answer. He put down the pile of plates he was carrying and walked back to investigate.

They were standing behind one of the book-stacks. Both had glasses in their hands. A half-empty whisky bottle stood on the table.

"Don't overdo it," he said.

"You said we could finish off the left overs," said Stuart.

"Food, yes. But take it easy on the drink. You know what they're like in this place about drink."

"Fuck... fuckin' hypocrites!" said Jon. "We're old enough to drink for Christ's sake!"

"Nonetheless it's in the rules. No drinking alcohol on the premises. If someone were to smell it on your breath at this time on a Sunday morning..."

"Not that they will," said Stuart. He raised his glass to his lips. "Cheers!" he said.

"I guess you're right," said Howard. He began to see things in perspective.

"And scotch   makes me really randy," said Stuart with a grin. "Jon too I wouldn't wonder."

"How do you know?"

"I'm not saying but it does. Go on. Have some."

Howard poured a small quantity into a glass and sipped it. It wasn't as bad as he feared it might be after being left out all night.

"Well.. bottoms up," he said.

"Bottoms up," Stuart replied and Jon giggled.

"A drop more?" asked Stuart.

"Well... just a drop. How's things going down at this end?"

"Just got to get rid of this bottle and glasses and take the cloths off the tables and then we're done. Apart from the buffet table, that is."

"We can leave that till later and use it for our lunch. Save going out in the rain," said Howard. He picked up his refilled glass. Stuart and Jon did likewise. That emptied the bottle. Howard looked around but couldn't see another which, he thought, was just as well.

"Did you do it last night?" Stuart asked.

"Do what?"

"Wank."

"Well, yes I did."

"What were you thinking about when you did it?"

"That's personal."

"You know what I thought?"

"No. What?"

"I thought I wouldn't be at all surprised to find my dear old friend Howard is planning a wild orgy in the library. Sunday. Library closed all day. Doors locked. Tutor librarian away..."

"Too smart by half," said Howard. "We could do though. You game, Jon?"

For a moment, Jon looked very dubious.

"Come on Jon. Be adventurous for Christ's sake. Let's have a bit of fun!" You said yourself it doesn't do any harm. It does you good to get your rocks off in a place like this," said Stuart.

"Oh... okay," said Jon.

They soon finished clearing the library. Howard took a look round. Apart from the buffet table, the place was back to its normal condition. He picked up the office key. Jon and Stuart grinned. He opened the door. They went in. He locked the door from the inside. Security hatch three sealed. Three heavy sets of doors separated them from the outside world! His cock jerked upward expectantly. It wasn't the only one. The lumps in their jeans certainly weren't handkerchiefs.

Stuart, always the leader, took off his shoes and socks. Jon followed his lead. Howard slipped off his shoes, his shirt and then his jeans.

"Shit!" said Stuart. "It gets bigger every time I see it." He tugged at his shorts. They slipped down to his ankles and he stepped out of them. "Yours is bigger than ever," he said.

"Watching you makes it bigger," said Howard. His voice sounded strangely husky and seemed to echo round the little room like the voices in a dream. It was true. Watching them undress was a delightful experience. He loved the scent of their excitement and the slight flush of embarrassed excitement on their cheeks.

They stood, naked, in front of him. Stuart still wore the gold chain round his neck. Howard didn't mind. It wouldn't get in the way.

"Did you know the gutter was broken, Howard?" Stuart asked, glancing towards the window.

"Sod the gutter!"

"It's hanging down. That's why there's all that water round the building."

"This isn't hanging down though," said Howard. He reached out and touched it. Stuart grinned. "You going to suck it like last time?" he asked.

"I may do."

"I like it when you do that."

"So does Jon. Don't you, Jon?" Howard asked. Jonathan blushed slightly. "It's okay, I guess," he replied.

"You liked it. You know you did. You were good too. Come a bit closer."

Warily, as if frightened that the floor might give way under his bare feet, Jon took a few steps forward. Howard reached out. A nineteen-year-old cock, stiff with anticipation, was enticing enough. Its silky texture made Howard's heart beat more strongly but he had other ideas that afternoon.

"You're as hard as hell already," he observed, sliding the foreskin back. The shiny purple head looked like a ripe plum.

"Guess so," said Jon.

"It seems funny for there to be three of us," Stuart observed.

"All the more fun," Howard replied and took Stuart's cock in his free hand. He could feel their pulses, racing and unsynchronised, in his fingers.

"Yours is really hard," Stuart observed. Cool fingers clasped Howard's cock. "I'll bet you come a lot this afternoon."

"Probably."

"So what shall we do?"

He let go of their cocks and, drawing them both closer, slid his hands down their backs to their soft, fleshy buns. Jon tensed slightly. He found their furrows and slid the middle fingers of his hands up and down inside them, pressing deeper and deeper.

"That's nice," said Stuart, giving his prick an affectionate squeeze.

"I know something much nicer," said Howard.

"What's that?"

"We could go the whole way."

"You mean...?"

Howard nodded.

"Let's just do what we usually do. You and me, I mean." There was a note of nervousness in Jon's voice.

"You'll like it. It's good." He pressed even harder into Jon's ass. "A really nice feeling," he added. The tip of his finger touched the tight orifice. The thought of actually penetrating; of feeling Jon surrender and hearing the boy groan was almost unbearably exciting.

Stuart let go of his cock. "Does it hurt?" he asked.
"No. I've got some special stuff." He reached over to the book shelf and retrieved the cream. "Here."
"How do you know it doesn't hurt?" Jon asked. "Has anyone done it to you?"
"Only one person."
"And you liked it?"
"Yes," he said, simply - and truthfully and then added "but if you don't want to..."
"We could try," said Stuart.
"Why not? Lean over the table, Stuart." He swept the few papers to one side. Stuart did as he was asked - and Howard was himself again.
"Eighteen," he murmured. The word had a musical ring like the beginning of a symphony; a symphony he was going to conduct and play for the very first time. Certainly, no musician ever had a more beautiful instrument to play on. Those perfectly symmetrical white hemispheres had been constructed specially for him; the master player. They had been left to mature for no less than eighteen years waiting for this moment.

He opened the tube. "This might feel a bit cold..."

There was a sudden loud bang. Both Jon and Howard swung round. Stuart straightened and turned to look at the window.
"Oh Jesus!" said Stuart.
"Oh no!"

A ladder had been placed against the wall but all they could see were the head and shoulders of a man gazing at them. His mouth gaped open for a moment. Then he disappeared down the ladder.
"Fuck!" said Howard. He went to the window and looked down. A small van was parked there, its wheels awash with flood water.
"Burroughs Roof Repairs," he read. His heart thumped and his mouth felt dry. "Now we're for it," he said.

CHAPTER SIX

The summons came, as Howard knew it would, at six o'clock that evening. He was to report immediately to his tutor. The three of them had dressed as rapidly as possible and cleaned up the office. Jon, pale and shaken and Stuart, tight lipped and angry, had gone back to the Beaumont building.

Howard wondered if he should pack immediately; decided against it and lay on his bed contemplating a ruined career and a shattered life. He actually cried a bit, dried his eyes; tried to read a book but couldn't concentrate and lay down again. It was almost a relief to get the little piece of yellow paper.

He walked across the road and knocked on Father Sebastian's door. Fr. Sebastian opened it. "Ah, Ainsworth. Come in." His voice was strangely cold. Fr. Sebastian conducted most of his interviews in his sitting room and provided cups of coffee. Not this time. Howard followed him into his study. The tutor sat at his desk. Howard was not offered a seat.
"I want to say one thing," said Fr. Sebastian. He spoke slowly and deliberately as if he had learned the speech by heart. "If what I have heard from the workmen who came to repair the gutter is true, I think what you have done is utterly disgusting. To abuse a position of responsibility as you apparently have done is the lowest, most depraved thing I have ever heard of. Is it true?"

Howard nodded dumbly.
"Well, I'll hear your side of the story. The rector will want to see you of course to decide what to do with you. My job is to hear the sordid details."

Howard explained that that all three of them had been drinking. "One thing sort of led to another. We were pissed. I mean we were pretty tipsy," he said.
"Did you actually offer the other two anything alcoholic?"
"No, Father, but when I saw what they were doing I didn't stop them. The whole thing was my fault."

"And who suggested the sexual orgy in the office?"

"Me. I'm entirely responsible."

"Indeed you are. Consider yourself removed from the Library Committee as from this moment. You are to have absolutely no contact with any of the Beaumont students. The rector will see you at eight o'clock. You know the drill."

"Er... Shall I pack, Father? Am I to be expelled?"

"Knowing the rector as I do, I rather doubt it."

Howard couldn't stifle a huge sigh of relief.

"Now get out of here. I am disgusted and disappointed in you, Howard."

"Yes, Father. What will happen to Lynch and Calder?"

"We'll give them a talking to. I regard the sex bit as your fault but they should have known not to touch the drink."

At eight o'clock that evening, Howard stood by the bench outside the rector's study flanked on either side by the President and Vice President of the Students' Union.

They heard the rector's car come to a stop on the gravel outside. One of his escorts opened the door for him. He stepped in, unsmiling, nodded and vanished into his office. They waited. Five minutes passed. They heard him talking and the telephone being put down. Finally, the green 'ENTER' sign flashed. One of the escorts knocked and opened the door. Howard walked in alone.

The rector, robed and with a purple stole over his bony shoulders, sat behind his vast desk. "I shall not," he said, "discuss your offence. Mr. Walker has told me as much as necessary - indeed as much I desire to hear. What I want to know are the whereabouts of the two students you so shamelessly corrupted."

Howard wanted desperately to deny that allegation. Neither Jon nor Stuart had required any 'corruption'. However, he knew the rector all too well. He was not a man to argue with, especially when one's career was at stake.

"How do you mean?" he asked.

"I thought I had made myself clear. Apparently not. Where are Lynch and Calder?"

"They went back to Beaumont, rector. I saw them."

"Well, they are not there now. Father Ramburton informs me that they can't be found."

"You mean they've run away?"

The rector peered over his half-moon spectacles. "No, I do not," he said. "I think you know exactly where they are. Lynch has occasionally left the premises at times when he should be here. Calder never has and Father Ramburton assures me that he never would. Where are they?"

"Truthfully, rector, I don't know. I have no idea."

"Then I fear we have to consider the possibility of suicide."

Howard was aghast. "They would never... I mean it's impossible," he said. "I fear you know less of the workings of people's minds than I, Ainsworth. It is more than possible. Guilt can be a terrible burden as I hope you feel. You can make your confession now if you wish."

"Not now," said Howard. "Have you contacted their families?"

"The Lynch parents are apparently away on a cruise but the person I spoke to at their house says that she hasn't seen Lynch. Calder's home is in the United States but his father is in Scotland. It would be impossible for him to have reached Scotland in such a short time."

"But Jon might have called him."

"Allow me to know what I am doing. It would only cause distress. If they were, as you suggest, to go home, the parents would certainly notify me. If they are not here by tomorrow evening, I shall have to of course. I begin to fear the worst." He pressed a button on the desk and the two escorts entered.

"Under consideration for being sent down," said the rector. "In the meantime to have no contact with the Beaumont students."

"What did you do?" asked one of the escorts when they were outside.

"Tucked into some of the governors' drinks with two second muggers."

"Bit steep for that," said the boy. "When Atkinson got pissed he just got a rocket."

"You never know with the old man though, do you?" said the other.

Howard walked away from them into the dark, rainy night. There was nothing he could do. The news that he might be sent down would be all over the college in an hour or two. He went straight to bed.

He hadn't been there long when there was a knock at the door. Undoubtedly the first of the scandal mongers, he thought. "Come in!" he called, and in came Fr. Sebastian.

"I've just heard," he said. "Are you quite sure you don't know where these lads are?"

"Absolutely. I saw them go into Beaumont. That was the last I saw of them."

"Well, cheer up. If they are out in this weather, they'll certainly come back soon."

"I hope so. The rector thinks they might do themselves in. That's balls. Rubbish I mean. I think they'll probably go home."

"It isn't for us to question the rector's decisions and certainly not my place to criticise my boss but there is much in what you say," said Fr. Sebastian. "I think, strictly between ourselves that he is concerned for his - I mean the college's - reputation. Lynch's parents are extremely wealthy and therefore influential. Calder's father, I gather, is something rather high up and rather secret in the American Army. The sort of lad whose disappearance might well have international diplomatic consequences. I think he rather hoped you would produce them."

"I only wish I could," said Howard.

"Well, they'll probably be back in the morning. Try to get some sleep. Let us do the worrying, eh?"

"Thanks, Father."

The tutor went to the door and turned round again.

"Strictly between ourselves, Howard," he said, "Do you think you are gay?"

Howard caught his breath. Well... what the hell. People would have to know sooner or later. "I don't really know," he said, "but I think I am."

"Poor old chap. You have my sympathy," said Fr. Sebastian, and he left the room.

Howard lay awake for a long time. Was his tutor sympathetic to his condition or his suspension? He didn't know. He had no doubt at all that Mark was at fault. Mark, after all had suggested it - or as good as. Mark had a lot to answer for. Howard was glad that the break had come.

Convinced that the two boys would not return willingly to face a priestly board of enquiry, he puzzled over what to do. No ideas came. Fortunately, there was one person who would be sympathetic and helpful. He resolved to go to see Lord Charles in the morning. He hadn't visited the man since the weekend at the Lakeside but then, Lord Charles was a busy man. In fact, he thought, it had been considerate of him not to call.

Thus consoled he fell into an unquiet sleep and dreamt of naked boys who danced in front of him waving whisky bottles and of being chased by priests round and round a constantly expanding library.

At breakfast, his hopes were shattered. All lessons for the school had been cancelled. The entire school was mobilised into search parties. Being under suspension, Howard was not included.
"One of them has a dad in high places. Something to do with secret weapons. They reckon he's done himself in somewhere in the college grounds," said one student. "I hope to Christ I don't find him. I've never seen a dead body before."

Howard watched the various groups assemble. Even the priests wore jeans and anoraks. Some students had cut sticks from the thicket. Mr. Harding's dog, a normally idle hound, had caught some of the excitement and barked at everybody. One contingent stayed to search the school buildings. The others fanned out over the campus. Howard waited for some time, then changed into jeans, slipped into his bomber jacket and went out.

The drive which bisected the college was weirdly silent. At that time on a Monday morning, tractors and cultivators were usually being warmed up and Brother Adams' explosive anger should have been echoing back from the chapel walls. All Howard could hear were the shouts of the students in the search party as they beat at the undergrowth round the sports fields.

The lane to the village was wet. He wished he hadn't worn his trainers. By the time he reached the cottage they were covered with mud. Charles' garage door was closed. That was a relief. It usually meant he was at home - unless he had gone abroad. That was possible. Howard wished he had kept in closer contact. He pushed the gate open, walked up the path and rang the bell.
"Howard!" said Lord Charles as he opened the door, "This is a pleasant surprise. What on earth is going on? I've just had one of your more officious priests here demanding to know if I had seen two students yesterday evening."
"It's about that, actually, Charles," Howard replied. "May I come in?"
"Of course, but I can only tell you what I told him. Innumerable students walk past this place every day and I really don't pay much attention to them."

Howard pulled off his trainers and left them by the door. He followed

Charles into the lounge. A huge fire blazed in the fireplace.

He accepted a coffee gladly. Charles and he sat down opposite each other by the fire. "So... what's this about?" asked Charles.

"I'm in the shit and I don't know what to do," said Howard. Haltingly, he told Charles the whole story, holding nothing back.

Lord Charles sat back in his chair, put his empty cup on an occasional table and looked across at the unhappy young man.

"Is this in any way connected with the row you had at the Lakeside? he asked.

"What do you know about that?"

"Nothing, except that it was obvious that you had fallen out."

"I suppose in a way it is. Mark told me to stop doing it. I wasn't going to let him dictate to me. I'm the biggest fool. I let him do what he liked with me. I thought he was a friend."

"And what is that supposed to mean?"

Charles smiled. "You're not known, dear Howard, for talking rubbish but I'm afraid that is."

"No it isn't!"

"Howard. Mark thinks the world of you. He tried to give you advice. Whether the advice was good or bad is not for me to say or even know. As for letting him do what he liked, you liked it too so don't come up with yarns like that. However, this is not the time to get into lengthy psychological discussions. Neither of us is qualified to do so. The important thing is to get these two lads back to college and for you to be reinstated. Have you any idea where they might be? Be honest now."

"None at all really. I thought they might have gone home."

"Has the rector telephoned their parents?"

"The Lynchs are on a cruise. Jon's American but his father is in Scotland. He's going to call him later."

"Hmm. I should think they'll be pretty upset when they know that their sons absconded and they were not told about it immediately but that is his problem. What are you doing for lunch?"

"There isn't a college lunch. The search parties have got sandwiches."

"Good. Let's go to the George. Nothing like a good meal for giving one ideas. They are sadly lacking at the moment."

An hour later they were in the George, being fawned over by the staff, all of whom knew Charles and seemed determined that the other diners should know of their intimacy with him. It was 'Is everything to your lordship's satisfaction?' and 'Certainly my lord', throughout the meal. Some of this exaggerated respect reflected onto Howard who rather enjoyed it.

"I wish I hadn't sent that letter," he said.

"What letter?"

"I wrote to Mark about the Beaumont students and the library. That's what started the row at the Lakeside."

"But that was some time ago. How long had it been going on for?"

"Not long but yesterday was the first time I had both of them in the office together."

"Hmm. That was, dare one say, slightly foolish. I don't think you know Mark as well as you think."

"But Mark's hardly in a position to take a high moral tone, is he? Look at him and Simon."

"Sssh! Keep your voice down. That's unfair. I know Simon. I've been friends with Simon for a good many years. The fact of the matter is that Simon loved Mark deeply. I think he still does. But when Mark fell for you, Simon did the honourable thing and stood back. He was genuinely delighted that Mark and you had become so close. Mark made it quite clear to Simon that you were the sole object of his affection. Since then I happen to know that, er, they haven't if you know what I mean."

"Simon still does it with the other two students Mark lives with though. He told me."

"Adam and Ben are different. Anyway, let's put our heads together and think about these missing young men. Have you no idea where they might have gone?"

"Home."

"I don't think so. How old are they?"

"Jon's nineteen and Stuart's eighteen."

"At that age you don't go home and say 'I've got into trouble at college.' No. They are somewhere. Not in Combleton certainly. It was Sunday so there were no buses. To get to the station would have involved a long walk and they would have been seen by at least a dozen boys. Even on a wet day like yesterday the village teems with students."

"They just like to get away from St. Fred's for an hour or so," said Howard. "Everybody feels sort of shut in on a Sunday afternoon."

"So the station is ruled out."

"Not if they took the short cut."

"Short cut? To the station?"

"Through the woods. There's a cigarette machine and a condom machine in the station. It's the way you go if you don't want the priests to see you. You come out in the goods yard and from there you can go straight to the platform. It's risky though. You have to cross a farmyard and if the farmer catches you, you're in trouble."

"So that's the answer! Well done. Let's go to the station."

"They won't still be there."

"Of course not but if any of the staff on duty today were there yesterday afternoon, they may remember two students, especially if one of them is an American. Let's go."

Charles paid the bill. The waiters and waitresses, grinning and cringing, formed a guard of honour as they left. From the way Howard's coat was deferentially put on to his shoulders and brushed, it might have been the most expensive garment in the world. Nobody seemed to notice his mud - caked trainers or the flakes of dried mud under the table.

"The station," said Charles as their seat belts clicked. Howard switched on the cassette player and the big car sped away.

"Go slowly here," he said as they coasted down the hill. "I'll show you the path. It's just round this corner to the left. Christ! That's him! Stop, Charles!"

"Where? Who?" asked Charles, slamming on the brakes.

"Jon. He's just going into the wood. See? Up there."

"Are you sure?"

"Quite sure. He's sort of tall and has a peculiar way of walking. I'll catch him." He flicked the seat belt open and had a hand on the door handle when Charles restrained him.

"He'll probably run away from you. That would make it worse," he said. "Let's head him off. You say he has to cross a farm - yard?"

"Yes, but you can't go in there. It's strictly private."

"We'll see. How long do you estimate?"

"From here to the farm?"

"Yes."

"About fifteen minutes."

"Good. Show me the way. I don't want him to meet up with any of the search parties. He might well blurt out more than he should. On your own admission yesterday wasn't the only occasion. The college are only concerned with the events of yesterday."

"I hadn't thought of that," said Howard. His stomach seemed to sink.

Charles reversed the car. They were back on the main road.

"There's a lane coming up on the left," said Howard.

"I think I know where you mean. Here?"

"That's it. Go down to the end and then turn right."

They came to a sign. ASH FARM. STRICTLY PRIVATE. NO ADMITTANCE.

"We could leave the car here and go on foot," said Howard, nervously.

"Certainly not." The car bumped and skidded along. The tyres squelched in the mud. Charles swung the wheel from right to left but the car kept a straight course.

"Just about here," said Howard. "He should come out by that big tree."

Charles stopped the car. "In about five minutes," said Howard, looking at his watch.

"Here's company already," said Charles.

"Oh lord! That's the farmer." said Howard. "If he sees Jon there'll be trouble."

"No there won't. Just do what I say."

The farmer was a wiry little man with a weather - beaten face and small, pig - like eyes which peered from under a tweed cap. He strode towards them, splashing through the puddles.

"Can't you fucking read?" he demanded. "This is a private road."

"The answer to your strangely worded question is 'Yes'," said Charles. As to the subsequent statement, I know. Lord Charles Beresford. I live in Combleton."

"Oh. I didn't recognise the car, my lord," said the man, pulling off his cap.

"Understandable in view of the state of your road," Charles replied. "As it happens, one of the lads with whom I was driving thought he saw a sheep down near the station. I must say that I doubt it because neither Howard nor I saw it but he was so concerned that it might stray onto the railway line or the road that he determined to drive it up through the woods and we are waiting for him. Get out and see if you can see him, Howard. He may need help."

Howard smiled and got out of the car.

"Unlikely to be a sheep," said the man. "Sheep don't go off alone."

"Better be safe than sorry," said Charles. "You know what people are like where animals are concerned."

"Not all of 'em," said the man. "Some of those students are a bloody nuisance.

They seem to think they own the place. I've set the dogs on them many a time. And they reckon they're training to be farmers! They need to get their hands in a bit of cow shit once in a while. Farming! Ha! All they bloody do is stick bits of soil in tubes. They use bloody tweezers to do that with!"

To his left, out of the corner of his eye, Charles spotted Jon break out of the woods. Howard shouted something. For a moment, Jon stood as if transfixed. Then he turned and ran. Howard sprinted after him. Charles jumped out of the car. Howard caught up with Jon and held him fast.
"Was it a sheep?" Charles called.
"No. False alarm," Howard shouted.
"I thought as much," said the farmer, seemingly oblivious of the struggle going on. "Well, it's nice to have met you, your lordship. I must be getting back."

Charles shook the gnarled hand held out to him and ran down the slope. Jon was a powerfully built young man and it was all Howard could do to hold him.
"Take your fucking hands off me! You've done enough harm!" Jon shouted.
"Stop that!" Charles commanded. "You're safe now."

Somehow, they managed to get him, still struggling into the car. Once inside, he seemed to calm down.
"You'll feel better after a hot bath and a meal," said Charles when they arrived at the cottage.
"I can look after myself," Jon growled.
"Let me be the judge of that. I also strongly suggest that you get a good night's sleep at my place before going back."
"What about the rector? What about me?" Howard asked.
"Don't worry about that. I'll deal with him. You just show Jon the bathroom. His clothes are very wet. He can use my dressing gown. It's on the bathroom door."
"Don't worry. I'll find it," said Jon.
"Then leave your clothes outside the door. Howard can bring them down and we'll put them in the washing machine."

As Charles had predicted, the clothes were soaked. Charles made some coffee.
"Better do some sandwiches too," he said. "I'll bet he's starving."

They worked together. Howard buttered the bread. Charles produced a cold roast chicken. Just as they finished, they heard the bath water running away.

"Feel any better?" asked Charles as Jon entered the kitchen, shyly fastening the dressing gown.

"A bit," he said.

"Good. Now then, the first question is where is the other lad?"

"He's staying with his uncle," - and Jon gulped.

"Okay. Let's talk about him later. Have a sandwich. Come on. We'll take them into the lounge and eat them there."

As sandwich after sandwich disappeared, Jon seemed to recover his spirits.

"Jon. I want to say something. Are you listening?" asked Charles. Jon nodded.

"I know what happened yesterday. It wasn't your fault. Now I don't think you should go back to college until tomorrow but I do think we ought to let your father know you're okay. He's probably heard from the rector by now and under the impression that you're either missing or dead."

"Can I call him from here?"

"Of course you can."

"The number's in my purse in my jeans."

Howard went to the kitchen to retrieve it. "Here," said Jonathan, producing a card. Two fifty pound notes fluttered onto the floor. He scooped them up and stuffed them back in the purse. Charles took the card and walked over to the telephone. He dialled a number and handed the receiver to Jonathan.

"Hi dad," he said. "Yeah. I'm okay. Oh that? That was nothing. No I'm with a friend in his house in Combleton. Yeah he's er..." He turned, questioningly to Charles who mouthed his name. "Charles Beresford," he repeated. "Yeah, sure you can." He handed the phone back to Charles.

"Colonel Calder? Yes, Charles Beresford. Your son appears well able to manage his own affairs. He's certainly big enough but I wanted to suggest that he stay here overnight so that I can take him back to St. Frideswide's tomorrow. I know them all well up there. I'm anxious that, if he goes back alone, they'll make a mountain out of a molehill... Yes, I rather thought they may tell you that. Some would call it priestly zeal. More like crass stupidity. Suicide indeed! Good... Thank you, Colonel. No... No trouble at all. Goodbye."

He put down the receiver and turned to Howard and Jon. "What kind of idiot

Peter Gilbert

rings a man and tells him his son has run away from school and may well be suicidal?" he asked. "I shall have great pleasure some time when all this has blown over in speaking rather sharply to certain people."

They drank coffee and watched television. At eight o'clock, having eaten a huge meal cooked by Charles and Howard, they sat at the fireside. Charles spoke.
"Jonathan, something nasty happened didn't it?"

Jon nodded.
"I think you had better tell us everything. Every tiny detail. Can you do that?"

Jon nodded again. Charles produced his notebook and a pencil.

Jon cleared his throat. "Er, you know that some window cleaners or something saw us? Me and Howard and Stuart?"
"Yes. I know all about that bit. Carry on from there. Howard saw you go back to your house or whatever it's called. What happened after that?"

CHAPTER SEVEN

It had been Stuart's idea to get away. Both knew that if they stayed in the college, there would be problems. The drinking alone was regarded seriously enough to get them both suspended. Sex in the library office was likely to get them both sent down. Jon couldn't quite see how running away was going to help but Stuart had boasted often enough of his friends' and relations' huge influence. According to Stuart, this particular friend, a guy named Dennis, would certainly give them a bed for as long as they wanted: certainly as long as it took for the dust to settle. Jon knew enough of the ways of St. Frideswide's to know that might take a long time but it was just possible, he thought, that Stuart's friend might be able to fix things so he went along.

Dennis lived near London. The fare was no problem. Stuart had plenty of cash. Anyway, he said, Dennis would probably give them some money. He was very generous. Stuart had known him for years and years and regarded him as a sort of unofficial uncle.

They waited until all the other students had gone down to tea and then bolted, taking nothing with them. They dashed across the road and into the wood, slithering in the mud and squelching through the mulch of dead leaves. They arrived at the station just in time to catch the slow train to London.

They got off at the suburb where Dennis lived. It was still pouring with rain. Jon's only experience of living in a British town had been many years previously. His father had only been a Major then. It was a nice place. He remembered the Cadena Tea Rooms and the bank where the cashier always gave him a sweet. In contrast, the suburb where Stuart's uncle lived was an awful place. The rain made it even more depressing. Posters stuck on shop windows advertised extra cheap prices. Multi coloured curtains of streamers hung over the doors of innumerable betting shops and video parlours. Women in head scarves and men's raincoats pushed baby walkers adroitly round the piles of dog shit and fast-food wrappers on the sidewalks.

Dennis Singleton lived in a house at the end of a quiet side street. A powerstation nearby sent up clouds of steam from giant cooling towers. Stuart rang the doorbell.

Mr. Singleton was about forty - five. He was slim and had sandy hair. The first thing that Jon noticed about him was that one side of the man's mouth was lower than the other. It gave the extraordinary impression that everything he said had some sinister double meaning.
"I expect you'd like a cup of tea," uttered in that strange sidelong manner made even a cup of tea sound frightening. But that was offset by his jokes. Jon had never met anyone who knew so many jokes. Everything either of them said reminded Mr. Singleton of a joke. Some were good. Most of them were weak. All of them were childish and Jon had heard many of them before but, like Stuart, he laughed dutifully.

The house smelt musty, rather like an old church, and it was horribly untidy.
"Run away, eh?" said Mr. Singleton as they sipped the hot tea appreciatively, "Did you hear about the most amazing tortoise in the world? It ran away from the zoo. Ha Ha! Get it? Ran away?"

They told him about the drink. That reminded him of several more funny stories.
"It was a bit silly," he said, after a time, "but you won't get into too much trouble for that. You're both old enough to drink. Old enough for a good deal more, eh? Ha ha."

There seemed nothing for it. They had to tell him the whole story. He put down his cup and listened. There were no jokes now.
"So you were both naked?" he asked.
"Yes."
"And this other lad. This Howard. Was he undressed too?"
"Yes," said Jon, blushing.
"You had nothing on at all?"
"Only my chain. I never take that off," said Stuart.
"What were you actually doing?" Mr. Singleton leaned forward over the table.
"Well, I... er..." said Stuart.
"Howard was putting some cream in his ass," said Jonathan.

"He was going to...?"

Stuart nodded.
"And you were going to let him?"

He nodded again.
"Had he done that to you before?"
"No," said Stuart. "He wanted to but we both thought it was a bit dangerous to do something like that in the library office."
"Looks like you were right. How old is this Howard?"
"Nineteen."
"Mmm. Big lad is he? Well built and all that?"
"Pretty big," said Jon.
"He should have known better. And you, Jon. What were you doing?"
"I was just watching."
"It must have been quite a sight, especially if this Howard is as big as you say."

They both giggled and confirmed that Howard's cock was very large indeed. Mr. Singleton made a joke about a boa constrictor. When they had finished, he admitted that they were in a 'sticky position' which caused him to make mirthful reference to the cream and to add that they would have been even stickier if their activities had not been so suddenly abandoned.

Mr. Singleton said he would think over their plight and discuss possible action on the following day. It appeared that he was a photographer. He had an assignment at nine o'clock but, after that, he would be free.
"So... what would you like to do this evening?" he asked.
"Neither of them had any definite wish.
"We could go to the pool. It stays open till ten now."
"But we go to the pool every time I come here," Stuart protested.
"But you like it. And it's good for you. You don't get nearly enough exercise at that place. Except for just recently I mean." He sniggered.
"We haven't got swimming things with us," said Jonathan who hated swimming. "Anyway, it's a bit chilly."
"It's an indoor pool," said Mr. Singleton. "And there are loads of swimming trunks in the house. Stuart has a new pair almost every time he comes."
"You keep buying them for me. I don't ask for them," said Stuart.
"Same difference. Talking of trunks, did you hear the one about the elephant?"

Thus another five minutes passed. Five minutes which, in Jon's opinion, would have been better spent talking about their awful predicament. But when Mr. Singleton had finished he seemed to take it for granted that they were more than anxious to swim. A pair of trunks was selected for Jon and they set off in Mr. Singleton's battered old car.

"Aren't you going to swim too, Mr. Singleton?" Jonathan asked.

"Uncle Dennis never goes in the water. He just watches," Stuart explained.

The pool was part of an enormous leisure centre housing a bowling alley (which Jon would have preferred) squash courts, a restaurant and a bar. Mr. Singleton paid their entrance fees and made his way up the stairs to the bar.

They swam - or, at least, Stuart swam. Jon stayed in the shallow end. He hoped that Stuart's uncle would not stay too long. The windows of the bar overlooked the pool. He caught one or two glimpses of Mr. Singleton looking down at them. First he was alone and then he was with another man; a bald headed man with glasses. He saw them laughing and he reddened. Mr. Singleton was probably telling the other man the whole story.

"You could at least try to swim," said Stuart, sliding past him and hanging onto the rail.

"No thanks. When is your uncle likely to want to go home?"

"Who knows. He won't be too long. He'll wave when he's ready."

"He's with some other guy up there," said Jon gloomily. Experience of his father's fellow officers had taught him that men with drinks did not follow ordinary arithmetical laws. Two men might plough a field in half the time taken by one but give two men the same quantity of drink and you were in for a long wait.

"What other man?" asked Stuart.

"Bald headed guy with glasses."

"I've never seen him before," said Stuart looking up. He waved.

"Are you sure you don't want to swim?" he asked.

"Quite sure."

"Let's go and sit on the side then. We'd better stay within sight of the bar."

They clambered out of the water. There was really only one thing to talk about. Stuart maintained that his uncle would think of a way out. Jon, ever the more pragmatic of the two, couldn't imagine how. "I mean," he said, "He hasn't got any real influence, has he?"

"Don't worry. Just be nice to him and do what he says. He's really kind."

"He's just waved," said Jon, relieved. "Can we go home now?"

Stuart waved in the direction of the bar again. "That's it," he said. "Compulsory swim over. Let's get changed."

Mr. Singleton was waiting for them in the foyer. "Enjoy it?" he asked.
"Yes thanks," said Stuart. Jon said nothing.
"I expect you're both hungry aren't you?"
"Very," said Jon. Neither of them had eaten anything for hours.
"We'll get something on the way home," said Mr. Singleton. He stopped near a shabby looking restaurant with a sign: 'Take - Away - Pizzas'. "You'd better stay in the car," he said. "Try to keep your heads down. They might be looking for you already."

Jon shuddered. They crouched in the back of the car until Mr. Singleton emerged from the shop carrying three enormous boxes.
"There!" he said, passing them to the boys in the back of the car "Now for home!"

He drove the car straight into the garage which made it a bit difficult to climb out, but the boys were slim enough to negotiate the half-open doors.
"Don't want the neighbours to see you," he explained. He unlocked the door leading from the garage into the house and they trooped in. Jonathan carried the pizza boxes in front of him like some sort of ceremonial cushion.

They ate in front of the electric fire, breaking off chunks with their hands and stuffing the food into their mouths. Crumbs fell to the floor but Mr. Singleton didn't seem to mind.
"Nice to get something warm inside you, eh?" he asked, flicking his eyes from one of them to the other.
"You always say that," said Stuart, laughing.
"Well, it is. I know what lads like."
"Have you thought of a plan to help us yet, Mr. Singleton,?" asked Jonathan. Their predicament hadn't been mentioned for some time. He was afraid the man might not have understood the urgency.
"I was talking to a friend of mine about you only this evening," said Mr. Singleton.
"The bald guy with glasses?"
"Yes, that's him. He's going to think of something. He'll telephone tomorrow

morning. You'll go to stay with him for a few days and he'll sort something out."
"But that's too late!" Jonathan cried. "My dad will go crazy as soon as he hears I'm not at college. It's okay for Stuart. His folks are on a world cruise and they won't find out yet."

Mr. Singleton looked thoughtful. "I'm sure my friend will be able to pass them a message to say that you are safe," he said. He paused. "In good hands as you might say," he added, and smiled.
"I'll still be in the shit," said Jonathan, miserably.
"No you won't. Cheer up! Both finished? Good. We'll put the boxes in the bin and have something to drink."

The state of the kitchen made Jonathan very glad he hadn't eaten anything cooked at home. Dirty milk bottles were everywhere. A thickly encrusted deep-fat fryer stood on the cooker. Long brown trails ran down the refrigerator door and the trash can was overflowing.
"So, what do you want to do now?" asked Mr. Singleton when they were back in the lounge.
"Show Jon your photographs," said Stuart.
"Oh, I don't think he would like to see those," said his uncle. Jon caught the warning glance the man flashed to Stuart.
"I don't mind," he said. That look had made him curious.
"Oh, all right then. There are too many to see in one evening. I'll just bring down the latest ones."

He left the room and went upstairs. They heard a drawer open and a door slam. He re-entered the room carrying a large brown package. "When were you last here, Stuart?" he asked.
"About eight weeks ago."
"Then you won't have seen any of these. This one was nice. What do you think of him?" He passed a large black and white photograph to Stuart who studied it closely. Jon glanced over Stuart's arm, turned away and then stared back at the picture to make sure he wasn't dreaming. A young man stood with one foot on the floor and the other on a chair. He was smiling. He was also stark naked.
"He's a big lad isn't he?" said Mr. Singleton. "A very big boy. Take a look at this one." The same boy lay on a bed, holding his enormous, rigid cock. He was still smiling. His apparent lack of modesty made Jonathan blush.
"How old is he?" Stuart asked.

"Twenty one or twenty two. Here's another one of him, and another. I did about fifteen altogether."

Jonathan knew that he shouldn't look but couldn't help himself. One after another the pictures were handed to Stuart and then to him. The young man on a chair; the young man on the bed, facing the camera or sprawled on his stomach with his legs apart. The young man grinning and holding his gigantic cock. Then the same young man masturbating with his mouth open and, finally, grinning triumphantly as semen streamed down the thickly veined shaft of his penis.

"It's against the law to have pictures like this, isn't it?" asked Jonathan. Deep down, he was rather excited.

"Well, it is and it isn't if you know what I mean," said Stuart's uncle. "Providing nobody minds, it's all right."

"And Uncle gives them money and presents, don't you, Uncle?" said Stuart.

"I make sure they don't want for anything," he said.

"How much do you pay them?" asked Jonathan, genuinely curious.

"Peter got a hundred pounds for these."

"A hundred pounds!" A hundred pounds, to Jonathan, represented more than a month's allowance.

"Worth every penny," said Mr. Singleton. He gathered up the pictures. "Want to see any more?" he asked.

"I don't mind," said Jonathan. "Yes please," said Stuart.

The pile of photographs on Jonathan's side of the sofa grew. He began to feel strangely excited. He was quite sure that what Mr. Singleton had done was wrong but that was nothing to do with him. There could be no harm in looking at the pictures. At first he found Mr. Singleton's comments embarrassing but Stuart didn't seem to mind.

"How's this for a cock?" asked Mr. Singleton, passing a photograph over.

"It's huge!" said Stuart.

"And if you want to see a really classic ass, how about this one?"

"That's what you said about me in Yarmouth."

"Why... did you... er... I mean, did you have your picture taken?" asked Jonathan.

Both Dennis and Stuart laughed. "Hundreds!" said Stuart. "Show him, Uncle."

"They're upstairs. I'll get them." Once again, Mr. Singleton ascended the stairs.

"How much did he pay you?" asked Jonathan.
"Enough. And he gives me presents."

Mr. Singleton re - entered the room. "Here we are," he said. This time he was carrying three very large, thick books. "I keep Stuart's best pictures in an album," he said. "All bum in an album if you know what I mean."
"They're not the ones you took when we first met?" said Stuart.
"All of them."
"Don't show those to Jon. They're awful."
"No they're not. They're nice. Move over."

They made room for him on the sofa. "This is the very first set I did," he said, opening one of the albums. "He was pretty young then - and I mean pretty."
"Uncle came to the house to talk to my dad," Stuart explained. "That's how we met."

Stuart's face smiled shyly up from the photograph. He was standing, naked, by a vase of flowers.

There were many more. Stuart with a model aeroplane; Stuart on a deserted beach; Stuart bending over to smell a flower...
"Show him the latest ones, Uncle. I look awful in these," said Stuart.
"No you don't. They're good pictures."
"That's what you think. I wish you'd tear them up."
"Certainly not! Anyway, this is Stuart last year, Jon."

Stuart stood, naked, on a river bank. His penis pointed outward and upward, parallel to the rod. A row of trout lay on the ground beside him.
"We bought them," said Stuart. "All I caught was a cold. Have you got the ones you took in Yarmouth, Uncle?"

Mr. Singleton handed him an album. "We had to stay in a hotel, see?" Stuart explained. "This is a good one of me, don't you think?" The picture showed Stuart lying on his side on a double bed with his legs splayed apart. The gold chain was clearly visible as it was in all the subsequent shots. From the way Stuart was fingering it in several of the pictures, Jon guessed it had been bought that weekend.
"And we met Pierre. He was a French waiter in the hotel," said Stuart. "He

was nice. Look, this is him."
Stuart was lying on the bed. Next to him was a dark haired, smiling young man with a considerable erection.

A strange feeling of warmth came over Jonathan as he looked at the picture. It wasn't the electric fire. If anything, the room was a bit chilly. He thought Pierre looked nice. It would be nice to have a friend like that. Howard was nice but there was something about Pierre that fascinated him.
"Do you still see him?" he asked.
"No. He ran away from the hotel a few days after Uncle took the pictures. The hotel said he went without even collecting his wages. "
"Homesick," said Mr. Singleton. "That must have been the reason. You were a good boy that weekend, Stuart. Are you going to be a good boy tonight?"
"If you want. What about Jon?"
"That's up to Jon. I never force anyone."
"You mean... have my picture taken like these?" asked Jon.
"Yes."
"No. I'd rather not. I don't mind watching though."
"As you wish. What does Stuart think?"
"He's seen me starkers before. I don't mind," said Stuart. "Why don't you have a go, Jon? It's worth it. You'd pay him wouldn't you, Uncle?"
"Sure."
"A hundred pounds?" said Jonathan. He was already beginning to see his father in Scotland as a more effective saviour than Mr. Singleton. He would need money for the fare.
"More if you're really co-operative. What do you say?"
"Who would see them?"
"Only you and me and possibly Stuart. They're private."

Jonathan couldn't help wondering if he had said the same thing to Pierre and to the other boys. The man was obviously lying but a hundred pounds was a hundred pounds. He allowed himself to be persuaded and reluctantly followed Stuart and Mr. Singleton up the stairs. A hundred pounds would get him to Scotland. It was going to be an unpleasant confrontation but it had to be done...

What, in a normal house, would have been the back bedroom was a studio. True, there was a bed; a large one, but it was surrounded by lights, cameras and things like silver umbrellas on stands.
"You two get ready while I set up," said Mr. Singleton and he began to busy

himself with his equipment as if they were not there.

Another plan began to form in Jonathan's mind as he undressed. There was going to be trouble. There was no doubt about that but what if he went back to college first? Then he could say, 'Look Dad, I'm sorry I ran away. That was dumb. But then I went to the college and I faced the music...' And then what? 'I've been slung out?' He didn't know what to do...

They were both undressed. Only a few hours previously, they had both been in a similar state in the college library and everything was looking so good.

"My word! You are a big lad, Jon," said Mr. Singleton approvingly. "Turn round."

Jonathan did so. He flinched as a hand landed on his butt. "Hmm," said Mr. Singleton. "That Howard certainly knows how to pick 'em. " The hand slid down his thigh. "Nice hairy legs. Makes all the difference. You ready Stuart? I'll do you first."

Stuart climbed onto the bed. Jonathan watched, amazed, as Mr. Singleton produced a comb, combed Stuart's hair and then pushed him back on to the bed and began to comb his pubic hair. Stuart said not a word, seemingly accepting the process as quite normal. Mr. Singleton turned on the lights. They were blindingly bright. He moved round the bed adjusting them. He kept peering through the view-finder, making more adjustments, checking again. Stuart lay patiently waiting. Finally, everything was ready.

"Off you go Stuart. Give me some little wriggles first. Good lad! Nice one. Good. Oh yes!"

Stuart writhed around on the bed like someone suffering from convulsions. The camera buzzed and clicked.

"That's nice. Let's have your hand on it. That's it! Get it up for me. Nicely."

Stuart played with his cock and smiled at the camera. Slowly, it began to rise. Mr. Singleton stopped to change a film. Stuart didn't. By the time the camera was working again, his cock was steel-hard. Jonathan was fairly sure he wouldn't be able to get a hard-on when his turn came. Mr. Singleton would have to make do with a limp one.

"Oh yes! Don't finish it off. Turn over for me. That's right. Oh yes. Lift it up a bit. Nice one. Open your legs for me. I want to get right in there. Lovely.

Okay. That's enough. Jon's turn."

Reluctantly, Jonathan climbed onto the bed and Stuart stood near one of the lamps. They were so bright that Jonathan couldn't see anything beyond the bed. Mr. Singleton's voice came out of the darkness.

"Try and do what Stuart was doing Jon. That's it. Just fling yourself around. That's lovely."

It was rather like doing some strange form of physical exercise. Jonathan's arms and legs began to ache slightly.

"Lovely! Keep on doing that. That's a nice one. Good! Open your legs a bit more. Let's have a good shot of those balls. That's it. Now play with it for me."

"I don't think I can..."

"Yes you can. That's nice. Keep that left hand out of the way."

Jon closed his eyes for a moment. What should he think about? Well, there was Howard of course. He wondered what Howard was doing at that moment. Perhaps he was at home, having been sent down. He shuddered. No... forget college and expulsions but keep thinking about Howard...

Howard and Jonathan by a river like the one in the picture of Stuart... A hot day. Howard wants to swim. Helping Howard to undress. Taking off his jeans; sliding his shorts down. Howard's cock standing up.

"Aren't you going to swim too Jon?"

"No, I'll watch."

"Get undressed. The sun will do you good."

Howard undressing him. Howard kissing his stomach. Howard taking it into his mouth. Howard sucking it. Howard's fingers playing on his balls...

"Oh yes! That's nice. Keep on. Lovely. Don't finish. Turn over for me."

Jonathan did so. Now Howard was under him. Howard, the boy who had got him into trouble. Fuck Howard! Yes, that was it. Fuck Howard. Really drive it into him. Make Howard yell. Push it right into his ass. Show him who's boss! It wouldn't be long now. He felt himself sweating just as he had in the library office.

"Lovely. Well done. Thanks Jon."

Reality again. He turned over and blinked.

"What about a few of the two of you?" asked Mr. Singleton.

"I don't mind," Stuart's voice came from somewhere near Jonathan's head. "How about you, Jon?"

"Uh huh?" Jonathan wasn't really concentrating. He felt Stuart getting onto the bed and then Stuart's hand running down his front. It clasped his cock. The camera began to buzz again. He reached down and found Stuart's. It was still remarkably hard. Stuart moaned slightly.

"Shall we try the real thing?" Stuart whispered.

"What real thing?"

"You know. What Howard wanted to do."

"To me you mean?"

"Yes."

"No thanks."

"You could do it to me."

"We haven't got any of that stuff."

"Stop whispering. Let's have some action!" said a disembodied voice from the darkness.

Stuart knelt on the bed. Jonathan got into position.

"Aha! That's what we need. Oh yes! Lovely!"

Jonathan grasped Stuart's hips and pushed forward. He was nowhere near the right place but it felt good and Stuart was enjoying it. There was no doubt about that!

"Oh that feels good!" said Stuart.

"Nicely. Take it slowly." said Mr. Singleton.

"Do it to me. Do it to me!" Stuart moaned.

Mr. Singleton said nothing but the camera buzzed and clicked frantically, seemingly from several different directions.

Jonathan put his hands right round Stuart's middle and felt his friend's cock. He pumped away. Sometimes Stuart was Stuart. Sometimes he was Howard. Nothing mattered now. He was sweating. He felt it dribbling down his face. Any minute now... any minute. "I'm... I'm coming!" he gasped. It streamed out of him. He let go of Stuart and watched it dribble down on to the bedspread. There was nothing he could do to stop it. The bedspread would be ruined. "I'm sorry," he said.

"Don't be sorry. That was great. Finish Stuart off. Let's see the spunk running."

Jonathan didn't really want to. An awful feeling of guilt overwhelmed him. So much for the resolution he had made in the train never to do anything like that again.

"Come on Jon," said Stuart. Jon took his friend's cock in his hand again and did what was asked of him, as quickly as possible.

"Oh! Ah! Oh! Nice! Oh! Ah! Here it... comes!" Semen flooded over Jonathan's fingers and splashed on to the bed.

"Lovely. Well done both of you!" said Mr. Singleton.

"When do I get paid?" Jonathan asked.

Mr. Singleton laughed. "Mercenary young man!" he said. "Get cleaned up and come downstairs. I'll give it to you then."

They showered together, dressed and went downstairs. Mr. Singleton opened a steel box which he took from the sideboard and handed over a hundred and twenty pounds. A hundred and twenty pounds! It was more money than Jonathan had ever held at one time. Stuart received nothing but seemed quite happy. Jonathan guessed he would get a present later that day. Another gold chain perhaps? After all, Stuart didn't actually need money.

Mr. Singleton suggested that Stuart should sleep in the box room and Jonathan in the studio. "That bed is made up," he said. "Be careful not to knock anything over, won't you?"

Jonathan would have preferred them both to sleep in the studio. The bed was big enough. Stuart made no comment and he thought it might seem forward to suggest it so he, too said nothing.

"I'll be up till late developing the pictures," said Mr. Singleton. "I've got an outside assignment first thing in the morning so I'll be up before you. Sleep well."

They said good night. "He's not so bad, is he?" said Stuart as they parted on the upstairs landing.

"No.. Not bad. Look, Stuart, I need to talk to you. Come in the studio for a minute."

"No... I'd better not. Uncle likes me to sleep in the box-room."

"It won't take a minute."

"Tell me in the morning."

Jon went into the studio. He peeled back the bedspread carefully. The wet patches were all too apparent. Carefully avoiding the cables which snaked all over the floor, he climbed into bed. It had been an eventful day. He spent some moments thinking it over and wondering what to do. Then he was in a train heading for Scotland, being pursued along the track by a man with a camera. Men on ladders peered into the compartment and a bird with Howard's features flew overhead.

He didn't know what woke him but, aware of a need to have a pee, he climbed out of bed and went to the bathroom. On the way back he noticed that the box-room door was open. He peered in. The bed was empty. That was odd. For a moment he wondered if Stuart had forestalled him and run away but then he heard voices coming from the big front bedroom. It sounded as if Stuart was in pain. He heard Mr. Singleton's voice, speaking in comforting tones. Poor old Stuart, he thought. He was subject to nightmares at college and often cried out in the night. He must have had a bad one. Jonathan thought no more of it and went back to bed.

He woke early the next morning. Mr. Singleton had already gone. There were two bowls on the table, together with a packet of cereal, a bowl of sugar and a half-full milk bottle. A note propped against the bottle said 'Back about 11.' He ate some cereal. The house seemed eerily silent. A portable radio, obviously many years old, stood on a shelf but he couldn't get it to work.

He went upstairs. Stuart's door was shut now. He tapped. No answer. He knocked again.
"Who is it?" came Stuart's sleepy voice.
"Me. Jon. Are you getting up?"
"Not yet."
"Can I come in?"
"The door's not locked."

He opened the door. Stuart looked up at him through half-closed eyes. "What's the time?" he asked.
"Half-past eight. Your uncle's gone out. Stuart, I think we ought to go back to college."
"We can't. We'd only be sent down."
"Sure. But our folks are going to hear about it sooner or later, aren't they? We might just as well go back."

Jonathan was sure he was right. He'd spent a long time thinking about it. "My mum and dad are away on the cruise until the middle of August," said Stuart. "They won't worry anyway. They never did think much of St. Fred's."
"Well, mine will go frantic. I'm going back," said Jonathan.
"Uncle Dennis won't like it."
"I can't think why. He'll have one less runaway to worry about."
"He's made plans for both of us."
"Well, say 'Thanks' from me but I'm going back. What shall I say about you? They're bound to ask."
"Don't say anything. Tell them we split up in London."
"Are you sure you're going to be all right?"
"Oh, I'll be okay. You get used to anything in time."
"I'll see you when you eventually get back then," said Jonathan. He was still hoping that his friend might change his mind.
"Don't count on it. Don't start organising any parties for me."
"Well... er... I'll see you sometime," said Jonathan. He felt horribly guilty at leaving Stuart but then, he thought, Mr. Singleton was his uncle - or as good as. Stuart would be all right.

He let himself out of the house. Once again, he trudged past the dismal houses, the take-away food shop and the video shops, fearful all the time that the old Renault would draw up alongside him.

He bought a ticket and sat on a bench on the platform. The next train to Combleton was due in a hundred minutes. He had plenty of time to think things over.

He decided not to report to Father Ramburton. The rector was the boss of the entire college. When his dad visited the college he always went straight to the rector. "Always go straight to the top," he had said.

So... the rector it would be. He was bound to know what had happened in the library office but Jonathan wouldn't mention that straightaway. After all, he didn't know what Howard had said. Howard must have been sent for. If he had confessed everything, then Jonathan was in deep trouble; not only with the school. He felt terrible about letting his dad down but after all, the sex business had been Howard's idea, not his. Howard was a strange guy. It would certainly be better, he thought, to avoid Howard in future if they let him stay on at the college. That would be his dad's advice. It was a pity because he liked Howard and sex with Howard was considerably more satisfying than a lonely wank in a creaking bed. But, there was no doubt about it. He'd been stupid to have gone along with it.

On the other hand, he was sick of having his life run by other people. First his parents, then the priests at St. Frideswide's. It was time people knew the truth. He was nineteen now; old enough to know that this wasn't just a phase which people went through.

"I can't help being what I am. Whose life is it anyway?" he said, unconsciously mouthing the words that Colonel Calder was to hear. The rather dowdy old lady sitting next to him looked up from the magazine she was reading and then moved to another bench.

The train came in. A newspaper lay on an empty seat. Jonathan scanned it anxiously but there was nothing about missing students. He read the rest of it, even the advertisements, during the long, boring journey.

At Combleton he decided to take the short cut and headed up the chalk path to the woods. He pushed through the bushes, becoming more and more nervous with each step. He reached the PRIVATE sign, ducked under the barbed wire and froze. Somebody was coming down the hill towards him. Somebody from the college or the farmer?

"It's okay. It's only me," said an all too familiar voice. Howard! He was trapped. It was like a nightmare. Going back to college was a mistake. He wanted to go home. Home was the only safe place. He turned and ran, stumbling, down the hill.

CHAPTER EIGHT

"It seems to me," said Charles, putting down his pencil, "that our priority is to rescue Stuart - after returning Jonathan college and safety."

"But he doesn't want to be rescued," said Jon.

"Whether he wants to or not, he must be," Charles replied. "That lad is in danger."

"Do you really think so?"

"Indeed I do. Anyway, Jonathan, you look shattered. Why don't you go to bed? Don't worry about tomorrow. I'll run you back to college and sort out that fool of a rector."

"I think I will," said Jon, standing up. "Thank you very much, er... my lord."

"Charles will do. Let me show you where everything is."

They went upstairs, leaving Howard in the lounge. He looked over Charles' notes and was still browsing through them when the man returned.

"I see you think the same as I do about Stuart's so-called nightmare," said Howard. Charles had written 'Stuart yelled out from Dennis' room. Nightmare???'

"I'm afraid so. I think that was what Stuart was referring to when he said he would get used to it. Anyway, this needs our friend."

"Our friend?"

"Simon. He must have some acquaintance with the underworld to be able to turn out those books of his. Get him on the phone, Howard. Get him down here fast. Hunting down scum like Singleton and his bald headed friend needs his brain."

"Wouldn't it be better for you to speak to him?"

"Certainly not. I shall make some more coffee. I happen to know that he would appreciate a word with you."

Howard dialled the number. He waited for some time and was about to put the phone down when a voice said, "Yes?"

"Simon?"

"Howard!"

"I didn't disturb you, did I?"

"No matter."

"I'm ringing from Charles' house."

"Oh yes."

As briefly as he could, he gave Simon Charles' message and gave an outline of what had happened, omitting his own part.

"What's the time now, Howard?"

"Just after ten o'clock."

"Tell Charles I'll be there in time for breakfast. How are you?"

"I'm okay."

"Mark rang the other day. He's desperately worried about you. He hasn't heard from you for so long."

"Well, I've been quite busy."

"I see. Will you be around tomorrow?"

"You bet!"

"See you tomorrow morning then."

"Tomorrow," Howard repeated. He put the phone down.

"Is he coming?" Charles called from the kitchen.

"He says he'll be here for breakfast."

"He'll have to make it himself then."

"I could stay overnight and do it. The college wouldn't mind," said Howard.

Charles came into the room. "I trust you completely, Howard," he said, "but if that lad tells them that he spent the night under the same roof as you, it would look a bit questionable, don't you think?"

Howard blushed. "I suppose it would," he said.

"When you've finished your coffee, I'll drive you back. If you can get down here tomorrow, you're welcome here at any time."

"I'll be here. Where do you think Stuart is tonight?"

"God only knows. Come on. I don't want to be long in case Jonathan has second thoughts.

———

Howard learned before breakfast that the emergency meeting of governors to discuss his case had been called off. What the others said about Stuart must have been true. It was Jonathan the college was really concerned about. He was supposed to call on his tutor to hear the news officially but concern for Father Sebastian's prayer life prevented him from knocking at his door so early in the morning. One more day would make little difference. He set off down the lane. The sun shone between racing clouds. Dead leaves swirled round his foot, blown in eddies by the cool wind.

Simon's car was standing in the drive. The wheel arches were spattered with mud and the windscreen was covered in filth save for the semi - lunar eyes where the windscreen wipers had swept it.

He rang the bell. Simon answered the door.
"Howard!" he exclaimed. "No lectures?"
"I'll tell you in a minute. Is Charles up yet?"
"You must be joking. There are vague sounds of movement upstairs though."
"That's probably Jonathan."
"And who is Jonathan?"
"He's one of the lads who ran away. Charles is going to take him back this morning. Have you had breakfast?"
"I made myself a cup of coffee."
"I'll do you one. I expect Jon will want one too. One egg or two? Scrambled or fried?"
"Two. Scrambled please. Shall I go and tell this Jonathan person?"
"No. Better not. He's had a nasty experience. Another strange man might upset him. I'll go up when this is ready."

Howard went into the kitchen. In no time the smell of bacon, sausages and mushrooms permeated the house. Somebody flushed the upstairs toilet.
"How did you get in, Si?" Howard called from the kitchen.
"He leaves the spare key in the hollow stone outside. He always does."
"That's dangerous."
"Not round here. I wouldn't do it in Hardwick St. Mary but nothing ever happens in Combleton. Anyway, would you like to tell me why you're not in lectures?"
"Promise you won't get angry? The rector had a go at me. My tutor has and I don't think Charles is very happy either."
"Promise. Keep talking as you cook. I'll sit here and listen."

Howard told the whole story. He held nothing back. He told him about Jon and Stuart; about his night - time vigils at the library office window. And then, as he scooped Simon's breakfast onto a plate, he told him of the events of Sunday afternoon. Simon picked up a knife and fork and began to eat.

"Well?" asked Howard.

"It's delicious."

"I mean what do you think of me?"

"My opinion doesn't matter. It's Mark I worry about. I possibly shouldn't say this but Mark had a chat with me at the hotel. He was genuinely worried."

"He's so possessive," said Howard.

"And you both fly off the handle at a moment's notice."

Howard would have liked to continue the conversation but clumping footsteps on the stairs announced the arrival of Jonathan.

"Just in time for breakfast," said Howard. "Did you sleep well?"

"Yes thanks."

"This is Simon Spencer. He's a friend of Lord Charles."

Jon extended a hand. "Hi, Mr. Spencer," he said.

"Simon to you," said Simon, shaking his hand'. They ate in silence whilst Howard cleaned the frying-pan.

"I enjoyed 'Blood on his Hands', Si," he said. "It's one of your best."

"Thank you."

"Excuse me, " said Jonathan, putting down his knife and fork, "Are you *the* Simon Spencer? Did you write 'Murderous Mission'?"

"Yes, that's me. It wasn't one of my best I'm afraid."

"Wow! I mean...Gee!"

"Have you read it then?" Simon asked.

"Loads of times. And most of the others. You can't put them down, can you?"

"That's very kind of you to say so, Jon. Thank you. Which one do you like the best?"

"I think 'Clayton of the Corps'."

"Because it's about the U S Marines?"

"Not just that, no. I think I like it because Clayton is kind of awkward and he does loads of wrong things but then right at the end he rescues his buddies. I liked the bit about his dog too."

Howard smiled to himself. A few weeks ago he had been just as effusive when he first met Simon. Soon, Simon and Jon were chatting like two old friends.

"Is that your car outside, Simon?" Jon asked.

"Yes."

"Beautiful! It's a bit dirty though. I hope you don't mind me saying so."

"Not at all. It was a dirty night for driving."

" How about if I come down this afternoon and clean it for you." Jon hung his head slightly. "Actually, I might not be able to," he said and gulped. "I might not even be..."

Simon leapt to his feet and put both hands on Jon's hunched shoulders. "I know what happened, Jon," he said. "Nothing is going to happen. You might get ticked off for drinking but that's all. Charles is going to see to it. You can trust him."

At which point the man himself appeared.

"Good morning everybody," he said with a yawn. "I must say it's nice to have guests in the house. Did you sleep well, Jon?"

"Yes thank you."

"Have you had some breakfast?"

"Howard made it for me."

"That was good of you, Howard," said Charles.

"Nobody's asked me if I slept well or had my breakfast," said Simon with a laugh.

"I'm the only person here who has any concern for you, Si," said Howard.

"And me. I'm going to clean his car this afternoon - I hope," said Jon.

"Good for you. If you're ready, I think we should go straight up to the college and see the rector."

Jon nodded reluctantly and followed Charles out of the house. Simon and Howard stood at the window and watched the car vanish up the road.

"I hope he's going to be okay," said Howard.

"He will be - and that's the nicest thing you've said so far. Charles will put things right. We just have to find the other one. What did Jon say about him?"

"He told us the whole story. Charles made notes. Here they are."

Simon sat on the sofa, put on his little reading glasses and began to read. "I think you're going to have to fill me in on details," he said. "These are pretty vague."

Between them, they reconstructed Jon's story. "Do we have this Singleton man's address or telephone number?" asked Simon, flicking through the pages.

"I don't think Charles asked. We just know the name of the place."

"Typical!" said Simon. "A missing eighteen-year-old last seen in a house near London and he doesn't even bother to ask for the address."

"He was worried," said Howard. "He didn't know what to do. That's why he asked you to come."

"I'm glad he did."

"Do you think you'll be able to find him?"

"If he's still in that house, yes. If not, it'll be much more difficult. What do you know about Stuart's family?"

"Away on a cruise. Pots of money apparently. His dad runs 'Cut - Price'."

"Then we're in with a chance. The police wouldn't be in the least interested in an ordinary student going missing. In this case they'll suspect kidnapping for a ransom."

"And it's all my fault," said Howard ruefully.

"A disputable opinion. You didn't force them to do anything and, young as they are, they're old enough to make their own decisions as to what constitutes a pleasant way of spending a Sunday afternoon. Aha! Here's Charles."

They heard the car door slam. Charles stood at the front door for some time, fiddling with his keys.

"Well, that's done," he said when he had finally gained entry.

"How did it go?" asked Howard.

"Oh, all right. He got a rocket for drinking and a sermon about sex and now he's back in his tutor-group.. So, according to the rector, should you be. I said you were actively helping to get the other lad back, about whom, incidentally, he seemed strangely unconcerned. One gathers that Stuart Lynch is not his favourite student."

"Did Jon tell him about Mr. Singleton?"

"Jon, on my advice, said nothing. Your rector was so relieved to get him back that he didn't even think to ask where he had been."

"That's typical," said Howard.

"And is Jon coming down this afternoon?" asked Simon.

"Yes. At three o'clock."

"Good. We need Singleton's address."

"I didn't think to ask."

"I know you didn't. Now I suggest we all go into town. I've got some shopping to do and we can have lunch in the George."

It was an interesting lunch. Several times Howard found himself thinking, not about Stuart's plight but about Simon and Charles. They teased each other unmercifully and laughed both at each other and themselves and both seemed to exude an aura of total happiness in each other's company. His grandparents had the same effect on him.

"Do you think you and Mark will get together again, Howard?" asked Simon.

"I don't know. It's just that he's so possessive. I mean... I wouldn't mind if he did what I've been doing. Being with Mark is like being married to him."

"How would you honestly feel if he did have a lot of sexual experience with other people?"

"I don't think I'd mind - providing he told me about it."

"You've got your beady eyed look, Simon," said Charles. "May one enquire what's going on in your devious mind?"

"Ferrets."

"I beg your pardon?"

"Ferrets. It's something an old countryman told me once. If you've lost a ferret down a hole, you send another one after him. Assuming that friend Singleton has passed Stuart down the line - which I am sure he has - we are going to have to send someone young and attractive along the same path. Now it can't be Howard..."

"I don't see why not," said Howard.

"Because your parents are paying a vast sum to St. Frideswide's to look after you and keep you away from the seamy side of this world. Adam and Ben are out. They would want to be together and I think our man wouldn't like that. But Mark is single and unattached and remarkably good looking."

"He wouldn't help," said Howard. "He'd see it as doing something to help me get out of a mess. The mess he told me to get out of before this happened. All you'll get out of Mark is 'I knew this would happen.'"

Simon smiled over his brandy glass. "There are times," he said, "when I wonder if you and I know the same young man. He'd do anything to help you."

It was a nice thing to say. Howard was convinced it wasn't true but he found himself mulling over the words all the way home in the back of Simon's car.

At three o'clock that afternoon, Jonathan was at the door. "They let me come," he said. "Shall I start now? Do you have a hose or a bucket?"

"I've got a question for you first," said Simon. "Do you know the telephone number or the address of this man Singleton?"

It was obvious from his expression that Jonathan had temporarily forgotten all about Stuart. "Er.. Anscott Way. Number fourteen. I don't know the phone number," he said.

"Good. Now let's have a go at the car."

"No. I'll do that," said Charles. "You get on with your detective work." He went out with Jon.

Simon picked up the telephone and dialled Directory Enquiries. "Let's hope he's not ex directory," he said. He gave the name and address and waited and then wrote down a number.

"Your turn Howard," he said. "Putting on your youngest, most exuberant voice, call this number and ask to speak to Stuart. If he asks who you are, tell him you're a friend from college. If he asks you how you got hold of the number, Stuart gave it to you."

Howard looked out of the window as he dialled the number. Charles and Jon were laughing and chatting as, together, they washed Simon's car. Jon didn't seem to have a care in the world. The badly upset young man of the previous day might well have been someone else. Just those long legs and pert bottom remained the same... "Hello. Dennis Singleton here." The man's voice sounded thin and reedy. Howard repressed his thoughts and spoke.

Stuart, said Mr. Singleton, had indeed been there and stayed over Sunday night with a friend. The friend had left early. He had personally taken Stuart to the station and seen him onto the Combleton train on Monday afternoon.

Howard relayed the information to Simon.

"Just as I thought," said Simon.

"We could make enquiries at his local station. That was Charles' idea. He said the railway men would remember."

"He's made very certain they remember," said Simon grimly. "See the boy onto a train and provide him with a change of clothes. He changes in the train and steps out at an intermediate station where the next man in the chain is waiting for him. It's the oldest trick in the book. However, it's worth following up. I'll get Joan on to it."

Joan was Simon's indispensable researcher. Simon dialled the number. "Hello, you old bag!" he said. "Job for you. Very urgent. I'd like to know today.

Can you go to Southwood station for me? I'm on the trail of a missing student. Hang on..." He picked up Charles' notebook. "Age eighteen. I've got someone with me who can give you a better description than I can. Apparently seen onto a train bound for Combleton yesterday afternoon and didn't arrive. The man who put him on the train is described here as having sandy hair and something wrong with the side of his mouth. Thanks dear. Here's Howard."

As carefully as he could, Howard described Stuart. He heard a keyboard clicking at the other end. He opened the window and called to Jon who said that Stuart had been wearing jeans and a sports top.
"She shouldn't take long," said Simon. "She's got a car. How's mine looking?" He pulled back the curtain and looked out of the window. Jon and Charles were both working on it, getting thoroughly wet in the process and obviously enjoying themselves.
"I think your friend Jonathan has made a hit," he said.
"You don't think that Charles..."
"I don't know. It's none of our business."
"Charles wouldn't, would he?"
"Why should it worry you if he did?"
"Well, it would be wrong. Immoral."

Simon laughed. "I rather think I've given you cause for thought, old Howard," he said. "Do you fancy a pint down at the Green Dragon?"
"Sure. We can discuss plans."

Joan called just before they left. Howard took the call. Simon was outside admiring his gleaming car.
"He seems to have made a bit of a nuisance of himself," she said, referring to Mr. Singleton. "He asked loads of silly questions about the train. The ticket clerk, the platform supervisor and the woman in the newspaper kiosk all remember the pair well. He bought a platform ticket and a second class ticket to Combleton. The young man with him was carrying a blue sports bag."
"That's them," said Howard. "Thank you very much."
"Don't mention it. It all goes on Simon's bill. Give him my love."
"I will. Thanks again."
"Definitely and absolutely not," said Jonathan when they had come in. "He didn't have a bag. He told me not to pack anything. He said it would look suspicious. He said his uncle would buy any clothes we needed if we were away for longer than a day or so."

"Which uncle has done," said Simon grimly. "A complete new outfit."

Charles excused himself and Jonathan from going to the Green Dragon. He felt, he said, rather tired after washing the car and thought that he and Jon could spend the early part of the evening watching television. Howard tried to persuade him to come on to the pub later after dropping Jon off at college.
"No, I'll have an early night. It's going to be a busy day tomorrow."
"I wasn't thinking of doing much tomorrow," said Simon. "I'll ring the lads this evening but I don't expect they'll be free until the weekend."
"Oh, Jon and I have a lot to do," said Charles. "Haven't we, Jon?"

Jon grinned. "We sure have!" he said.

CHAPTER NINE

"This place must be the asshole of the world," Adam observed.
"Then I'm surprised you don't like it," said Mark.

Adam ignored the joke and looked down the length of the huge pool. "No, honestly," he said, "did you ever see so many unattractive people? The pool back home is worth going to but this... ugh!"
"Well, we have to stay here until Singleton turns up so we may as well make the best of it."
"If Singleton turns up."
"Simon said his research assistant has checked carefully and he always comes here on Saturdays."

Adam shaded his eyes with his hand and looked up at the windows of the bar. There were one or two people there; couples mostly. He guessed they were parents looking down at their children. There was no sign of a sandy haired man.

From his vantage point, further down the pool, Ben had come to the same conclusion. Lazily, he swam back to the other two.
"He doesn't seem to be there yet," he said.
"I know," Adam replied. Ben heaved himself out of the water. "Phew!" he said. "It's ages since I swam."
"It's very good for the muscles," said Adam. "You'll be more enjoyable than ever later on."
"That's if we get there. We can't leave Mark until he's made contact. That's what Simon said."
"Let's hope he makes contact soon. The idea of spending a night in the Bricklayers' Arms - even with you - is not pleasant."
"I've got to stay there all the time," said Mark.
"You haven't got to at all. Simon made that clear. You volunteered."

"Well, I can't let Howard down. This lad has got to be found."

"We'll think of you as we lie in our luxurious bed in our five star hotel," said Adam.

"Thanks a lot."

"Still no sign of him," Ben observed.

"Well, when he comes he can have a sight of the nicest ass in the world," said Adam, turning over on to his front.

"You always said mine was," Ben replied.

"Yours is   functional and comfortable but it lacks the compact tightness of mine."

One never knew with Adam whether he was serious or not. There was, thought Ben, much truth in what he said and the yellow swimming trunks Simon and Charles had bought for Adam that afternoon set it off to perfection. A thrill went through him as he thought of the forthcoming evening. Those perfectly toned muscles would be brought into action. He, too, turned over - not so much to show off his own broader buns as to disguise his excitement. Mark sat next to them glancing up to the bar every few minutes.

"That lifeguard is rather nice, don't you think?" Ben asked.

"Not bad," Adam replied.

"I should have thought he was very much your sort. Nice legs. A big cock too by the look of his shorts."

"The problem with very big cocks," said Adam, "is that their owners are all too often ugly."

"Speaking from experience?" Mark asked.

"You could say that. Some of the guys in the football team are well endowed but they're not very appetising. One day I shall write a book on the subject. Now, you see that chap standing on the side down there?"

"Yes," said Ben, who had been looking in that direction for some minutes.

"Now he would have a perfect cock. I can almost guarantee it. A good six inches of stiff bliss. He's pretty young so he doesn't drink much. I'll bet he tastes superb. Quite a nice little ass too. The awful shame is that it will probably never be used."

"You're disgusting!" Mark observed.

"I don't see anything disgusting about admiration. Now were I to..."

"He's here," said Ben, interrupting them. "I just caught a glimpse of him at the window."

"You're sure it's the right guy?"

"Well he has sandy hair. It's impossible to see his mouth from this distance."

Adam turned over again and spread his legs slightly. "Get a good look at that," he whispered. "Come and lie down, Mark. You're the bait. Not us."
"It would be funny if he took a fancy to that other guy instead of me," said Mark. In fact, he thought, it would be a great relief. He had said nothing to the other two but he was scared. He kept telling himself that he was doing it for Howard but that didn't stop his heart from thumping or his mouth from feeling dry.

He lay on his front and could just see the lower part of the bar window. The chairs were red. He watched as one of them was propelled nearer the window.

Ben sat up and crossed his legs "He's moved right up to the window," he announced. "He's got a beer in his hand."
"We'll give him about ten minutes," said Adam. Then, by the time we've changed he should have drunk it. Is he watching us?"
"Yes."
"Then here goes." He stroked Ben's back.
"Don't make it too obvious. There are other people around," said Mark.
"I couldn't care less. I shan't be coming here again and Ben likes it."

"He's interested," said Ben. "He's watching us."
"Give him a smile," said Adam. Ben did so.
"Ha! He waved," he said.
"Good. I'll have a quick swim and then we'll get changed." He stood up and dived into the water. Watching Adam swim was a revelation. It was, thought Ben, like watching something released into its natural element. Adam cut through the water. His speed seemed effortless. Several people turned to watch him. He swam six lengths and then climbed out of the water.
"Right," he said. "Let's go."

They got changed, rolled their new bathing trunks into the towels which Simon and Charles had also provided and made their way to the foyer. As Adam had predicted, the man was waiting for them. Not ostentatiously so; he could have been waiting for somebody else. He might even have been genuinely interested in the Rotary Club swimming gala, the poster for which he was reading but, as they crossed the foyer he came over.
"I saw you swimming," he said, addressing Adam. "You're very good."
"Thank you. I was school champion three times running."
"So you're an athlete as well. Ha ha. Get it? Three times running."

There was no doubt that this was Mr. Singleton. Jonathan had mentioned the awful jokes and the sidelong twist to the man's mouth confirmed the identification.

Adam laughed. "Got time for a drink?" asked Mr. Singleton.

Adam looked at his watch. "Could do," he said. "Is there a bar here then?" "Oh yes. They've got everything here. It's upstairs. Follow me."

The bar was brighter than the one in the Bricklayers' Arms where they had lunched with Simon and Charles but, nonetheless, it had the depressing, rundown appearance of everything in the area. Some of the plastic covers to the chairs had been torn and there were so many rings on the tables that they looked like advanced exercises in geometry. Mr. Singleton led them to one in the centre of the room. "Now then," he said, "what would you like, or should I say 'What's your pleasure?'"

They asked for beer. He went to the bar and returned with the beers on a tray.
"Here we are then," he said. "My name's Dennis Singleton."

They introduced themselves. "And what are you doing in this neck of the woods?" he asked.

Following the story they had thought up with Simon and Charles at lunchtime in the Bricklayers' Arms Adam explained that they were university students; that Mark had come down to spend a few days with his uncle and that he and Ben had come with him but were actually on the way to London to spend a weekend there.
"You want to be careful in London," said Dennis. "There are some pretty funny people there. Stick together."
"We do, all the time," said Adam. Ben blushed.
"Now, what's that supposed to mean?" asked Dennis, putting his glass down.
"What I said."
"You're..er... close friends?"
"Yes."
"Good for you. You believe in moving with the times as the mouse said when it climbed onto a pendulum." He turned to Mark. "And what will you be doing while these two are seeing the sights and I don't know what else?"

"I shall have to stay with my uncle. He's here on business. We're staying at the Bricklayers' Arms.

"Nice place. I do a lot of wedding receptions there. I'm a photographer. What sort of business is your uncle in?"

"Office furniture," said Mark. "Cash registers, computers, that sort of thing."

"Doesn't sound very interesting."

"It isn't. Neither is my uncle but my parents insisted."

"How long will you be here?"

"I don't know really. As long as it takes my uncle to clinch the deal he's working on."

"Perhaps we could meet again?" said Dennis, staring hard at Mark.

"I'd like that."

"What we could do..." He turned to Adam and Ben. "When will you have to leave here?" he asked.

"Soon actually. We want to see a show if we can get tickets."

"I was wondering if you'd like to come back to my place, Mark. We could get something to eat on the way."

"Sounds a good idea," said Mark. He took a large swig from his glass but his mouth still felt horribly dry.

"How long can you stay out?"

"There's no limit really. My uncle is out with business friends."

"And we'd better be off," said Adam. "We've got to get our bags out from downstairs. Where's the nearest tube station, Dennis?"

"Turn left as you leave here. It's about two hundred yards down the road. I wouldn't leave it too late or you'll get caught in the rush hour."

Adam and Ben stood up and shook hands. Dennis helped retrieve their towels from under the table. "See you soon," said Mark. He suddenly felt very alone and, if the truth is to be told, rather frightened.

"We've got time for another one," said Dennis, after they had left. "Same again?"

"Yes please." Dennis went back to the bar. For a moment Mark experienced a sensation of panic. If Dennis had not been served so quickly, he would certainly have made a dash for the door.

"Here we are then. One for the road as the man said when he ran over a hedgehog."

Mark took the glass. "Cheers," he said.

"Bottoms up! Your two friends are a strange couple."

"How so?"
"Well, are they really, er gay?"
"Yes. Does that shock you?"

No... Not at all. It's just that they were so open about it. I mean to say, they're pretty young."
"I don't think I would describe either Ben or Adam as 'pretty' or 'young', said Mark.

The remark had the desired effect. "No. They both looked younger from a distance. Now you - you really do look young. How old are you?"
"I'm twenty-two."
"You don't look it."
"That's what everybody says."
"Perhaps you lead a pure and unblemished life."

Mark laughed. "Far from it," he said.
"You get around, eh?"
"You could say that."
"With those two?" Dennis leaned forward over the table.
"God, no!" Mark thought carefully for a moment. "I tend to prefer something a little less.. er... ripe," he said.
"Why not?" Dennis leaned so far forward that he nearly upset his beer. "Drink up," he said. "I've got something at home that might interest you."

Mark finished his beer. It was, he thought, pretty obvious what Dennis meant. Young Stuart was still at the house. All that was necessary was to establish the fact, go back to the Bricklayers' Arms and tell Simon. It had been easier than he had imagined.

Dennis' beaten-up old car was in the car park. They got in. Dennis stopped at a 'take-away' pizza restaurant and bought two pizzas. "Good place that," he said, placing them on the back seat, "Their son is on my list. Nice lad. Just joined the army."
"Oh yes?"
"Beautiful cock on him," Dennis continued. "Anyway, here we are. Home again."

The car had drawn up in one of the shabbiest streets Mark had ever seen.

The house itself was one of the larger ones and had its own garage. Everybody else in the street appeared to have adapted their small front gardens into private parking lots. He followed Dennis into the house. There was a distinct smell of sour milk.

"Just eat these with our fingers in the lounge, eh?" said Dennis. Mark sat on one of the two threadbare easy chairs. Crumbs from previous meals were everywhere. From where he sat, he could see a quite large piece of a pizza under the sofa. He wondered where Stuart was. There was no sound, apart from Dennis' munching.

"I had a lad in here earlier who you'd have liked," said Dennis.

"Oh yes?" Mark wiped his fingers on his handkerchief.

"Boy Scout leader of some sort. Talk about clean in mind, word and deed! Ha! That lad does just about everything. And you should see him come! I caught him just at the right moment. More luck than judgement to be honest as the condemned man said when the rope broke. Here! I've got a video you'd enjoy. I haven't seen it myself yet."

He stood up and, in so doing, scattered more crumbs onto the floor. He slotted a cassette into the machine and took up a position on the sofa. "You can see it better from here," he said, patting the upholstery. Mark declined the invitation and watched the screen with wide open eyes. He'd never seen anything like it.

"He's really enjoying that!" said Dennis with a chuckle. From the expression in the boy's eyes, Mark had a different impression. He said nothing. Dennis continued to give a running commentary that came more from his imagination than from the cassette.

"He's had it several times before." "He wants a bit more of it. You can tell. That's right. Nibble his nuts. They love that! Go on. Get right up him! He can take it." The tape came to an end. "Good eh?" said Dennis.

"Very good," said Mark. He looked at his watch. "What about this lad you mentioned?" he asked.

"I've got loads. Hang on." Dennis left the room and went upstairs, returning with an armful of large envelopes. Mark's heart sank. He might have known the man was talking about photographs! Still, with Stuart's description so clearly in his memory, he should be able to pick him out.

"John," said Dennis, handing over an envelope. "Nice lad. Met him on holiday last year."

The photographs were good. There was no doubt of that. John grinned at the camera from almost every position the human body is capable of. So did Alan and Tim and David and Simon. To hurry the man would have been disastrous so Mark examined each print carefully, congratulating Dennis from time to time and showing what he hoped would seem (and which sometimes was) genuine interest.

"He looks nice," he said. The boy had fair hair. His height was right. It was just possible that Dennis gave them false names. "Where did you find him?"

"In Scotland. I did a commercial job up there for a forestry concern."

"And this one?"

"Andrew? He's German strangely enough. Apparently his father was English. He was over here on an exchange of some sort and ran out of pocket money. Nice lad. The funny thing is that most of my stuff gets published there. One day, somebody's going to recognise him but that's not my concern."

The envelopes continued to be passed over. Dutifully, Mark examined the contents of each one, replaced the photographs and took the next. It was already eleven o'clock. He wondered when the Bricklayers' Arms closed the doors. He hadn't thought to ask for a key and he was no further forward. "Let me show you the others," said Dennis. "Have you got time?"

"I'd better phone the Bricklayers' Arms first," said Mark. "I don't want to be shut out."

Dennis indicated the telephone. The handset felt horribly greasy. Mark dialled the number. They put him through to Simon's room. It seemed odd to address Simon as 'Uncle'. Mark explained that he had met an extremely nice man; a Mr. Singleton and that he would be back shortly. He hoped that his uncle would not mind and hoped that uncle's meeting with the people about office equipment had gone well. Simon, quick off the mark as ever, said that it had been reasonably successful and that he was pleased Mark had found such congenial company.

"What did he say?" Dennis asked as he entered the room bearing an even greater number of manila envelopes.

"I shouldn't be too late," said Mark. "I don't think there'll be time to see all those."

"Better start with the first ones then. Let's see now. These are all from the nineteen - eighties. I'd just started."

"Wouldn't it be better to see the latest ones first? I mean to say, an eighteen-year-old in the nineteen eighties is almost middle aged by now."

"I hadn't thought of that! What a horrible thought! Good idea. Well now...Let's see. Here's Richard. As you see, I like to get them in action. It's all good practice."

Richard, a tall, dark haired young man, was pictured with a young man of about Mark's age, gazing admiringly at the young man's erect member, holding it, sucking it and finally succumbing to it with a fixed and artificial grin.

"This is a good one," said Dennis, handing him yet another envelope. "Jonathan. He's an American."

There was no doubt about it. Mark had not met Jonathan but, he thought, there couldn't be many Americans with that name in England and the other one; the lad on the receiving end, was fair haired and had a gold chain round his neck. He had found Stuart at last!

"Oh yes!" he said. "He's really nice."

"Isn't he?"

"Where did you find him? In America?"

"No. He fell into my lap. Sheer luck. Sure you've got time?"

Mark looked at his watch. "I think so."

"Well, you see the other one? The one with the gold chain?"

"Yes."

"He, believe it or not, is the son of some very rich people indeed. Went to a posh private school and all that. A spoiled little sod but I first met him when I went to their house to talk about some commercial work. Well, there was this conceited kid. I offered to do some studies - mostly to convince his father that I could take photographs. I did some in the garden; some in the house..."

"Not naked?"

"Oh Christ no! Well, I sent them off. Got a nice letter back and the contract I wanted. I signed the contract and that was it as far as I was concerned. Then he failed his A levels. Not just bad grades. He blew it completely so that was Goodbye to his parents' dreams of Cambridge and all that. Blow me down. His dad asked me to take him on as assistant."

"And did you?"

"Well, I took him on but not as an assistant. He's as thick as two short planks but he's got looks."

"He certainly has," said Mark, gazing at the photograph. "Well endowed too." He suddenly felt horribly guilty. It was small wonder that Howard had succumbed.

"I did loads of studies with him. We got on pretty well but he's a spoiled bastard. A real mummy's boy. He even took to calling me 'Uncle'. Then the parents heard of some Catholic place which guaranteed to get the thickest kids

through exams so I lost touch with him. Then... You won't believe this. Only a few days ago it was, he turned up again - with Jonathan. They'd scarpered.
"What for?"
"That's the laugh of the century. You know what these Catholic places are like. Every student screws every other student and gets screwed by the monks...

Mark would have liked to stop him there and tell him the truth but kept quiet. "There's this bloke there - name of Howard. Don't know whether that's his surname or family name, not that it matters. He decides to screw them both - in the library would you believe? So he gets them pissed and is just about to shove his cock into young Stuart when a window cleaner appears outside and sees them. Of course they were both in a panic so they ran away and came here."
"And then what?"
"Well, Jonathan was short of the ready stuff so I got photos of both of them as you can see. Jonathan pissed off early the next morning back to college."
"And what about Stuart?"
"He wasn't in much of a condition to piss off anywhere. He earned a lucky charm to hang on his chain that night all right!"
"You mean you...?"
"Too right I did. I wasn't going to wait any longer. If he was prepared to let the unwashed cock of some randy student in there, he could let his dear uncle be the first."

Mark could hardly contain his anger. Randy! Unwashed! This was Howard the man was talking about.
"So you did?" he said.
"Of course. Took him into my bedroom. Did the 'It's all going to be all right' act. You know. Off with the shorts. 'You like this don't you? Let uncle show you how much he loves you.' Warm them up, grease them up and then it's just up... all the way!" He laughed.
"So he went back to college?"

Dennis gave a long wink which, in conjunction with his lop-sided mouth made him look positively deformed.
"Well, he got on the train," he said, "but I should be very surprised if he got there. You know what they're like. Once they've lost their cherries they worry about it for a few weeks, then their asses start to itch for another cock... Here, I've said too much already."

"Yes, and I really ought to be getting back to my uncle," said Mark.

"You want to watch these uncles," said Dennis.

"Ha! No chance. It's been a great evening. Thanks a lot and thanks for the drinks and the pizza."

"You're welcome. Any chance of seeing you again?"

"Of course."

"What are you doing tomorrow?"

"Nothing much."

"Why don't you come round in the morning? You could give me a hand if you like."

"I'd like that, but tomorrow is Sunday and I don't know much about photography."

"You don't need to. I've got a couple of baptisms to do. What you might consider..."

"What?"

"I'd like to get some pictures. I pay well."

"Sure. I don't mind. What time shall I come round?"

"I could pick you up at the Bricklayers' Arms."

"No. I'll come here. What time?"

"Say half-past nine?"

"Sure." Dennis let him out. Mark heard chains being fastened behind the door. He trudged along the darkened streets. Empty drink cans rolled along, clattering in the brisk wind. In one street a boy, framed in the bright light of an open door, bent down to put an empty milk bottle on the step. He closed the door again. A light appeared in an upstairs window. Unseen hands closed the curtains.

"Sleep well. Stay safe," Mark muttered.

CHAPTER TEN

Mark was beginning to think that photography was the most boring job in the world. In three days he had attended four weddings and eleven baptisms. He had offered comforters to crying toddlers, arranged innumerable vases of flowers and polished second hand cars to make them look slightly more attractive to susceptible buyers.

The annoying thing was, he thought, that he was not much nearer Stuart's trail. He had followed Simon's advice to the letter. "Inspire the wretched man's confidence," Simon had said. "Do what he wants and don't tell him any lies he can check up on. It's the bald headed man we're after. Sooner or later he'll lead you there. Just stick with him."

Thus Mark spent the days behind the camera and the late afternoons or evenings in front of it, lying on a bed in Dennis' home studio or over a damp tree stump in the corner of a field. It was as well that Simon didn't want sex when he returned to the Bricklayers' Arms late in the evenings. He was beginning to wonder which would wear out first: Dennis' imagination or his seminal vesicles. He had spurted it into the air; onto the bed; over the open pages of a magazine; into a wine glass and onto a mirror. That didn't really worry him. Simon had promised that the photographs would be destroyed. What concerned him was Dennis' next project

"We'll have to find you a partner," he said. "Someone dark. A bit on the swarthy side. The two of you together would make a lovely study."

On the way to different assignments, Dennis would point out potential co-stars. "How about that one?" he would ask. "Nice ass. Looks like he's got quite a lot up front too."

The remarks revolted Mark but what worried him was that, deep down, he agreed. The lad they saw on the corner of the street really did have a 'bottom like a balloon'. He really would like to have 'pricked' it. The greatest worry of all was that he knew that, once naked with such a boy in Dennis' studio, he wouldn't have the strength to resist. His criticism of Howard's behaviour would be revealed as the hypocrisy Howard claimed it to be.

"How about that one in the photo you showed me? Stephen... or was it Stuart? Some name like that." said Mark one evening, after Dennis had gone through his little black book for the third time.

"No chance. I wonder if Antonio is available. I could ring him in the morning. I must think of some excuse."

But Antonio was not available to help Mr. Singleton in any way. His anger at being asked was detectable at a considerable distance from the telephone. Another reprieve.

It was the fourth morning of his stay. The grease of the Bricklayers' Arms breakfast made his mouth feel unpleasant. It was raining. He turned into Anscott Way and kicked an apparently empty fast-food packet into the gutter. It burst apart and released a cascade of cold chips all over the pavement. It was not going to be a good day! Charles, he thought, was no fool. Charles had gone back to Combleton almost immediately. He felt he should be there to liaise with the college authorities and attend to pressing business.

The steam from the cooling towers hung around, driven downwards by the rain. He reached number 14 and rang the doorbell.

"Ha! Bright and early as ever!" said Dennis, as he opened the door. "It's a good thing you're not taller."

"Why?"

"You'd lie longer in bed! Ha! Get it?"

"What's on today?" Mark asked.

"A special. A church job. Interior, so we need to take a lot of lighting. I'm going to need about three halogen floods and we'd better take a couple of pups as well. Oh! And filters. Pack the lot."

In the last few days, Mark had learned a lot of photographers' jargon. He went upstairs, got the necessary lighting, lugged it all down to the garage and stowed it in the Renault. Dennis collected the burnished aluminium boxes which housed his cameras and they were soon rattling along streets which seemed seedier and dirtier as the journey continued.

"Is this a wedding or a christening?" asked Mark, interrupting yet another of

Dennis' jokes.

"Neither. We're doing shots for a Christmas card."

"In July?"

"That's when the Christmas business starts to come in as Santa Claus said when he put a condom in a boy's stocking."

All Saints church stood on a triangular island flanked by three busy roads. It towered above the grey terraced houses and run down shops like a remote giant, loftily unconcerned with the day-to-day lives of the thousands who lived at its feet. The rectory stood close at hand. Like the church, it had been built in the days of Victorian opulence and was much too big, even for a large family.

The Reverend Cuthbert Kelvin, or 'Father Cuthbert' as he preferred to be known, did not have a large family. Not of his own anyway. Mark had never seen so many boys in one house before. There were boys in the hallway, boys in the kitchen and boys in the lounge. Boys could be heard upstairs. The noise was incredible.

"Come in. Come in!" said Father Cuthbert after Dennis had introduced Mark. "Don't mind the mess," he added. "It's always like this."

He reminded Mark of one of those skittle men which can't be knocked over. He was a very short, rotund little man. In the old days he would have been described as a 'portly priest'. The old leather belt round his cassock was at the last hole and looked as if it might burst apart at any moment. He seemed to glide, rather than walk. One got the impression that if one were to give him a hefty shove, he would glide to the wall and bounce back again.

"We'd better go into the study," he said. "There won't be any boys in there." They stepped carefully over the four who were sitting in the hallway. Mark stepped aside to let a radio controlled model car hurtle past him.

"We won't be disturbed in here," said Father Cuthbert, opening a door. Contrary to his forecast, his desk had been commandeered by three little boys for a board game.

"Shoo!" he said. "These gentlemen have come on business!" Protesting, they packed up their game and left.

"Little scamps!" said Father Cuthbert with a chuckle. "They know they are not allowed in here."

"I've brought some sample cards with me," said Dennis. He produced a cardboard folder. "This holly and mistletoe motif is rather nice or would you prefer the robins?"

Mark was not at all interested in Christmas cards. Indeed, he considered Christmas to have become a commercial racket of which Christmas cards were a prime example. He walked round the room studying the pictures on the walls. He had never seen anything like them. They were hideously gaudy water colours and each depicted a naked, very small boy. The first; Mark guessed him to be about nine, trailed a teddy bear. The picture was captioned 'A Little Bear Behind'. A picture of a boy sitting on a boulder was entitled 'Rock Bottom'. There were twelve of them in all and each had a title making play with the words 'behind' or 'bottom'. He thought them the most tasteless things he had seen in years. Rather than the theological textbooks one would expect in a clergyman's study, Father Cuthbert's shelves were filled with statuettes and china models of little boys.

"I'm not at all sure about the wording," said Father Cuthbert. "I send them to...er...very close friends if you know what I mean."

"Don't worry about Mark. He's one of us," said Dennis. Mark winced.

"Oh! How nice! And are you learning the trade?"

Mark was at pains to explain that he was merely helping Dennis out for a few days whilst his uncle was engaged on business.

"Lovely! And so nice for Dennis to have company. Nice for you both I am sure. You look like a very helpful young man. Energetic too, I shouldn't be surprised."

Mark shuddered and would have said something had Dennis not butted in.

"Do you want these done in the rectory or the church?" he asked.

"The church is the obvious place. I've chosen the boys. Absolute cherubs! Wait till you see them." He got up and went to the door.

"David, love, do you think you can find Neil and Tony for me?"

"They're upstairs, farve."

"Go and get them, dear."

"I brought your videos with me," said Dennis. 'Boys' Hobbies' was nice."

"Isn't it? I've got some more that you can have. 'Camping for Boys' and 'Camp Fire Frolics'. There are some delightful things in that. Are you going to Harry's tonight?"

"Christ!" said Dennis. "I must be getting senile. I'd forgotten all about it."

"It should be a good show." Father Cuthbert seemed not to have noticed the blasphemy. "Is Mark going?"

"Depends on Mark."

"What goes on there?" Mark asked guardedly.

"Harry stages tableaux vivants parties," said Father Cuthbert. "Terribly artistic and rather lovely."

Mark was none the wiser but didn't have time to ask any more questions. Two breathless boys of about twelve burst into the room as if they were being chased.

"Did you want us, farve?" asked one of them. He was a very pretty little boy, as was his companion. Both were blond and had the sort of open, friendly faces which appealed to Mark. He smiled. They smiled back.

"Yes boys, I did. You know Dennis. This is his assistant, Mark. They've come to take those photographs we talked about."

"I'm only a temporary assistant. Just helping out," said Mark, anxious that these little lads should not get the wrong impression.

"We'll go and set up. Bring the boys when you're ready," said Dennis. "It shouldn't take long."

Mark was worried and didn't know what to do. It looked as if he was to be an unwilling accomplice in something so illegal and so revolting that it made him feel almost physically sick. He wanted to get away but couldn't. There was only one way to get to Howard and that was to stay with Dennis. With a heavy heart he helped carry the equipment from the car. In prison, he thought, he'd probably have to carry heavy loads. Maybe it was good practice.

The interior of the church was pretty hideous and the scent of incense hanging in the air made his eyes water. Father Cuthbert and the two boys went into the vestry and returned with a Christmas crib which they set up by the altar. Mark concentrated on getting the lights focused on to it. Dennis wanted the stained glass window behind the altar lit. That was difficult. Finally, they were ready. The two boys dressed in red cassocks and long white surplices appeared and knelt meekly in front of the crib. Dennis looked through the view-finder.

"The one on the left," he said. "His hair's slightly untidy." Father Cuthbert glided forward with a comb in his hand as if he had been waiting for the cue. Lovingly, he combed the boy's hair down. Neither lad seemed to find this strange. Mark guessed they were used to acting as models.

"That's it.. Wait for it... Now!" said Dennis. "Now another. Can the boy on the left look a bit more pious? That's it. Good lad. Now!"

Then the boys had to stand in the choir stalls, holding hymn books.

"Whilst shepherds washed their socks by night," sang one.

All seated round the tub..." the other rejoined.

"Oh! You naughty little imps! Not in the church. Not in the church!" said Father Cuthbert. "I shall have to smack your bottoms!"

He didn't. Dennis took another series of them holding candlesticks. "That's enough, boys. Go and get changed," said Father Cuthbert.

"Is that it?" Mark whispered as he helped Dennis dismantle a floodlight.

"That's it."

"I'd invite you to stay for tea but I've got a prayer meeting and I must send the scamps home," said Father Cuthbert as they packed up the gear. "See you tonight at Harry's."

"Extraordinary man," said Dennis when they were on the way home.

Mark agreed. "Writes books," said Dennis. "All about the charm and innocence of little boys. Their parents think the world of him. It's a funny old world."

"It certainly is," said Mark.

The photographs, he had to admit when they were hanging up to dry, were good. The crib was bathed in coloured light reflected down from the window. The boys' hair shone gold and the scarlet material of their cassocks made a perfect contrast with the whiteness of their surplices.

"They're really artistic," he said.

"So I should hope. You'll find this evening even more artistic. That reminds me. We ought to start out." He packed a couple of cameras and several rolls of film into a burnished aluminium case and they were soon on their way again. It started to drizzle. Dennis turned onto a motorway.

"Are you photographing boys tonight?" Mark asked.

"Yes, but if you've got any thoughts about getting your end away, forget them."

"I wouldn't. You know I wouldn't."

"I just thought I'd mention it. Harry's shows are strictly eyes only. I even have to hand him the exposed films so that no stray copies of the prints get about."

"What is it? A sort of strip show?" Mark asked.

"Harry would have a fit if he heard you say that! It's an artistic experience."

"What's he like?"

"Harry? It's difficult to describe him. He worships youth. Puts 'em on a pedestal somehow. To Harry, a boy possesses all the virtues. He never lays so much as a finger on them. Most of his guests wouldn't agree but they pretend to and that keeps him happy. It's not far now."

They left the motorway, drove through a small town and turned into a narrow lane.

"It's down here," said Dennis. "I hope we don't meet anyone coming the other way as the man said when he had a wank on the bottom bunk."

The house was very large and looked as if it might have been built for a retired sea captain. It was very long and very white. A series of balconies, wide on the first floor and narrower at the top gave it a tapered, streamlined look. The marine motive was enhanced by portholes. A flagstaff stood at the entrance, surrounded by parked cars. The front door opened and they stepped inside.

"Dennis dear! How lovely to see you but who have you brought with you?"

The speaker was a middle aged man, tall, slim and dark haired. There seemed to be something strange about his eyes but his clothes were even odder; bright yellow pants and a pink, silk Cossack shirt.

"This is Mark, my temporary assistant. He's one of us," said Dennis.

"And how old are you, Mark?" said Harry, extending a hand which felt like a half inflated rubber glove.

"Twenty-two."

"As old as that! You don't look it. Poor love! You must miss being a boy terribly! All those good times, gone for ever."

Mark's boyhood memories were mostly of miserable school days, relieved only by furtive sessions in his friend's attic.

"Such a pity!" said Harry, and looked for a moment as if he might cry. "But come in and meet everybody," he said, cheering up instantly. He beckoned to a good looking young man. "Peter," he said, "can you get drinks for Dennis and Mark?"

"Sure," said Peter. "What will you have?"

In any other circumstances, Dennis would have capitalised on the question. He didn't at Harry's. He merely asked for a scotch. Mark asked for a beer. Peter went to get them, and returned. "Here you are," he said, "What's your name?."

"Mark." Mark would have liked to have talked to Peter. He was extremely beautiful. His eyes shone under long eyelashes. There was just a trace of hair on his upper lip. Otherwise his face was perfectly smooth. When he laughed, his lips drew back to show a row of gleaming white teeth. He laughed a lot. Dennis' jokes came like bullets from a machine gun, with just an occasional pause for appreciative laughter as the magazine was changed.

"I said sew it, not show it!" said Dennis apparently directing the punch line at Peter's groin. Mark stared ahead and caught a glimpse of another lad. There were plenty of young men in the room but all except this one were talking to the other guests. Father Cuthbert had no fewer than four clustered round him. Mark left Dennis and Peter and walked across the room.

"Hi! I'm Mark," he said.

"My name's Lance," said the young man. He was more handsome than Peter.

"Not short for Lancelot?"

"No, thank God. Lance is bad enough."

"It's rather a nice name."

"I'm glad you think so. I don't. What are you doing here? You're much younger than the others."

"I've come with Dennis Singleton, the photographer."

"Poor sod," said Lance. "When I saw him come in I kept out of sight. I couldn't stand another session of his jokes. I see he's trapped Peter. In a few minutes it'll be 'You must get in touch with me. Here's my card.' Harry gets cross when he does that."

"Tell me about Harry. He's interesting," said Mark.

"He's great. Everybody likes him. When he first moved here it was different. You know; ex window dresser, suddenly come into a lot of money; funny clothes. You get the idea?"

Mark nodded.

"Then he gave the village a cricket pitch and a pavilion. He badgered the council for a safe crossing by the school. He provided a mini bus to take the little kids to and from school. Have you seen the pool?"

"No, not yet."

"It's fabulous and he lets us use it whenever we want."

"And in return you pose in the nude?"

"It's not like that at all. These parties are artistic, see?"

Mark nodded but wondered about the motives of the guests. Father Cuthbert had his hands on a young man's hips and was apparently studying the label on his jeans. Another had been pulled on to a seated guest's knee.

Harry tapped a glass.

"Time for me to get ready," said Lance. "If you like, I could show you the pool afterwards."

It was a perfectly innocuous invitation but there was something in the way it was said; something about the look in Lance's eyes, that made Mark's heart miss a beat.

"I'd love to see it," he said.

Lance grinned. "I'll make sure you do," he said, and disappeared through a door on his left.

When all the boys had left the room it was as though some essential catalyst had been removed. Guests seemed not to want to talk to each other and behaved like naughty schoolboys who had been caught and were waiting for the inevitable punishment. A full half-hour passed before Harry put his head round the door. "Ready at last!" he said. "You've no idea how long it takes to get them ready."

They filed into a much bigger room. The seats had been arranged round the walls. There was a large empty space in the centre. Dennis took up his position in a corner, camera in hand.

"Everybody ready? Here goes," said Harry's voice and the room was suddenly darkened. Mark was aware of some activity in the centre but could see nothing.

'The Bathers' Harry's voice, amplified, rang round the room. Bright lights in the ceiling came on. Like everybody else, Mark rubbed his eyes and stared. Three young men; three beautiful young men, stood naked in front of him. One stood, with upraised arms on a small step ladder, as if about to dive onto the blue sheet spread on the floor. Another stood with arms akimbo at the side of the sheet and the third sat next to him, pointing at the 'diver'. None of them moved a muscle. Mark concentrated on the diver, unable to take his eyes off the boy's taut buttocks - and then the lights went out.

More scuffling and then "A Summer Picnic." This time there were seven boys. Mark recognised Lance at once. He knelt as if turned to stone, next to a picnic basket and held a sandwich out to another boy. Lance with clothes had been attractive but Lance naked was utterly beautiful and the kneeling position set off his bottom to perfection. His front was slightly in shadow but there was enough light for Mark to see what he wanted to see. A thick cock hung from a shield of soft looking hair. The light made it look as if the boys really were basking in sunlight. Mark looked up at the ceiling. A great battery of lamps hung there, each contributing its rays to the tableau. The green of non existent grass reflected perfectly onto one boy's back. The glint of running water sparkled on another's white thigh.

"Perfect! Quite beautiful!" said the man sitting next to Mark, clapping ecstatically.

The show went on. 'Tales Round a Camp-Fire', 'The Water Hole' 'Eden', 'Summer Dreams', 'Midday in Summer', 'Bath-time'.

The atmosphere in the room became charged with the exciting scent of youthful perspiration. The lights had a lot to do with it. The 'actors' seemed to shine more brightly as the show continued. Matt, white skin began to glisten and, all the time, the heady odour drifted over the audience. It began to affect their response to the tableaux. They continued to applaud but "Magnificent!" "Quite beautiful!" and "Bravo!" gave way to "Just look at that ass!" and "What wouldn't I give for a mouthful of that!"

Lance was in most of the tableaux; standing, sitting, kneeling, lying on his back - and Mark was enthralled. 'Midday in Summer' enabled him to appreciate the perfection of Lance's perfectly rounded butt and the golden fuzz on his legs. 'Athenian Gymnasts' afforded a glimpse of a tight scrotum and a mysterious and inviting darkness behind it. Mark crossed his legs. The audience reaction became more and more explicit. Harry, somewhere out of sight, was presumably also out of hearing range. The stars of the show must have heard but made no sign of having done so but posed still as statues with wide, unblinking eyes, only smiling if the subject of the tableau required it.

The show closed with 'After the Match' in which all the boys were shown in a dressing room after a most improbable football game which they had played without getting the slightest fleck of mud on their clothes or themselves. Some stood naked, either towelling themselves or in silent conversation with friends. Lance sat on a bench with his back to Mark. His shorts had already been removed and he was pulling a muddy jersey up over his long back. Mark gazed at his flattened rump and clearly delineated spine. He was glad, for Lance's sake, that the show was over and that Lance need no longer exhibit himself to a lot of dirty old men. It was quite wrong, he thought, that Harry should thus exploit people, however aesthetic his motives.

The audience left the room, chatting excitedly. The drinks table had been replenished. Mark saw Dennis give several rolls of film to Harry and then open the camera for Harry to look inside.

Mark took a drink and went to a chair in the corner. A certain bulge at the groin made standing slightly embarrassing and he didn't feel inclined for conversation.

"Well? Did you like it?" Lance had returned. Strangely, he looked just as attractive in jeans and T shirt as he had a few minutes previously.

"It was terrific!" said Mark. "You were good. I liked you in that Greek thing."

"I moved in that," said Lance. "Harry was cross. Did you notice? I was supposed to balance on one foot."

"No. I never noticed," said Mark. In the tableau in question he had not been concentrating on Lance's feet.

"When you've finished your drink, I'll show you the pool if you like," said Lance.

Mark put down his glass. "Let's go now," he said. "I was waiting for you."

"I'll go first," said Lance. "Through that door and then you turn left. I'll wait for you by the patio door."

"Why the secrecy?"

Lance grinned. "Harry doesn't approve of over socialising with the guests," he said.

"I don't want to get you into trouble."

"You won't. See you in a minute. Don't be too long." As he spoke, Lance rubbed a hand over the front of his jeans and grinned. Then he was gone.

Mark sat sipping his drink. Outwardly he might have appeared calm but instinct and conscience fought such a battle in that short time as they had never waged before. He stood up, shrugged his shoulders and slipped through the door. He found himself in a long corridor lined on both sides with circular windows. At the end was a pair of frosted glass doors. There was no sign of Lance. He pushed the doors. They opened and he stepped out into darkness. The click of a light switch came from somewhere nearby and he saw that he was standing on the side of an extremely luxurious, glass roofed swimming pool. Long, white reclining chairs were ranged round the edges.

"This is it. Smart eh?" said Lance.

"Fantastic!"

"It cost him millions apparently."

"Where did all the money come from?"

"His mum ran off when he was young and she divorced his dad. Harry trained to be a window dresser and he was working in London when he heard that she had married a multi millionaire and that they had both died in a car crash so he got the lot."

"Very nice too," said Mark. He paused. "Is this all you're going to show me?" he asked.

"There's the changing cubicles..." Was it his imagination or was Lance's voice huskier?

"Let's see one of those."

"Over here. When there's a lot of us, we usually share one. They're quite big as you can see." He opened the first door in a row.

"They're luxurious!" said Mark, looking at the hair drier on the wall and the electric heater. "Who do you share with?"

"Depends on who's here."

"No girls?"

"Oh no. Harry won't have them. We swim in the nude."

"Nothing wrong with that. I've done it myself. It's more fun than wearing trunks."

"I think so too."

"It's a pity we can't have a quick dip now," said Mark. It would be more healthy than being inside boozing with a lot of old men."

"We could. If I turn the lights out, nobody will know we're here."

"Towels?"

"In the drawer. There are always plenty of them."

"Okay then. But just two lengths. A race if that's all right with you."

"Great!" Feverishly, they both undressed. Mark watched Lance and Lance watched Mark. They smiled at each other as two half-hard cocks sprang into view.

They stepped out onto the poolside. Lance switched off the lights. It took some time to get used to the darkness but the moon flashing between racing clouds gave just enough light for them to negotiate round the pool furniture.

"We'd better not dive in. Someone will hear us," said Lance. They climbed in at the shallow end. The water was cold. Mark shuddered.

"When I say 'Go!'" he said, between chattering teeth. "One - two - three - go!"

Lance was a good swimmer. Mark thought he would have no trouble in beating him. In fact he won by a short head.

"Again?" said Lance.
"I'd better not. I'll have to be going soon."

They climbed out of the pool and walked, shivering, to the cubicle. Lance opened the door. Mark followed him, closed the door and bolted it.
"I'll put the heater on. Should have done it before," said Lance. "That was good fun." He opened a drawer and produced two enormous towels. He passed one to Mark.
"We could dry each other," said Mark. "Fun of another sort if you know what I mean." He couldn't keep his eyes off Lance's cock. Drops of water from Lance's dense bush ran down it, hung for a second and then fell to the floor.
"If you want," said Lance with a grin. "If you're in a hurry I'd better do you first."
"Okay. If I lie on the bench, you can do my back first." He lay down and felt his cock slip through the wooden slats. Lance began vigorously to towel his back. "That feels good!" said Mark. The towel moved down to his butt. That felt even better! He parted his legs slightly and shivered as the towel moved between his buttocks. "You've got hairy legs, haven't you?" Lance observed. Mark didn't answer.
"Right. Your back is done," said Lance.

For a moment, Mark hesitated. Then he turned over.
"Wow!" said Lance as almost seven inches of hard cock came into view.
"You can touch it. It won't bite you," said Mark.
"It's huge!"
"Go on. Touch it." Lance's own prick, still limp, was only a few inches from Mark's face.
"I'll do the rest of you first." He wiped Mark's face and then his shoulders. Then it was the turn of his chest and his abdomen. Mark held his breath as the towel touched the top of his pubic bush. Then it happened. A towel-covered hand grasped his cock.
"Sure you don't mind?"

Mark grinned and shook his head. Mind indeed! He closed his eyes. The towel fell over his legs. For a moment he thought Lance had had second thoughts. He opened his eyes again. Lance's prick was rearing up. He felt Lance's long fingers on his cock head. They slid up and down the shaft, fingered his balls and once, to his intense pleasure, reached behind them. There seemed to be no method in his approach but it was enjoyable and - more important - it had an effect on his young manipulator whose cock now stood right out. Six inches of uncut, succulent flesh!

Mark reached out and touched the inside of a wet thigh. Lance took a step nearer. Mark slid his hand upward. Lance gasped as the side of Mark's hand made contact with his balls.

"Are you going to do it to me?" he asked.

"What do you want me to do?"

"I don't know."

"But you want something?"

Lance nodded, blushed furiously and then averted his eyes.

"I think I know what you want," said Mark. He placed his hands round the boy's superbly rounded butt. The soft flesh in his hands felt cold and wet. He drew Lance forward. Lance offered no resistance. Indeed, he stepped rather too far forward and Mark, who wanted to feel that cock on his lips first, had to take most of it at once.

The pure taste of young masculinity filled his mouth. The slightly sour element of perspiration mingled with the clean flavour of the pool. It was too late now to think about what he was doing; too late to ponder over questions of morality. He pulled his head back, letting go of the rigid, pulsating shaft and then, gripping Lance's buttocks and kneading their soft flesh, he licked and kissed through silky hair to smooth skin and from the underside of the upward pointing cock down to the coolness below. Lance began to quiver in his hands.

Mark looked up. "Ready?" he asked. He gave the cushions of flesh an affectionate squeeze. Lance nodded. Mark took a deep breath, opened his lips slightly and let the young man push it into his mouth. Lance put his hands on the wall above Mark's head to steady himself.

Mark worked his lips up and down the shaft, sucking rhythmically as he did so. He worked his fingers round the smooth buttocks - pushed them into the damp cleft and tickled. Lance shuddered with pleasure. His breathing became louder and louder. His cock head hammered against the back of Mark's throat. His ass cheeks tightened and relaxed with each thrust. Mark pushed his middle finger further inwards. Instinctively, Lance moved his feet further apart. Mark could feel it; a soft, crinkled little spot. His pushed his finger tip against it and felt it tighten to resist the pressure. Lance's movements became more and more frantic. Mark, trying to play his tongue against the rigid cock, found it impossible to do so.

"Mmm! Oooh! Aah! Ah! Ah! Ah! I'm..." Semen flooded Mark's mouth, tasting slightly bitter and with a tinge of chlorine. He felt it in his throat; under his tongue and washing round his teeth. He pressed harder against the rosette. It was slightly more relaxed. If only there was more time... He leaned back against the wall, releasing Lance's cock. Warm drops landed on his legs. He took it in his hand and squeezed it affectionately - and came! It wasn't entirely unexpected but he had hoped to make it last a little longer. The first gush landed on Lance's abdomen; the second on his right thigh. Mark managed to catch the rest in a towel.

Lance laughed for the first time since they had started. He picked up a towel and wiped himself. "You must have been saving that up for days!" he said.
"You didn't do too badly yourself," Mark replied, wiping his mouth with the back of his hand. "Did you like it?"
"I wouldn't have let you do it if I didn't, would I?"

They dried themselves and began to dress. "Shall I see you again?" asked Lance.
"Do you want to?"
"That's why I asked."

There was a long pause. Mark fastened his belt, put on his shoes, tied the laces and then looked straight into Lance's eyes.
"Honestly, Lance," he said, "I don't think it would be a good idea but I shall always remember you."
"And I'll remember you," said Lance.

Mark picked up the towel and went to hang it on a hook. As he did so, the label caught his eye. 'HOWARD & COMPANY'. He flung it to the floor and dashed out.

The anteroom was much less crowded. Most of the guests had obviously gone home. He looked round for Dennis and, for the second time in almost as many seconds, he was almost overwhelmed by guilt. Not only had he seduced one of Harry's young men but he had forgotten the reason for his being there. Dennis was talking to man; a bald headed man! He was not just bald. There was no hair on his head at all. Mark went over to them.
"Oh! Here he is. Where the hell have you been?" asked Dennis.

"Outside. I needed the fresh air. It was stuffy in there."

"He'd do," said the man.

"I'll ask him. He's at university though."

"I only need him for weekends. They don't study at weekends."

"Ask me what?" said Mark, feeling slightly affronted.

"I'll tell you in the morning. We ought to be getting back. We're late already. Your uncle will be wondering where you are."

Dennis shook hands with the bald man and sought out Harry who came out to the car to wave them off.

"Lovely to see you!" he said. "What did you think of it, Mark?"

"Very artistic. It was quite an experience!" said Mark. Harry beamed with pleasure.

"Hm! Experience it certainly was not!" said Dennis crashing through the gears. Mind you, there were some I wouldn't say no to experiencing. That one you were talking to for instance. He was nice. Did you see his cock? Imagine having that in your mouth!"

"Mmm. Quite a thought!" said Mark and the stickiness behind his teeth and on his tongue suddenly tasted horribly bitter.

CHAPTER ELEVEN

Another police car went up the road to the college, passing Howard as he tramped down into the village. It was the third he had seen that day. Things were certainly hotting up. He had been interviewed and, following a 'script' prepared by the rector and another man whom he had never seen before, he said nothing about the sex or the wine. He had last seen Stuart enter the Beaumont building after Stuart had helped him clean up the library he said.

It was what Jonathan might say that worried him. Jonathan would almost certainly tell them about Dennis Singleton and that would result in a police raid on the man's house where they would almost certainly discover Mark. Mark was irritating, possessive and hot tempered but the thought of him being arrested as some sort of accomplice was worrying. Howard walked faster.

The village telephone box was on a corner near the post office. There was a pay-phone in the college but it gobbled coins at a frightening rate and, being situated on a landing, was totally unsuitable for private calls.
"Shit!" Howard muttered. A woman was in the phone box and another was waiting. There was only one thing to do - ask Charles if he could use the phone in the cottage. Passing one of the many posters headed 'MISSING' over a not very good picture of Stuart, he went round the corner, along the street, past the shops to Mill Cottage. He rang the bell.

Charles opened the door. Briefly Howard explained his worry.
"I rather think," said Charles when they were in the lounge, "that you underestimate the powers of the establishment to protect itself. Sir Rodney Murley is up at the college now is he not?"
"There was a man with the rector, yes. Who is he?"
"Chairman of the governors and one of the country's top legal brains," said Charles. "It's bad enough that they have lost one student but he, apparently, is a bit of a skate and often cuts lectures. To admit that Jonathan also ran

away must worry them sick. But you have a point. Better safe than sorry. Don't ring Mark though. Ring Simon. He's at the Bricklayers' Arms. I have the number here."

Howard dialled and was put through to 'Mr. Black'. Mark, it appeared had got up late after a very late session photographing somewhere out of town and was at that moment at Dennis' house. Simon would warn him.
"How is he?" asked Howard.
"Singleton or Mark?"
"Mark of course."
"Oh, he's fine. He's doing a good job. I've got enough here on three people to send them down for a long time but I'm doing nothing until we've found the other lad. Your Mark is a good detective. Can I have a word with Charles?"

Howard handed over the receiver. "Your Mark." The words made him feel curiously elated. He would have felt even happier, he thought bitterly, if Mark were a more reasonable person.
"... very well," Charles was saying "I enjoy playing with it myself. Three times and my back is still aching. He's here at the moment as a matter of fact. Oh good. Let me know, won't you? Bye!"

Howard was slightly surprised that Charles didn't offer him a drink as he usually did. They chatted for a few moments. Howard said that he ought to go back to college. He was standing on the path. Charles had closed the door. "Charles, can you come up here for a moment?" Howard heard the words distinctly. There was no mistaking that drawl. Jonathan! What the hell was Jonathan doing in Mill Cottage?

Things fitted together with every step Howard took up the hill to the school. The afternoon when Jon and Charles had washed the car together. Charles' sudden return from London and now "I enjoy playing with it myself."
"I'll bet you bloody do!" Howard muttered and he kicked a stone into the woods. He didn't know who was the worse of the two. Charles, for enticing Jonathan, or Jonathan for allowing it. But Charles of all people! He knew Charles was gay but the man was nearly forty years old! It was disgusting!

———

"What did that man want last night?" asked Mark.

"What man?"

"The bald headed guy you were talking to."

"Oh him. Here, hold this a moment." Dennis passed over another clip of photographs. The red light of the dark-room made his face look even more satanic. "That's Chris," he said. "He runs a club. He's after staff."

"Gambling you mean?"

"You could call it that. Give that one another thirty seconds."

"I can't see myself as a croupier," said Mark.

"That's not what he had in mind. He's a worried man at the moment. Not that he need be. He's the guy Stuart went to."

"I thought you said you'd put him on the train back to school."

"I also said that I doubted if he would get there. There's no way on Earth that anyone could link Stuart with Chris. I'm in the clear. Friend of the family. Seen putting the lad on the train. The ideal concerned uncle that's me. What the silly sod did after that is no concern of mine. 'Yes, officer, I suppose I should have driven him back but have you seen my car? London to Combleton? It wouldn't have made it. I told him off, gave him money for the fare and put him on the train.' What more could I do?"

"And what happens if the other lad tells them you took nude photographs of them and the police come here with a search warrant?" Mark asked, trying to make the question sound casual.

"Photographs? You won't find any pictures of either of them here. I made sure of that the moment the posters went up. They're all in a safe place some way from here. Anyway, nobody in the world will admit to that. It's a funny thing. You could show a lad his photo and he'd deny to his dying day that it was him. No... Like I told Chris, if he keeps Stuart out of sight for a few weeks till the heat's off, he's got nothing to worry about. Is that one ready yet?"

Mark handed over the wet print. "Good. That's the lot then. Let's get out of here."

They were in a pub some miles away when Mark found an excuse to re-open the conversation. They had been photographing the members of a pop group; teenage boys in glitter suits. It hadn't been an easy session.

"That drummer was a pretty little thing," said Dennis. "I like blonds. They get dirty quicker."

"I'll have the singer. He was good," said Mark.

"Musically, yes. I just hope they succeed. Being the official photographer to a pop group means money. Big money."

"You could speak to your friend Chris. Get them a contract to play in his club," Mark suggested.

"I don't think there is music there. I'm not sure. I've never been there at weekends. That's when he's busy."

"Yes, I remember him saying that we don't study at weekends. What did he actually want me to do?"

The corner of Dennis' mouth dropped further. "Keep it under your hat," he said. "You know these London clubs with hostesses? You know. A bottle of champagne at an extortionate price gives you the right to a bit of a feel around? Two bottles and she's yours?"

"I've never been to one but I know what you mean."

"Well, the Fare and Fowl is the same. With blokes instead of girls."

"And he wanted me to do that?"

"It was suggested. Don't worry. It's only that he was desperate."

"Thanks a lot!"

"No. I didn't mean that. Christ, you're a stunner. You'd send the profits sky high but with Stuart under wraps and another three have left, he's short staffed."

Mark thought quickly. He was on the trail at last!

"What's the plan for this afternoon?" he asked.

"Wedding at three at St. Matthews. Reception at the Bricklayers' Arms. Extras of the page - boys for aunt in Australia. That bit might be interesting. I wonder if it's going to be kilts or satin pants."

"If it's to be at the Bricklayers' Arms there might be a chance for you to meet my uncle," said Mark. "He's dying to meet you."

Simon had, in fact, suggested it. It was the sort of thing an uncle would want to do. He had even bought a briefcase and stuffed it with office equipment brochures.

"Could do," said Dennis. "If there's time."

"I'll call him," said Mark.

Fortunately, the telephone was in the other bar.

"You can't go," said Simon, when Mark had told him about the job offer. "It would look too suspicious. You'd better stay with Singleton. Tell him that Adam and Ben are interested."

"They wouldn't do that!"

"I think they would, just to help you - and it's only likely to be a weekend. Two of them can get him out of the place much easier than just one. I'll call them."

"We've got a wedding reception this afternoon at the Bricklayers'. Do you want to meet him?"

"It might be an idea. Just to establish that you really do have an uncle. Just in case he gets suspicious."

"He's too thick," said Mark. "See you this afternoon."

————

"Your uncle reminds me of somebody," said Dennis as they drove out of the confetti strewn parking lot.

"The most boring man in the world?"

"He does go on a bit, doesn't he? What do I need a new filing cabinet for? I've already got two. As for a desk - what does a photographer want with a bloody desk?"

"You could pose a boy on it. A blond. Call it 'A Fair Bit to do in the Office.'"

"Hey that's good! I like that. I might use that."

"You're welcome. Hey! I know what I wanted to tell you. I thought about it when you were doing the pages. You know that job at Chris' club?"

"Yes."

"Adam and Ben might be interested."

"What? Those two friends of yours? The ones I met at the pool?"

"Yes. Why not? They're gay and they're both broke."

"They didn't look very broke to me."

"They are now. That weekend in London cost them a bomb and they won't get their student grants for months."

"Mmm. I don't know. Can they keep their mouths shut? When there's nothing in them I mean."

"Sure."

"I could mention it I suppose. They're a nice looking couple. How could he get in touch with them?"

"Let me know. I can get a message to them."

"Are you quite sure they'd do it?"

"I would say yes. Like I said, they're both broke and it would hardly be a new experience."

The corner of Dennis' mouth dropped even further. "Do they do it with other people then?" he asked.

"You bet they do. How else do you think they manage to dress so well? It's a question at the moment of working for Chris or hanging around in the local gay pub and hoping for a quick well - paid session in the toilets."

"That's a dangerous game," said Dennis. "I'll have a word with Chris and let you know."

———

Adam's first instinct was to say 'No' very firmly but Simon pointed out that it would help Mark. It may possibly, he said, bring Mark and Howard together again and last but by no means least, they would be doing a public service by rescuing Stuart. All they had to do was to establish where he was. Simon and Charles would take over at that point. Strangely, Ben seemed to accept that it would have to be done.

"Get down there on Friday afternoon if you can," said Simon. "He wants to look you over first."

In fact, being 'looked over' was the worst part. They were both very nervous. They had to undress and stand in front of Chris' desk in their undershorts.

"You'll do," he said. "Peter will show you what to do."

Peter was twenty-three and had been with Chris for four years. He and his fiancee were saving to buy a house. That was the first surprise in a weekend full of surprises. The phrase 'all sorts and conditions of men' used everyday in the chapel at Combleton school was a perfect description of the Fare and Fowl's clientele.

There was the man who booked them both - and one of the curtained alcoves. By the time he arrived they had both realised that these little recesses were danger areas. The other hosts called them the 'groperies'. All the hosts were required to wear very brief and very tight satin shorts and, apart from a pair of sandals, nothing else. Once inside a 'gropery' with the thick curtain drawn shut, it was like being in a cave with an octopus.

Earnestly, as they helped him through a bottle of wine for which he had paid more than five times its value, he warned them of the dangers they faced. Homosexuality, he explained, was clearly forbidden by the Bible. He quoted text after text to prove the point. Failing immediate repentance, all they could look forward to were millennia of agony. Hellfire was hottest for homosexuals.

Halfway through the second bottle, his attitude had changed and the hand which had been thumping the table stroked Adam's thigh.

Ben went to fetch a third bottle and was delayed, as one often was, by a customer who wanted to slip a bank note into his shorts. That third bottle was never opened.
"Then I'd fuck you silly; get right up your tight little ass!" the man was saying, as Ben pulled back the curtain. Then he burst into tears. Adam managed to disentangle himself. They closed the curtain on him and left him to his misery.

Much more dangerous than the groperies were the upstairs rooms, the keys for which hung invitingly behind the bar. One after another, long legged hosts with satin - clad bottoms climbed the stairs followed by a grinning customer rattling a key. Late on Saturday night Ben was just congratulating himself on avoiding the ascent when, after tucking into Chris' excellent Boeuf Wellington his customer, a diplomat of some sort, collected a key. Ben, who had been about to fetch the man's coat and send him on his way, was terrified. He need not have been. For about three quarters of an hour he lay over the man's knees having his behind alternately slapped and fondled.
"You're a very naughty little boy!" said the man. Ben, five feet nine inches tall and weighing over eleven stone, agreed that he was and received six slaps.

To invent, and then to confess to sufficient misdeeds took considerable imagination. Further, they all had to be the sort of misdeeds that a very young boy would commit. By the time he had owned up to riding his bicycle on the pavement; riding it at night without a light; smashing his mother's favourite vase; breaking a window; cheeking a teacher and playing truant, Ben was at a loss for further ideas. His backside was stinging slightly. He was horribly uncomfortable.
"Are you sure you have told me everything? You know what I do to naughty boys who don't own up."
"I drank some wine," said Ben, wishing he hadn't. He had, in fact consumed quite a large quantity with various customers. His bladder was uncomfortably full and his present head - down position made him feel slightly nauseous.
"Ha! Another Stuart! When will you boys learn?"

Ben was hardly aware of the twelve slaps which ensued. The paper on Stuart which Charles and Simon had prepared was clear in his memory. He had to get the man to talk. If only he had known earlier when, between mouthfuls of Boeuf Wellington, the wretched man had held forth on the importance of disciplining small boys. Ben had assumed the existence of a miscreant son in the family!

"It's no good," he said, trying to make his voice sound as deep as possible, "I shall have to have a pee."

Reluctantly, the man let him stand up. He went into the adjacent bathroom. Somehow, he had to destroy the man's small boy fantasy and then get down to some questions. How?

University life and hairy legs did it. He embarked on a description of one of the professors and followed that with the not too surprising fact that the hairs on his legs seemed have grown much more dense since his twentieth birthday. "Look at this one!" he said. "It must be half an inch long!"

The man looked at his watch. "I should be getting back," he said.

"Oh must you? I was hoping we could talk."

"I don't expect to be here again for some time," said the man.

"I hope my crimes were up to Stuart's standard whoever he may be," said Ben.

The man smiled. "A very bad boy," he said.

"Somebody here?"

"He was. He got drunk and ran away."

"I don't know him but this is my first weekend."

"You ought to have done. He's quite beautiful and has such a cheeky bottom! Here. This is for you. I must be off."

Ben took the money and stuffed it, with the rest of his earnings into the genuine pocket of his shorts. The other looked like a pocket but was, in fact, just a slit. Adam called it the 'access hatch'.

Adam was even luckier. Chris had made it clear that they didn't have to do anything which they found unacceptable.

"Felt and fondled but never fucked," he said when, at three in the morning, they were in the room Chris had assigned them as a private bedroom. "I'll tell you one thing Pudge."

"What's that?" asked Ben from the comfort of the bed.

"I'm going to fuck the ass off you tonight. I've had six successive hard-ons and my balls are aching." He continued to pull folded banknotes out of the hem of his shorts.

"Hmmm. Not bad for a night's work," he said, smoothing them out on the dressing table. He pulled his shorts down. Ben laughed.

"You won't think it's funny when it's up you," said Adam.

"It's not that. Come here."

Adam approached. "Turn round," said Ben.

"What..." Adam felt Ben's fingers between his ass cheeks.

"This," said Ben. "It was sticking out of your ass. A fifty quid note."

"I'll spend that one first," said Adam. "Move over a bit."

———

"I don't think he's here now," said Ben an hour later.

"Who?"

"Stuart of course. He was here. That well dressed bloke told me."

"Must tell Simon in the morning," said Adam. "He'll know what to do."

"Not as well as you do."

"Enjoy it did you?"

"What do you think?" Ben leaned over, planted a wet kiss on his friend's forehead and fell asleep.

CHAPTER TWELVE

"Excuse me, rector," said Howard running up to the bat - like figure ahead of him.

"Ah! Ainsworth."

"I wondered if there was any news of young Lynch," said Howard. He was quite certain there wasn't. Nobody within a twenty mile radius of the college could have failed to notice that the frantic activity of the police was continuing. There were posters everywhere; the duck pond had been drained. The local and national newspapers carried banner headlines and the Lynch limousine had been seen in the visitors' car park several times.

"Regrettably not."

"Couldn't Calder give any clue?"

"No. Calder went with Lynch to see a friend of the family but didn't stay. Lynch was put on a train to Combleton the next day. The supposition is that he was kidnapped by somebody he met on the train. The police are investigating of course. The number of times we tell you lads not to speak to strangers! You no longer see Calder of course?"

"No."

"I'm glad to hear it. Lord Beresford has taken an interest in him. I'm delighted about that. It's very good of him. Good for the college too."

Howard had his own ideas as to why Lord Beresford had taken an interest in Jonathan. The whole business was disgusting. Middle aged men and nineteen-year-old students! The odd thing was that Charles had never made even a suggestion to him. He had to assume that Jonathan was more attractive.

Howard decided to take a short stroll to think things over. Yes, he thought, that was it. One couldn't really blame Jonathan. He was young. It was Charles' fault. Jonathan must have confessed that he enjoyed the sessions in the library office. The feel of his butt muscles tensing in Howard's hands and his cock head pushing against the back of Howard's mouth were extremely pleasant memories.

Undoubtedly, Jonathan had told Charles how much he enjoyed it and Charles had suggested that they carry on. He wondered how far Charles had got. It had been pretty easy to persuade Jon to accept a hand and then a mouth. Surely Charles wouldn't have progressed further but it was possible. If it hadn't been for the workmen, Howard would have got there first.

He suddenly realised that his thoughts had taken him into the village. He had no memory at all of the walk down the hill. The windows of Mill Cottage sparkled and the antique brass door knocker gleamed. The garage door was closed which meant that the car was inside. He opened the garden gate. One of the upstairs windows was open. Howard stopped to pick up a small piece of paper which had got caught in a rose bush and then stopped.
"Ah! Ah! Ah! Ah!" The sound came from the open window. Someone gasping. Someone young. No need to guess who it might be. Well, it was going to have to stop. He rang the bell.
"Ah! Ah! Ah! Ah!" Typical of Jonathan. He was taking his time to come. The sound stopped. Howard waited. They would have to dress. That would take time...

The door opened. Jonathan stood there. Not smart Jonathan with his school suit and house tie. This was Jonathan as Howard had seen him in the library. Jonathan in athletic shorts. One couldn't really blame Charles for falling for those legs...
"Hi Jon. Is Charles in?"
"No. He's gone to London."
"Come off it! The car's in the garage."
"I know. It's much more sensible to take the train to London. All that traffic. That car drinks gas."
"What's he gone to London for?"
"Business of some sort."
"So what are you doing in the house?"
"He gave me the key."
"You're quite certain that he isn't here?"
"Of course I am. Hey! We shouldn't be talking here. If one of the monks comes by, you'll be in the shit."

A problem, Howard thought, which could be easily solved by inviting him in but, of course, Jonathan couldn't do that. There was obviously some sort of incriminating evidence; possibly even Charles himself, undressed and obese, fondling his rigid tool and waiting for Jon to fend off the unwelcome visitor before they got down to it again.

Howard shrugged his shoulders. "When will he be back?" he asked.
"After the weekend some time. I'll leave a note to say you called, shall I?"
"Don't bother. It's not important." Howard turned away and the door closed behind him. He stopped, hoping to hear voices but heard nothing. He could imagine what they were saying well enough.
"Who was that, Jon?"
"Howard. I told him that you'd gone to London."
"That was clever of you."
"Do you fancy Howard?"
"Not really. You're much nicer. Let's have those shorts off again shall we. Let's start where we left off."

Imagination gave way to reality. There was no mistaking those gasps. "Ah! Ah! Ah! Ah!"
"Bloody liar!" Howard muttered. "I hope he hurts you!"

———

"This is quite an honour, my Lord," said Chris. "We don't have any members of the aristocracy - or we didn't."
"I'm sure you would if some of my fellow peers knew about the place," said Charles. "Meeting that diplomat chap was pure chance."
"Mr. Burton?"
"I don't think that was the name. I met him at one's club and he was, I fear, rather the worse for wear and discoursing upon the pleasures of slapping bottoms. Every man to his own pleasures but I can think of better things to do with a bottom. A university student, he said. Imagine that!"

Chris laughed. "That would be Mr. Lanz," he said. "The student is working here temporarily. I've got two of them. Nice class of lad too. Well spoken, clean, polite. They're doing well. I'll make sure you meet them on your first visit. Drinks on the house for your first evening of course."
"Actually," said Charles, "I was wondering if you might have something a little...

shall we say less sophisticated? Students, I find, are prone to discourse upon the world's ills when one wants them to be... well, ...just prone."

"Someone who uses his mouth for what mouths are best at, you mean?" said Chris with a leer. "I'll see what I can do. When were you thinking of?"

"Well, this evening is out. I have a reception at the Royal Academy. Tomorrow perhaps - or is that too early?"

"No. I should be able to manage something. They do come expensive though."

"I'm not terribly concerned about that. One is used to paying well for one's pleasures."

"About how old?" asked Chris. They were alone in the office but he lowered his voice.

"Oh legal. I'm not one who goes for green apples."

"Hmmm. Wait a bit."

Chris went out. Charles cast an eye over the papers on his desk. An invoice from a drinks supplier; another from a butcher. Certainly nothing incriminating.

"Take a look through this," said Chris on his return. He handed over a photograph album. Charles opened it. The first page showed a picture of a bearded young man squatting in a yoga position on a mat.

"No thank you," said Charles, repressing a shudder. He leafed through the pages.

"And this one?"

"That's Tony."

"This one is quite nice," said Charles, turning the page.

"He is. I get a lot of good reports on him. Timothy. He's a railway plate layer by trade."

Slowly, Charles turned the pages. The photographs themselves were aesthetically pleasing. Chris' commentary, on the other hand, was revolting. "You wouldn't know he'd had a cock in him." "Takes a while to get worked up but goes nicely when he is."

Mentally counting as he turned the pages, Charles came to number thirty-nine. Stuart! There was no doubt of it. He had never actually seen the boy but the picture fitted Jon's and Howard's description perfectly. Not only that but Jon had mentioned the long, thick curtains in Dennis' studio and there they were in the background. To top everything else, a gold chain glistened against the young man's white skin.

"Oh yes!" said Charles enthusiastically. "That, one could say, is very much my ideal boy."

"Keep going," said Chris. "There are plenty more." There were. Another seventy-six faces grinned up at him from successive pages.

"Now, he's the same age as Stuart who you liked," said Chris. He's only just eighteen. Michael. He's never actually been fucked. You might like to do the honours. You won't get any high falutin' talk out of him. He's hardly ever been to school."

"Mmm. Possible. But on reflection I think I'll have the other one. Stephen was it or Stanley?"

"Stuart. And unfortunately he is the one lad I can't produce."

"Already booked?"

"No. He left just recently."

"That is a pity. Why did he leave?"

"Oh.. just a little difficulty. What about Michael? I can get him. He lives locally. No problem."

"If you would. Shall we say eight o'clock tomorrow?"

"Sure. Look, I'll give you a key now. Save you being stared at and possibly recognised by the other customers. Room five on the second floor. He'll be there waiting for you when you're ready. Just have a drink and pop out the back. It'll look as if you've gone for a pee. Gone to the toilet I mean."

He handed Charles a key with a plastic tab. In return Charles handed him a very large sum of money indeed and left, glad to be in the fresh air again. "Jonathan is not going to like this," he murmured as he waved to a taxi.

———

Michael parked his bike between the dustbins. He had intended to go over to Regents Park that evening but his mother said Chris had rung to ask if he might be free to help with the washing up.

He pushed open the back door. The smell of food made his mouth water. A tin of sardines was all he had eaten that day.

"There you are!" said Chris. "About time!"

"Sorry. I had to help me mum."

"Shovelling coal by the look of you," said Chris. "Go up and get a good bath and then get changed. You're going to be a lucky lad tonight."

"Why?"

"Because you're going to meet a real life, genuine lord, that's why."

"What, with a castle and all that?"

"His brother's got the castle. This one's got two houses; one here and one in France."

"Bloody hell!"

"Don't you use language like that to him. You be polite - and if you'll take my advice, you'll let him do anything he wants. Off you go. Get yourself properly clean and don't leave a tide line round the bath."

"Any chance of something to eat?"

"Here, take this." Chris handed him a chicken leg. Gnawing it greedily, he went up the stairs.

Half an hour later he lay in the bath enjoying a pleasant reverie about lords. Lords who took a fancy to eighteen-year-old boys and adopted them. It was a pity that this one didn't have a castle but two houses would be considerably better than a tenement in Raymond Buildings. He would ask for a horse first. He had always wanted a horse...

Chris burst in. "Aren't you ready yet?" he asked. "He'll be here in half an hour. Stand up. Let's have a look at you."

Michael clambered into an upright position.

"Mmm. Not bad. Dry yourself and put these on. Room five."

"What's he gonna want?"

"How do I know? You just let him do what he wants. None of your bloody blushing innocence act tonight. If he wants your ass, you let him. Understand?"

"Sod that! It hurts," said Michael, towelling his shoulders.

"That's life. Hurry up now. Here's the key. Lock yourself in. And no rabbitting afterwards. He's the sort of client I'm after and if you so much as breathe a word about him I'll have you sorted out. Understand?"

Room five was the best room. Michael sat in the only easy chair and looked round. He felt frightened and terribly alone. In the old days the Fare and Fowl had been fun. The clientele had been younger and more fun loving. More often than not, a customer would take two or three of them upstairs together. It had all been a bit of a lark. Being alone and locked in was different. The bed seemed threateningly huge; much bigger than the one he slept in at home. It was cleaner too; much cleaner. The cover had been folded back to reveal snow-white sheets. He hoped he wouldn't do what he did last time. Not that Chris seemed to mind. Michael's mother would have gone mad if he made a stain like that at home. The customer had been pleased too. Michael remembered how the man had patted his backside and congratulated him. Gay men, he decided, were odd.

He heard a key turn in the lock and jumped.
"Michael?"
"Yes, er.. sir."
"I'm Charles."

He wasn't at all as Michael had imagined he would be. Michael's knowledge of the aristocracy came from films and television. Lords were old, decrepit creatures who walked with the aid of silver-topped walking sticks and punctuated their speech with 'Eh?' and 'What?' This man was youngish - certainly not more than forty and had a friendly sort of face without the moustache Michael expected.
"Pleased to meet you," said Michael, standing up. He gave what he hoped was a polite bow. Charles laughed and held out a hand. Michael shook it. He had shaken hands with a lord!

Charles sat on the bed. "So, tell me all about yourself," he said.
"What do you want to know?" Michael had three carefully rehearsed life stories for various customers. There was the abused boy story. That went down well with the sentimental types. There was the boy scout story. Quite a few of them enjoyed that - especially when he got to the bit about the summer camp. Lastly there was the 'I think I'm different from other people. I seem to like men' one. That was a sure winner.
"What school did you go to?"
"Springfields. Round the corner from here. I never went there often."
"So I've heard. Do you have a job?"
"Nah! I keep looking out though. I wouldn't mind being a butler or something like that."
"Family?"
"Mum, two sisters and three brothers."
"Six of you, eh? What about your dad?"
"Never had one. I've always wanted a dad. I wouldn't mind being adopted."

Charles laughed. "And what brings you to this place?" he asked.

Aha! Playing the customers was a bit like playing with an old fashioned radio set. It took time to find the right wavelength.

"I like men," he said. "Dunno why. I mean, all my mates have got girlfriends. They're just not my scene somehow. With a man you can have long talks and he can advise you what to do and... er... punish you if you do something wrong if you know what I mean. And if a man wanted you to do something - anything - you'd do it because you like him so much. Know what I mean?"

Charles smiled. "I think," he said, "that we should start being honest with each other. Then we'll get on better. I just want you to do me one favour."
"Sure. Anything. Like I said." His mouth went dry. It had been unbearably painful when the last man had tried.
"There was a boy here recently named Stuart Lynch. Did you know him?"
"Stuart? Course I did. Posh voice."
"What happened to him, Michael? Where is he now?"
"No idea."
"Did you know him well?"
"Yeah. We was mates. We worked together sometimes."
"How?"

Michael's opinion of the aristocracy went down slightly. They, of all people, were supposed to know about life.
"You know," he said, slightly irritably, "customer books two of us. Brings them up here. Works on one and the other has to watch. It's supposed to be a turn-on, see? Like 'I'm going to suck your mate dry and I want you to watch so you can do it better when it's your turn.' Things like that."
"Extraordinary!"
"The customers like it."
"And you?"
"Oh, it's okay. We don't mind. Not mostly. The sados are a pain. Chris doesn't let them come on too strong but some of them try to smuggle whips in."
"Did anything like that happen to Stuart?"
"Not as far as I know. It was just smackers and suckers when we was together. There was one bloke who wanted us to do it together so he could watch."
"Do what?"
"Screwing. We didn't though. We can always say no. That's what Chris says.

Mind you...I wouldn't mind if someone really nice wanted to try."

"You need have no fear. In truth, Michael, I need your help and not your body. I want to find Stuart."

"Are you a detective or something?"

"Nothing like it. I'm a friend of a friend - and Stuart has to be found."

"I don't know where he is. There was the night of the panic and I never saw him after that."

"Tell me about that."

"I don't know what happened. Chris said us part timers shouldn't come again unless he asked us to. Like tonight with you. He don't want the place to be too obvious, see?"

"And Stuart? He wouldn't have had a home to go to. Where did he live?"

"Here. He had a room upstairs."

"So he could still be here?"

"No. Definitely not. I'd know if he was."

"So go through that last evening for me, Michael."

"It was quiet. I had a smacker first. Then I was in a gropery with a Japanese bloke."

"A what?"

"Those alcoves with curtains downstairs. There was this bloke coming on strong about my cock. He wanted me to shoot a load over his dinner. It was funny really."

"Sounds pretty revolting to me. What was so funny about it?"

"Well, he'd ordered his dinner and there he was tossing me off dead slow so that I'd come just at the right time but I came before the dinner did - all over his suit. Of course! I remember now."

"What?"

"That was why his dinner came late. Chris was with another bloke and Stuart in a gropery."

"Chris and another man?"

"Yeah. I thought it was odd. Chris usually stays in the kitchen."

"What did the other man look like? Do you know anything about him?"

"I've seen him here before. Not very often. Foreign - looking. Rich."

"Describe him for me."

"Well, he's about fifty I should think. He's tall. He's got black hair. Wears a suit."

"What makes you say he's rich?"

"Got a chauffeur. When he comes the chauffeur eats in the kitchen. I've seen him in there. Chris used to give me bits and pieces to take home. Mum's out of work, see?"

"No idea of the car registration number or names, I suppose?" said Charles.

"The chauffeur's called Harry. That's all I know."

"Well, that's enough to go on. Now, let's do a bit of deception, shall we?"

"How do you mean?"

"Well, friend Chris will want to be reassured that you have done what I was supposed to come here for. Stage number one is to ruffle the bed. You can do that. Make sure it looks as if it's been thoroughly used. I, in the meantime, will attend to the accessories which must be somewhere."

He found them in a cupboard beside the bed. He tore open a contraceptive packet, dropped the torn paper on the floor, squeezed the cream tube into the rubber which he wrapped carefully in his handkerchief and pocketed it carefully.

"How's that?" asked Michael triumphantly, throwing a pillow onto the floor.

"Looks as if there were about six of us," said Charles with a smile. I wouldn't have credited myself with so much energy. Now, let's deal with you."

"How?"

"Financially. Now, I want you to make it quite clear to Chris that you are my personal boy from now on. Here's fifty pounds..."

"How much?" Michael's eyes were wide open.

"Fifty pounds. I'll deal with Chris downstairs. Now then, have you eaten?"

"Chris gave me a chicken leg."

"Not enough for a man with your build. Where's your favourite eating place?"

"The Hungry Hussar round the corner. It's not your scene though. Rock music and all that."

"With good company, everything is my scene. I'll meet you in there in half an hour, okay."

"Sure. Thanks a lot."

"And if Chris asks, I. ...er.. did it, if you know what I mean."

"Screwed me?"

"Yes."

"What if he asks me what it feels like?"

"If one's school-days are anything to go by, I should say 'uncomfortable' and if he asks anything personal about me, you didn't see it."

"He won't. He never does."

"Just as well. I'll see you shortly."

Charles took off his jacket, crumpled it slightly, put it on again and left.

"All right?" said Chris who was standing in the open kitchen doorway at the foot of the stairs.

"Superb!" said Charles. "You certainly know how to pick them!"

"He obliged then?"

"Oh yes. It took a little persuasion but we managed."

"Good for you! When we get back to normal, he'll be a good earner. Once they've had one cock, they'll take others."

"I wanted to talk to you about that. He's such a nice boy that I'd like to have sole rights."

"Oh, I don't know about that."

"Would this help?" Charles handed him a thick envelope. He opened it.

"Well, certainly for the next few months, my lord. After that, I couldn't say."

"A few months will be enough," said Charles.

"Those two students are in tonight, my lord, if you'd like to meet them."

"Very much but not tonight. I have a dining appointment elsewhere."

"Of course. House of Lords is it?"

"Not exactly no. Good night."

"Good night, my lord and thank you."

"Jon isn't going to like this at all," Charles muttered as he left the building and set off for the more congenial atmosphere of the Hungry Hussar.

CHAPTER THIRTEEN

Howard wasn't really surprised to hear that Charles had gone to London again the following weekend. He would have been very surprised if it was true. Charles hated London. Jonathan was so obviously lying. At least he had invited Howard in. That was something. There was no visible sign of Charles' presence but then, thought Howard, there wouldn't be. He was upstairs waiting impatiently. Well... Howard would make him wait.

"They're well on the track of Stuart," said Jonathan.

"Good. That's why he's gone to London, is it?"

"I guess so. He's had several phone calls from Simon in the last week."

"I hope they weren't at inconvenient times."

"No. Why?"

"Well, when you're busy you don't want to be interrupted by phone calls, do you?"

"I guess not."

"Did Charles mention Mark at all?"

"Yeah. He's kind of a key player. I don't know how. He's with Simon."

"And Charles has gone all the way to London to see them, has he?"

"I guess so."

"By train?"

"Yes."

"I thought he hated train travel. He always used to."

"It's more economical."

"So you said last week. Do you think I could have something to drink? It's a long walk down that hill."

"Oh sure. Wait there." Jonathan went into the kitchen. There was no doubt about it. He really did have a perfect ass. Howard watched as he opened the refrigerator and bent down to take out a bottle. If he had done that a few times in Charles' presence one couldn't really blame the man for falling for him.

"You having one yourself?" Howard asked.

"Not yet. I'll have one later on." He came back with a bottle of beer and a glass.

"Thanks," said Howard, I needed that. What do you actually do down here? It must be a bit lonely surely, with Charles away."

He had no doubt at all that the question had gone home. Jon shifted awkwardly from one foot to the other and blushed slightly. "Not really," he said. "I get more lonely at college. Now that Stuart's gone. I like coming down here. There's things to do."
"Such as?"

He was fairly sure that Jon would have told him everything. Unfortunately, there was a loud and peremptory knock on the door. Howard jumped. Some of his drink splashed down onto his jeans.
"No worry. It's only the odd job man," said Jon.
"We seem blighted by odd job men," said Howard. "They always seem to arrive when things are getting interesting."
"He's only come for his money," said Jon. He went over to the desk in the corner, took some notes out of a drawer and went to go to the front door. It really did look as if Charles was not at home after all. He was probably shopping, thought Howard.
"I'd better slip out through the back door," he said. "Don't want anyone to see me here. It'd get us both into trouble. We're not supposed to have any contact at all."
"No. Stay. This won't take a minute. The college can't stop us seeing each other in someone's private house."
"They'd have a bloody good try." The door knocker rapped again.
"They couldn't in the States," said Jon. "What goes on in a private house is none of their business."
"Maybe so, but we aren't in the States now. Anyway, I'd better get back to college. What about you?"
"Oh, some time yet."

Some considerable time, thought Howard as he closed the back door behind him. Time for Charles to come back with the shopping and unwrap that. Or would he unwrap Jonathan first?

––––

"As far as we can make out, he's not often here. Peter says he's a nasty piece of work," said Adam.

Charles sipped his brandy and looked over the rim of the glass. "That's not surprising in this place. Who's Peter?" he asked.

"The tall one in the green shorts. He's the sort of senior host."

"What did Peter say about him?"

"His name is Tom Gonzalez. He lives somewhere down in the New Forest. He's South American. He's a porno - king. He's always after boys to star in videos. That's why he comes here. Peter said it's best to stay well clear. They're the real hard stuff. Watch out. Here comes Chris again."

"... but I don't think I know Professor Gregory," said Charles, loudly.

"Getting on well?" Chris asked for the second time that evening.

"Very well. A nice couple of lads," said Charles. "Forgive me, once I start on recollections of my university years I can't be stopped."

"Oh, that's all right. We're not busy. Er.. that package is waiting for you, my lord."

"I'll be along in a moment." He turned to Adam and Ben again. "There was a professor... Professor Jenkins or some name like that. Extraordinary man. Quite mad..." He waited until Chris was out of earshot.

"Anything else about him?" he asked.

"I don't think so. How long is this business going on for?" said Adam.

"If Simon can trace this man, we should be able to tie it up. Unless Tom whatever his name is has passed Stuart on already. I'd better be getting on. I now have to spend an hour in the company of a young man upstairs and try and convince your boss that I have done everything in the book. In fact we shall sit and talk."

"I'll bet Simon wouldn't just sit and talk," said Ben.

"Possibly not. I have long said that one day, Simon will compromise himself badly," said Charles. They stood up. "Well, have a good and profitable evening," said Charles. "Tell me, aren't those shorts uncomfortably tight?"

"Yes, but we don't wear them all the evening," said Ben with a laugh. "They're more off than on."

"You both deserve a medal," said Charles.

"Everything okay, my lord?" Chris was again waiting in the kitchen door.

"Very much so. He's a really nice obliging young man."

"I'm glad. Will you want him next weekend?"

"I'm not sure. Can I call you?"

"Of course you can. You know the number?"

"Yes. Can I have a very private word with you?"

"Of course. Come into the office." Chris led the way through the kitchen.
"Money problems?" he asked when the office door was closed behind them.
"No, no. Nothing like that, thank God. I know that you're a man of great discretion."
"Have to be in this line."
"This is about a great friend of mine. Have you heard of Simon Spencer?"
"The writer? Yes of course."
"Well now, I know Simon very well. We've been friends for years. Simon has a problem. I knew something of it before but meeting those two lads has confirmed how serious it is."
"What?"
"You will keep this under your hat?"

Chris nodded.
"Years ago, about four years ago to be exact, Simon had a fling with a boy. A nice lad. I've met him. I thought then that he was somewhat indiscreet. The affair with Simon is all over now. I don't think they have slept together for years. Now it happens that the boy is at the same university as your two youngsters. My stupid fault. I boasted about being a friend of Simon's and they told me that the news that he is gay is all over the university. The young man brags endlessly about the days when he was the light of Simon Spencer's life. I need hardly tell you what would happen to Simon's reputation if it were to go further. You can't write macho war stories and go on manoeuvres with the army and be openly gay. His public wouldn't take it."
"I see. Adam and Ben shouldn't have mentioned it to you."
"Oh it's as much my fault as theirs. I boasted about knowing Simon. Don't tell them I mentioned it to you."
"I don't really see where I come in," said Chris.
"What is needed," said Charles, "is for this young man to vanish. It shouldn't be too difficult. He's twenty-two. There isn't a family to make a fuss. Let him go abroad for a nice long time or..."
"I see what you mean. I might be able to help. I do have a contact. Is this lad good looking?"
"I would say yes. Rather too old for my taste of course."
"Can you give me full details? I really need full details. This acquaintance of mine will want to check."
"Of course."
"I thought you'd never get here," said Michael shouting over the noise of the music.

"Sorry. I got held up with Chris."
"No problem?"
"No. If I had really done all the things to you I said I'd done, you wouldn't be able to sit down!"

Michael laughed. "He told my mum I was doing well."
"Doesn't your mother wonder where all the money comes from?"
"She doesn't stick her nose into my business. I don't stick mine into hers. It's the same sort of business if you know what I mean. Mine is better paid though, thanks to you."

They ate their way through the Hungry Hussar's usual oily cuisine. Michael was good company and if any of the youthful clientele of the Hungry Hussar thought it strange that a lad in tattered jeans should be sitting there with such a well dressed and distinguished looking man, they said nothing.

––––

"That's where your friends are working. That place on the left," said Dennis.

The Fare and Fowl private dining club looked respectable enough from the outside. It was brightly lit and freshly painted. Two ornamental box trees flanked the steps.
"Do you want to pop in and see them?"
"No. Better not. They'd be a bit embarrassed. It looks okay."
"Oh it is. High class clientele. Only place in London with ass on the menu. Good quality ass too."

Mark laughed "I'll pass on the compliment to Adam and Ben when I see them again!" he said. "Can you drop me somewhere near the Bricklayers?"
"Not coming back for a coffee?"
"No. Not tonight. I'm a bit tired."

He wasn't so much tired as bored. They had spent the entire day photographing houses and cars. That, and Dennis' dreadful sense of humour had taken its toll. Dennis dropped him off at the corner. "See you at the crack of dawn, as the hangman said to the condemned man," he said. Mark managed to raise the last laugh of the evening and the aged Renault clattered off.
Simon was waiting for him in the bar. "A good day?" he asked.

"Don't talk about it. It was dreadful. I don't think I can take much more."

"You don't have to. I've just had Charles on the phone."

"Oh yes?"

"He thinks he knows who's got Stuart."

"So I can go back to university?"

"Correct, but let me get you a drink and tell you a story."

"We passed the place where Adam and Ben are working," said Mark, after the first delicious sip of the first beer of the day. "It looks okay. We nearly went in."

"Thank Christ you didn't!" said Simon. "That would have blown things. Anyway. Story time. Once upon a time, a struggling writer met a boy in a bus station. He took the boy home and, after a few weeks, they had what the books call a meaningful relationship..."

Mark laughed. "Was the boy incredibly good looking?" he asked.

"He still is. In fact the struggling writer still occasionally has the hots for him. Anyway, the boy grew up and fell in love with somebody else and that was the end of that. Then this incredibly handsome, good looking youth went off to university."

"... to study computer science?"

"Correct. But then he started to spread the story that the struggling writer was gay."

"I never said a word!" said Mark, aghast. "I've never once mentioned your name to anyone except Adam and Ben! Who told you that? I'll kill him!"

"Calm down! It's a story. It's all being fabricated. We are going to need you as a sort of bait. Don't worry. It'll all be safe and well planned."

"Just as well!" said Mark. "I don't like people making accusations like that, even in a story."

"No... I'm sorry. Charles felt it was necessary."

"So what do you want me to do?"

"Finish with Singleton tomorrow. Tell him that your kind uncle has finished down here. Then you go back to university. It's possible that our friends might do some checking. Tell me, is there anyone there who is really outrageously gay? There's usually at least one in every senior common room."

"Ha! Only the theology prof. Everybody knows about him."

"Excellent. I want you to make friends with him. Don't worry. You don't have to do anything. When our friends do their checks I want you to be seen in that man's company. Tell him you've seen the light or something. Then, when you hear from me or Charles you go down to Combleton and hole up there. Don't draw any attention to yourself. We'll contact you there."

Mark sipped his drink again. "I won't be sorry to get out of this place," he said

"Nor me. I'll have to be here for a day or two to work things out with Charles."

"Was it all a story?" asked Mark.

"How do you mean?"

"About the handsome young man and meaningful relationship?"

"Certainly not! Only the last bit about the rumour was false. The struggling author is still keen on him."

"I thought he had Adam and Ben."

"He has them when he can but they're not a match on the handsome one. He was first and always will be. But, as I said, he fell in love with another boy..."

"That's all over," said Mark bitterly.

"Which is a pity. Another beer?"

"Yes please."

Simon went to the bar and returned with a scotch and a beer.

"What this author, who could hardly be described as 'struggling' doesn't realise," said Mark, "is that his handsome young friend still occasionally has the hots for *him*."

"Really?"

"Really. It's funny. You and I got on so well. We argued sometimes but they were soon over. Not like me and Howard."

Simon laughed. "Remember the rose bush? I wanted it in the front garden. You wanted it in the back. In the end I had to go out and buy another one."

"That's right! And what about that time when I lost my temper with the spade and threw it at the car?"

"And you used the entire draft of a chapter to start a bonfire! Oh, there were times when you got right up my nose!"

"And there were times when you got right up me," said Mark. "They were good times though."

"Do you mean that?"

"Yes."

"What about another for old times' sake?"

"I haven't finished this one yet."

"I wasn't thinking of beer. Come up when you're ready."

"I'll come upstairs with you. I can leave this. You're sure your reputation will

allow it? Going upstairs with an incredibly handsome young man, I mean?"
"Who cares? I'm an office equipment salesman. They can get away with anything."

———

The nice thing about Simon, thought Mark, was that he was so gentle. He lay cradled in the man's hairy arms. That old, familiar stretched feeling in his ass was strangely comforting.
"Do you still hate Howard?" Simon asked, twining a lock of Mark's hair in his fingers.
"No, I don't hate him at all. I miss him. But it's all over. We could never get on with one another."
"Let's wait and see. I'm sure Howard misses you. This especially." His hand went round Mark's cock.
"Mmm. I wonder. Keep doing that. It feels good," said Mark.

CHAPTER FOURTEEN

"Not far now," Mark panted. "Nearly there."

Stephen started to sing again. "Four and twenty virgins came down from Inverness..."
A taxi drew up alongside them. The fourth since they started out from the Leather Bottle. "You all right, mate?" said the driver and then, "Oh it's 'im." The taxi sped off into the distance.
"That's right. Fuck off. Fucking cunt!" Stephen shouted. "You too," he added, as he spotted two women on the other side of the road. "You can fuck off too and..." He grasped a lamp - post, did a sort of dance around it and then stopped to vomit violently in the gutter. Mark just managed to get out of the way in time.
"Jesus fucking Christ!" Stephen choked, and another gush splattered over the pavement.

There was no doubt that 'our Stevie' as Professor Carpenter called him, really did have a problem. Sadly, it wasn't the problem Mark had thought it was but there was no way he could leave Stephen in that condition. He'd never get home unaided. Mark was stuck with him. Until that evening he'd entertained such high hopes. Now they were all dashed. He should have found out about Stephen first. Possibly he could have asked the professor himself.

The professor held open house every Monday evening for people who had 'problems'. Mark hadn't specified any problems when he made the appointment to go round there. It was common knowledge that, in fact, the professor was only interested in one and it became pretty obvious after being in the house for only a few minutes that the five other students were gay. Outrageously so. Two sat on the sofa. Two were on chairs, leaving Mark to sit on the floor with a young man named Matthew who, it appeared, was destined for the Church - as were two of the others.

Professor Carpenter sat in a high backed wooden chair with a peculiar brass reading stand in front of him. It even had a candle holder and must, like most of the rest of the furniture, not to mention the house itself, have dated from Victorian times.

"Identification of the problem is so important," he droned in that strange ecclesiastical voice. "St. Paul himself acknowledges the thorn in his flesh and we can - ah - judge to what he was referring in his exaggerated concern for Timothy."

"Oh I say! Perhaps he put his thorn in Timothy's flesh!" one of the others whispered. "Lucky Timothy!"

The professor ignored him. "That is what we all must learn to do," he said. "We must acknowledge our weaknesses and be open."

"I'm open any time for the right man," said Matthew. Mark looked at him and wondered how anybody in their right mind could fall for a twenty-year-old with a hawk-like nose, thick glasses, legs like match-sticks and, from what he could detect, a cock to match. It wasn't only his appearance that was against him. Mark was so close to him that Matthew's repeated but silent farts were going right up his nostrils.

The professor had launched into another homily, this time quoting Michaelangelo as the example all should follow when the doorbell rang.

"That'll be dear Stevie," said the professor. "Perhaps one of you would let him in."

The others stayed put. Matthew got to his feet and, with an expression of extreme distaste, left the room.

He returned followed by none other than Stephen Marshall! Mark had seen Stephen around and heard about him often enough at home. Both Adam and Ben had raved about him - with good reason. Stephen Marshall wasn't just attractive. He was gorgeous. He was very tall - almost as tall as Lord Charles. He had beautiful and immaculate blond hair; a smiling face and the most attractive lips Mark had ever seen. They were thick and exactly like the cupid's bow that romantic novelists wrote about. Mark's heart speeded up as Stephen found a space on the floor and went to sit down.

"Late as ever, Stevie," said the professor. "How is your dear father?"

"He's okay," said Stephen. He lowered himself gracefully into a squatting position. Mark took in the bulge in the front of his jeans and quickly looked away again.

"I really must get down to Porchester some time and visit the dear man," said the Professor. "We're talking about St. Paul and Michaelangelo tonight."

"Oh yeah?" said Stephen - and the boredom continued. Mark, who felt like screaming 'What the hell does it matter if they were gay?' sat and contemplated Stephen out of the corner of his eye. Was it possible? Adam and Ben reckoned it was. "I'll bet old Carpenter screws his delectable little ass more times than he has hot dinners," Adam had said. The thought of Stephen naked, and spread out on a bed upstairs was enough to turn anyone one on but with Professor Carpenter? Mark shuddered. The man was at least sixty, emaciated and wrinkled. Mark turned away from Stephen. The professor's fingers were draped over the edge of the reading stand. The ghastly amethyst ring which he wore on his little finger and claimed to be a present from the Patriarch of somewhere glittered as he droned on. Had that bejewelled finger caressed Stephen? Surely not.

The professor closed the book he'd been quoting from. "That must be enough for today, my dears. I think you'll find that Mrs. Hutchinson has excelled herself again," he said. The rush to the door should have told him that seven young men had been bored out of their minds.

In the back room was a huge table. Mark had rarely seen so much food. The sideboard was similarly laden but with bottles and cans. Mark took a beer, loaded his plate with cold chicken and salad and moved over to Stephen. That wasn't difficult. He stood by himself, ignored by the others.

"What are you doing here?" Stephen asked. "You're computer studies aren't you?"

"'S right," Mark replied, speaking with a mouth full of lettuce. He swallowed. "Somebody told me it was worth coming for the food," he said.

"And the drink," said Stephen. He frowned. "I wouldn't have thought it was good enough to come just for that though. You don't look as if you've got any problems."

Remembering Simon's advice, Mark said he thought Professor Carpenter a most interesting man..

"He's a fucking lunatic. That's what my dad said."

"Does he know him then?"

"My dad's a bishop."

"Odd language for a bishop to use."

For the first time that evening, Stephen laughed. His face seemed to light up and he stopped being merely attractive. Stephen Marshall, Mark decided, was the most beautiful young man he had ever met. Just looking at that smiling face made his legs feel weak.

"Why are you here, come to that?" he asked. "What's your problem?"

"Me? I have to come once a week. If I come on the night when he has his fairy ring meeting, it gets it over quicker, that's all." He took a can of beer from sideboard, clicked it open and put it to his lips.

At which point, just as the conversation was getting interesting enough to make up for the hour and a half's tedium earlier, the Professor entered the room again. From the sounds which had come from the front room, Mark guessed he'd been putting the furniture back in order. He made a bee-line for the two of them.

"You two know each other then?" he asked.

Mark explained that they had just met.

"Splendid. Don't overdo it will you, Stephen?" he said. He might as well have been talking to a brick wall - or a sponge. Stephen stared at him insolently, put down the can and picked up another. He opened it. His lips seemed to reach out to connect with the hole.

"Better come with me now," said the professor. Stephen scowled but he put the can down again and followed the professor out of the room leaving Mark alone. One or two of the others tried to get him into conversation but the latest image of Stephen filled his mind to such an extent that he found himself nodding; saying 'Yes' and 'No' automatically. The professor had left the room first, followed by Stephen. No jeans shop in the world, Mark decided, could possibly have sold a pair like that off the peg. They had to have been made specially for him. It was almost as if the material had been sprayed on to his behind and left to set. Two beautiful denim clad globes; a maker's label on the right one; a seam that ran straight down from the exact centre of Stephen's back and vanished into his crotch. Just that momentary glimpse was enough to make Mark feel light headed and strangely happy. Adam's narrow, muscular behind and Howard's pert jutting bottom were nothing compared to what he had just seen. It was a revelation.

He suddenly felt strangely alone and afraid; as if surrounded by alien forces. He'd never felt like it at Father Cuthbert's or Harry's. Momentarily he thought he heard Stephen's voice raised in some sort of protest. He went to the door but then decided he must have been mistaken. All round him, the members of the professor's 'circle' continued their chatter.

"They have it in mind to make him Dean. Anything to get him away from parish youth work. That's what I've heard," said one.

"Oh my dear! They'll never manage that. You'd need a crowbar to prise him away from his boy scouts," said his companion. "I should know. I was one. Oooh! Those summer camps - and I do mean camps!"

"He's got the most lovely little church you ever saw," said one of the others. "I went there in the vac with my friend."

"And I'll bet you stayed overnight," said another; a young man with a hawk-like nose and thick glasses.

"We did actually. Had a lovely time."

"I'll bet. I say, these sausages are rather 'more-ish' don't you think?"

"They certainly put me in mind of something similar that I wouldn't mind more of."

Mark had had enough. He put down his plate and his half-empty glass and sidled round the half-open door. He padded along the dim hallway, reached the front door and emerged, with a sigh of relief into the open air. He got into the car, started it and was about to drive home when an idea struck him. He drove down the road, turned left, left again and drove right round the block until he was back in Professor Carpenter's road. He parked near the kerb, switched off the engine and waited.

Half an hour went by before the door opened and the one called Matthew came out, closely followed by another. Then, for a long time, nothing happened. He fell to thinking. His acquaintance with the clergy was minimal. Father Cuthbert, he thought, wasn't really evil. It was unlikely that he ever actually did anything to his young 'scamps'. The chaplain at school had been a wet character who tried desperately to be one of the lads and, in so doing, managed to alienate them all. According to Howard, the monks at St. Frideswide's hadn't the slightest idea of what went on in the place but were well-meaning enough. The Reverend Professor Carpenter was a different kettle of fish altogether. All that phoney theology was a defence. He had some sort of hold over Stephen...

Two more students came out of the house and then the last. Now just Stephen was there. Mark wondered what he was doing but found the thought so distasteful that he picked up the computer magazine from the passenger seat and propped it up against the steering wheel. Anything to take his mind off those withered hands in contact with any part of Stephen's body.

He'd barely read the first paragraph when the door opened yet again and Stephen emerged. Mark put down the magazine and stared out through the windscreen. There was something about the way Stephen was walking which wasn't quite right. He looked a bit like a puppet being manipulated by a not very skilled puppeteer. Every foot-fall looked too deliberate. Mark started the car and drove down to where Stephen stood shaking his head.

"Lift?" asked Mark, opening the nearside door. Stephen didn't reply but managed, with some difficulty to get into the car.

"Thank God that's over," he said.

"A painful experience eh?" said Mark as he started the car.

"It always fucking well is. Still, I got stacked up with enough loot for the week."

So that was it! The poor sod was doing it for the money. In some ways it was a relief to hear that. The thought of a person as beautiful as Stephen having any sort of affectionate relationship with Professor Carpenter was too horrible even to contemplate. Stephen obviously needed someone like Mark to put him on the right lines and to love him properly.

Stephen lived in digs in Greig Road, a run-down street of Edwardian terraced houses. Mark hoped he might be invited in but no such luck. Stephen thanked him for the lift and he watched as his new friend walked unsteadily up the garden path, found the key and let himself in.

"Been fucked silly!" Mark muttered, and shuddered slightly at the thought.

He said nothing about Stephen to Adam or to Ben. They were too occupied with their sordid adventures in London and with work they had to catch up with. Mark, too, had a lot of catching up to do but found himself wandering in and out of various university buildings several times during the following week, hoping to catch up with Stephen again. It was Adam he had to thank for their next meeting. Adam wanted the car to go to a football practice. Mark wanted it to go to his computer club. They compromised. Mark would drive Adam to the sports ground and then go on to the club. He would leave there at a reasonable time and pick Adam up on the way back.

They had just arrived at the sports centre. Adam pulled his bag out of the boot and disappeared through one door when Stephen appeared coming out of another. They must have missed each other by split seconds. Mark leapt out of the car.

"Hi!" he said.

"Oh hi!"

"Didn't know you were a sporting man."

"Badminton," said Stephen. "What are you doing here?"

"Same question last time we met," said Mark with a grin. He explained the situation.

"I was wondering if you'd like to come out for a drink some time this week," he said.

"Love to but I can't afford it."

"No worry. I'll pay," said Mark. Ben, he thought, should have topped up the household petty cash. He could borrow a bit from that."

"I'd feel guilty," said Stephen.

"No reason why you should. I never do if you know what I mean."

Stephen smiled. "Okay then," he said. "When and where?"

"Do you know the Leather Bottle in Ancton Lane?"

"Sure. Been there several times."

"Let's go there then. I won't bring the car so we can both drink. Tomorrow?"

"Sure. About eight o'clock?"

"I'll be there," said Mark. "Want a lift?"

"No. The walk will do me good. It's not far."

Mark didn't sleep that night. He lay in bed with one hand on his rampant cock, making up delightful little phrases about Stephen. 'Glorious, globular gluts' was a good one he thought - so was 'A pretty, pulsating prick'. It looked at last as if his life was going to get some sort of direction. Howard was in the past. So were all the sordid people he'd met in the last few days. He had a new partner; a really good looking young man of about his own age who he could relate to properly. Simon would be pleased. It would be great to take Stephen to the next Lakeside meeting. Adam and Ben's noses would be put out of joint but they had each other - and he had Steve.

It didn't give him time to reach for a tissue that evening. He cursed, got out of bed, stripped off his sodden shorts and then went back under the covers. After that, he slept.

The Leather Bottle was a nice pub, much frequented by students and had the advantage of being about half-way between Greig Road and Mark's place. A couple of pints in the Leather Bottle and then... It would be better, he thought, to get Steve to take him back to his digs. One never knew about Adam and Ben. There was always the chance that one of them might disturb them. Sooner or later they'd have to know that he was fucking Stephen. Later better than sooner. He opened the pub door and went in. Every table was full. He looked over to the bar and there was Stephen, sitting on a bar stool at the corner of the bar next to a fruit machine. For a second or two Mark feasted his eyes on Stephen's behind. It projected over the top of the stool like an apple on an egg-cup.

"Ready for another?" he asked. Stephen's glass was almost empty.

"Thanks."

The barman served two drinks; a beer for Mark and a beer for Steve. Mark queried the price.

"He's already had two," said the barman.

"Hope you don't mind," said Stephen.

"Oh no. Sure. No problem." It was in fact, he thought, a bloody cheek. Perhaps Stephen knew what he had in mind and was determined to make him pay for it. It had been a bit stupid of him to offer to buy the drinks anyway. That sentiment intensified as the evening progressed. By the time they found a table in a corner, Stephen had drunk four beers and was on his first rum. Mark was still on his second pint.

"I don't think I'll be going to any more Carpenter evenings," he said.

"You're lucky."

"All that balls about St. Paul and Michaelangelo. What the hell does it matter if they were gay?"

Stephen nodded. Mark lowered his voice. "Quite a lot of famous people are gay," he said. "Ever heard of Simon Spencer?"

"No. Who's he?"

"You must have seen 'Murderous Mission'. He wrote the original book."

"No. Never heard of him. Mind if I have another one?"

This was hard going, Mark thought as he went up to the bar for another rum.

"He's had just about enough," said the barman, nodding in Stephen's direction.

"He'll be okay. I'll take him home," Mark replied. He looked back to where Stephen was sitting. He looked okay.

"I still can't understand why you have to go round there every Monday," he said when he'd got back to the table. "I mean... due respect and all that but they're a bunch of weirdoes."

"Don't tell me. I have to. My dad arranged for him to shell out my allowance in weekly instalments. It's this stuff." He held up the glass, stared at it for a few seconds and then downed the contents. Mark felt like a child whose favourite toy has been snatched away from him. He'd been quietly assessing this particular toy ever since they sat at the table. It looked pretty big; the sort of toy which worked well once it had been wound up.

"I could introduce you to Simon Spencer if you're interested," he said.

"Who?"

"The writer."

"No thanks. How about another drink?"

And so the evening wore on. Stephen became more and more aggressive as he downed successive drinks. The funds Mark had borrowed declined at a frightening rate. He had made a hideous mistake. There was going to be no chance whatever with Stephen - unless...

"One last one for the road," he said, picking up Stephen's glass.

"Yeah, okay. I'll just nip out again."

He'd been to the toilet about five times. This time he had trouble opening the door and almost fell in.

"Your mate's had far too much," said the barman. "You're going to have problems with him."

Mark wondered. He hadn't given up hope. "Can you call for a taxi?" he asked wondering, as he did so, if he'd have enough money for the fare.

"You won't find a taxi firm that'll take him. They all know him of old. So do we. He's caused more damage in here than a hundred regulars."

Stephen hadn't been too bad in the pub. Once they were outside in the fresh air, the trouble started. Stephen shouted obscenities at a group of girls; kicked a parked car and raised a threatening finger at a group of men.

"Take no notice. I'll get him home. I'm afraid he's a bit pissed," said Mark as two of them came over.

"Pissed? Whose fucking pissed? I'll show you who's fucking pissed!" Stephen shouted. Mark put an arm round his waist and shepherded him out of the car park. It was funny, he thought. In any other circumstances, having an arm round Stephen's waist would have given him an erection in seconds.

Not that night. Every step was murder. The total distance to Greig Road wasn't more than a mile. It seemed like ten.

Stephen was almost a dead weight. He was also an embarrassment. Several people were told to fuck off or that they reminded Stephen of some personal item of anatomy. Mark hoped that he would sober up after he'd been sick but even that didn't seem to do any good. By the time they got to his doorstep with Mark panting heavily from the effort, Stephen's head was slumped on his shoulder.

"Key?" Mark asked. There was no response. There was nothing for it but to reach into his pocket to find it and that wasn't very pleasant. A vomit soaked handkerchief had to be got out of the way first. Stephen giggled as Mark groped. He found the key and opened the door. Stephen slumped across the step and would have fallen if Mark hadn't held him tight.

"I'd better come in and look after you," he said. There was a pervasive smell of cabbage made Mark feel queasy. Strangely it seemed to revive Stephen. He managed to climb the stairs, putting one foot deliberately onto each tread and then bringing the other up. Mark followed him closely and placed a steadying hand on Stephen's backside.

"You're after my ass," said Stephen, and he giggled.

His room was a pretty typical student pad. There were posters on the wall. A computer stood on a desk in the window. There were books and papers everywhere but no bed.

"Where's your bed?" Mark asked.

"Thish. Folds down. Bit fucking diffi - difficult," said Stephen collapsing onto the sofa.

It was. He heaved Stephen up and onto the floor and, for some moments groped round the thing trying to find some sort of lever. Finally, more by luck than anything else, the sofa extended. He put down the legs and sat on it to test it.

"Right!" he said. "Let's get you undressed and into bed."

That was easier said than done. Stephen appeared to have gone to sleep on the floor and there was no way Mark could lift him. He knelt and managed, with great difficulty and not without tearing something, to pull his shirt over his head and away from his arms. Stephen had a remarkably hairy chest. Then he began to undo Stephen's laces. The trainers came off and then his socks.

He had extraordinarily long toes. Next was his belt buckle and then the zip fly. Stephen just lay there. Mark might as well have been undressing a corpse. He managed, somehow to pull the jeans down to Stephen's ankles and then manoeuvre them an inch at a time over his feet. In other circumstances, he thought, he'd have been almost beside himself by this time.

Stephen's boxer shorts were black. There was some sort of pattern on them. He put his fingers into the waist-band and Stephen opened his eyes. "Got to go and have a pee," he said and, with a series of extraordinary body contortions he clambered unsteadily to his feet. One leg went out, a hand pressed down on Mark's shoulder; the other leg straightened - and Mark was left with a close up of two of the whitest, hairiest legs he'd ever seen - not to mention a pair of boxers, one leg of which had ridden up to the top of Stephen's thigh.
"Sure you'll be okay?" he asked.
"Think so. Not far," said Stephen and he left the room.
"Now what?" Mark said, voicing his thoughts aloud. A phrase drifted into his brain. It was a chapter heading from one of Simon's books. 'A Friend with a Flaw'. It described Stephen exactly. Not that his body was flawed; far from it - and people with his problem could get help. That was all that was needed. Stephen needed a friend - someone like him. Someone to take control of him and point him in the right direction. Someone he could relate to and who would show him affection - in return for which of course... Mark smiled and got to his feet again.

A long sausage-shaped textile object which had been draped over the sofa turned out to be a duvet. Rapidly, Mark stripped off, lay down and covered himself. He shivered slightly and then continued to think things over. Stephen was almost certainly not gay after all. He'd been a fool not to have found out more before going out with him. Could one have a relationship of any sort with a person like Stephen? Probably not but with someone quite so good looking, it would be worth a try.

There was a retching noise, followed by the sound of a lavatory being flushed. Then a clatter as something was knocked over, followed by an angry "Fuck!" from Stephen. The door swung open and he appeared - naked. Mark lifted his head. "I thought I'd better stay the night," he said and, as he spoke, he feasted his eyes on the longest limp cock he'd ever seen. It hung down almost to the middle of Stephen's thighs. It was slightly thicker than a broom handle and tapered to a puckered point. Framed by those powerful thighs and crowned by a dense patch of hair much darker than that on Stephen's head, it swung slightly from side to side as he approached the bed.

"Pleash yesself," he muttered and Mark moved as near the wall as he could to avoid being crushed as Stephen fell onto the bed. Mark managed to pull the duvet out from under him and covered them both.

Sharing a bed - no matter with whom - always did things to Mark. The warmth of the other person and the sound of someone else breathing had a remarkably rapid effect. His cock twitched slightly and then began to rise. It wasn't that he was afraid Stephen might notice it, though he thought it unlikely that Stephen would have noticed if he'd put a python in the bed. Prudence dictated that it would be better to turn and face the wall so he did. This had the added benefit of keeping his nostrils out of the stream of rum-laden breath which emanated from Stephen's gaping mouth.

He lay like that for a long time, alternately thinking what a fool he was; how he was going to repay the money from the petty cash and what sort of explanation he was going to give Ben for spending so much in one night . The pattern in the wallpaper seemed to change as the moon moved across the sky. A wank would be the answer but that was impossible in the circumstances. A wank always sent him to sleep. He made out the shape of a knight in armour peering round a clump of plants. Then it turned into an elephant tearing down a tree. For a second or two (or so it seemed) he dozed off. A distant clock struck three quarters of an hour. Then he was the knight rescuing Stephen from an enraged elephant. Adam and Ben stood in the distance laughing. He got down from his horse and tried to lift Stephen up into the saddle. Then the barman from the Leather Bottle appeared and explained that Stephen was in no condition to mount any animal. Mark looked down to the ground and found that he was standing in an ants' nest. They were crawling up his legs. He put his hand down to brush them off - and woke up again with a considerable start. That part wasn't a dream. There really was something climbing up his leg. He felt it against his thigh, an extraordinarily light, silky touch.

"Bloody hell!" he muttered. Bed bugs or something similar were all he needed to top off an evening of disasters. He slid a hand down his thigh. For a moment he felt nothing apart from his own skin but there was something on the back of his thigh. He reached down for it and, for a moment, lay quite still as if paralysed. Insects didn't grow that big. Insect bodies were not hard and insects didn't have bunches of wiry hair at their tails.

He had to be dreaming - but he wasn't. He tried to squeeze it. He might as well have tried to compress a steel rod. He ran his fingers up the shaft to the warm and already damp head. Stephen let out a long sigh which stirred the hairs on the back of Mark's neck. He smiled. So he had been right after all! At that moment he felt more sorry for Stephen than he had ever felt for anybody. He was sorry for Howard but, when all was said and done, Howard had brought his problems on himself. Stephen hadn't. It wasn't his fault that his well meaning bishop-father had deposited his son's allowance with Professor Carpenter. He had no idea, and Stephen couldn't tell him, that Professor Carpenter demanded his pound of flesh before handing it over. It probably did weigh a pound too, he thought, as he caressed it. But he'd seen the way Stephen had left the professor's house. It wasn't just Stephen's cock that the revolting old man had abused. No... Stephen had been fucked; roughly too. Well, it was up to him, Mark Lee, to show Stephen was sex was really like.

It slipped out of his hands and between his legs. There was no doubt what Stephen wanted. It wasn't in the plan but why not? There were many experiences worse than being fucked by someone as good looking as Stephen Marshall...

Then he remembered. The condoms he always carried were in his wallet. And where was his wallet? In his clothes on the other side of the room. The gel he'd bought specially for this occasion was in his jeans pocket and there was no way; absolutely no way that a cock the size of Stephen's was going to get in there un-lubricated and unprotected.

"Got a rubber?" he whispered but Stephen didn't answer. Instead he put both hands round Mark and began to tease his nipples. That felt good. Stephen's cock moving up the inside of his thigh felt even better. Stephen's chest pressed against his back. The hairs tickled slightly. Stephen kissed the back of his neck; a long, wet kiss. Mark wanted to turn over and let Stephen have access to everything he had but Stephen's arms were holding him tight and his fingers continued to tweak Mark's nipples. It would have to happen as he was.

That beautiful cock continued to move upwards. He felt it against the back of his balls. Stephen gave a shove - which hurt. Then it was pressing upwards somewhere between his balls and his ass. That didn't feel so bad.

Stephen kissed the back of his neck again and gave another push. Then another. He murmured something but Mark couldn't make out what it was. He was still inwardly cursing himself wondering whether to say 'Stop for a minute. I need to get something out of my pockets,' but to do so was all too likely to break the spell. And he'd have to climb over Stephen to get out of the bed. No... it was better this way. When morning came it would be different.

Another shove, then another. Stephen snorted with each one. If only he had the sense to take his hands off Mark's nipples and play with his cock. That was where Mark wanted them. There was a danger that Stephen would come, fall asleep and Mark would be left to deal with a very frustrated, erect cock himself.

Desperately he thought about the following morning. Stephen would be sober then. How would Mark have him? Lying down? Possibly. Kneeling? No. That didn't appeal at all. Lying on his back? Ah yes! That was it. Those long, hairy legs over Mark's shoulders. Stephen grinning and saying "I said you were after my ass. I knew all along."

That did it. Mark's balls ached. Stephen's cock continued to ram remorselessly against him. He could feel Stephen's pubic hair against his backside and Stephen's balls flopping against the inside of his thighs.
"Ah! Ah! Ah!" Stephen gasped. His grip became so tight that Mark could hardly breathe. He felt the first jet; felt it running down his thigh. Then another. Then another and this time it was Mark's turn to gasp as his own load cascaded out of him and, presumably, onto the wallpaper.
"Great!" he sighed. Stephen let go of his nipples.
"Better than being with the prof, eh?" said Mark but Stephen didn't answer.
"I said better than the Prof," said Mark but the only answer he got was a long drawn out snore. Stephen had fallen asleep. Mark lay awake for a long time making plans. In the first place, he'd have to get Simon and Charles to agree to Stephen sharing the house. That might be a bit difficult. Both seemed to assume that it was Howard's rightful place. Well, to hell with Howard. He was a nice enough guy but living with him would be impossible. Howard wasn't a man to take advice. Not like Stephen. Stephen must know the damage he was doing to himself with the drink. He just needed a metaphorical hand to hold onto him. Mark smiled. Not so metaphorical actually. There was plenty of space in his desk in his bedroom for another desk for Stephen to study at. He wondered what sort of music Stephen liked. They probably had the same

tastes, he thought and if not there were always headphones. That was no worry...

Stephen's alarm clock woke them both.

"Christ, we supped some stuff last night," said Stephen.

"You did, you mean."

"Did you bring me home? I guess you must have done."

"I did. And very worthwhile it was too." He put out a hand and felt Stephen's right thigh. He slid it upwards. Stephen's skin felt delightfully cool. Then his fingers made contact with Stephen's cock. It was rubbery which was always a good sign. It wouldn't take long to get it hard again.

"What the fuck do you think you're doing?" Stephen moved away as if he'd been in contact with a live wire.

"Tit for tat," said Mark.

"What?"

"You screwed me last night. Now it's your turn."

"Are you out of your fucking mind?" Stephen got right out of bed.

"Course not. You screwed me..."

"You must have been dreaming, mate. I never did anything of the sort."

"But..." Mark was about to prove it. That would be easy enough. Steve's spunk was still wet on his thighs.

"You fucking nasty little queer," said Stephen "I should have known. Going to fairy circle meetings and going on about bent writers. Here. Get dressed and get out before I put one on you." He threw Mark's clothes at him. "By the time I come out of the bathroom, I want you out of here. Understand?"

Furious and disappointed, Mark took a bus home. There wasn't enough money for a taxi. Ben and Adam were just getting ready to leave.

"Where the hell have you been?" asked Adam.

"Had a few drinks too many so I stayed over at a mate's place."

"He didn't have a spare razor obviously. We've been waiting for you."

"Why?"

"Simon rang. You're to go down to Combleton and get there this afternoon. There's somebody in the house to let you in. He'll pick you up from there. Where are the two of you off to?"

"Search me. Does it have to be today. I've got a hell of a lot of work to do."

"Simon said it was important. Ben can come back and take you down to the station if you like."

"Would you? I'm a bit broke at the moment."

Peter Gilbert

Ben's face was a study. "I'll come back for you straight after lunch," he said. "You coming in with us this morning?"
"No, I don't think so. I'd better get shaved and packed.

CHAPTER FIFTEEN

Jon opened the door, put the key back in its hiding place and stepped into Mill Cottage. He closed the door behind him and, for a few seconds, stood in the tiny hallway breathing deeply. He loved the smells of Mill Cottage. Old leather and furniture polish with just a trace of wood smoke were the authentic smells of the England he'd known as a small boy. To a person forced to spend the major part of every day amidst the smells of an agricultural college, stepping into Lord Charles' house was like walking into the Garden of Eden.

There were just five letters in the box. Two were the manila ones he'd gotten accustomed to in the last few weeks. He took them into the lounge and put them onto the desk next to the computer. Finance first or fitness first? That was the question. Duty called. He switched on the computer and then looked at his watch. The mystery guest would be on the train at that moment. It wouldn't be a bad idea to get changed... Leaving the computer to boot up, he went upstairs and returned a few minutes later in his shorts. He'd put on a white T-shirt as well. Shorts alone might be too obvious...

He opened the two brown envelopes. All thoughts of the mysterious Mark Lee were soon forced to the back of his mind. It was inconceivable that Charles of all people was losing his marbles but the spending spree of the last few days defied all logical explanation. The Hungry Hussar. One hamburger with chips and one full English breakfast. The Hungry Hussar again. Two cheeseburgers and another full English breakfast. He entered the figures and picked up the next receipt. "Nothing like contrasts!" he murmured. The Fare and Fowl Private Dining Club. One plate of oysters and one steak and one bottle of wine at no less than thirty pounds. The Fare and Fowl again. Deposit. Two hundred and fifty pounds.
"Deposit for what, Charles? Deposit for what?" he asked - but there was nobody to answer him. He put it under 'Miscellaneous' and drew a huge question mark on the back of the paper. For weeks, ever since he gladly

volunteered to do Lord Charles' book-keeping for him, he'd badgered the man for proper, detailed receipts. It just didn't seem to register with Charles. Jon was perfectly certain that there had been other expenses that Charles hadn't recorded but Charles wasn't a man you could get angry with. Charles was just about the nicest guy in the world. He was immensely generous and so sensible. There was the business of the letter for example. Life would sure as hell be very different if Jon had sent it. He stopped work for a few minutes to remember the incident. Charles had been sitting in his usual chair by the fireplace...

"Not finished yet? Need any more information?" the man said.

"Oh I've finished the finances. I'm writing a letter."

"Ah! Who to?"

"My dad."

"I see."

"Yeah. It's time he knew the truth. I've made up my mind. I'm not living a lie any longer."

"The truth about what? What lie?"

"That I'm gay. I guess he'll take me away from St. Fred's and there'll be one hell of a row but he's got to know sometime."

"I see. Tell me, Jon. Does your father discuss his sex life with you? Do you know exactly what your father and mother get up to when they're together in bed? Has he told you every detail of his teenage escapades?"

"Of course not. No American parent would."

"So why upset the man with yours?"

"Because he's got to know. That's why."

"Why? Sex is something private. I don't talk about my sex life to other people. I never ask you or anybody else about theirs. Why do you want to upset Colonel and Mrs. Calder with yours?"

"It's like I said, Charles. I feel like I'm living a lie."

"If a man doesn't talk he can't be telling lies. Take my advice. Just live your life as you want to live it and don't upset or bore other people with the details. Work on the 'need to know' principle. If there is one thing Colonel Calder does not need to know it is that his son and heir is gay."

And so the letter had been deleted which was just as well because just two days later he'd received the nicest letter his dad had ever written him. Jon would have liked to read it again but it was upstairs in his pocket. '... hear you got into some sort of scrape in London... I don't want to know the details. The great thing is that you got yourself out of it again and I'm sitting here feeling real proud of you, son! Wish I'd known when you called that your friend is a real English Lord! You sure are mixing with all the right people...'

That letter made up for a lot but not for Jon's loneliness. Charles said the right person would come along and he ought to be patient. Apart from the business back in the States, there had been Stuart. Sex with Stuart had been fun but that's all. Stuart was not a really likeable guy. Then there'd been Howard. He was a nice guy but that was in the past. People like Charles didn't realise how miserable he really was.

"Snap out of it!" he told himself - and continued to enter Charles' horrendous expenditure.

The sound of the doorbell was so unexpected that he almost fell off his chair. He looked at his watch. He'd spent no less than a hour in that reverie! He went to the door, opened it.

Suddenly to be confronted by an angel has always been a shock ever since that surprising visit just before the start of the present millennium. Jon's spine went rigid. His heart fluttered and then began to beat more strongly. Standing on the path in front of him was a tall, boyish-looking young man with dark, curly hair and laughing eyes.

"Hi!" said the visitor in an unexpectedly deep voice. "I'm Mark. You must be Jon."

"Yeah. I... er. Yeah. Come on in."

All Charles had said was that a friend, Mark Lee, was coming down to spend the night before going off the following morning with Simon Spencer. There was plenty of food in the house and Mark was well able to look after himself, he said. Jon had been on the point of asking 'Is he gay?' but didn't. Charles wouldn't have answered.

Mark dumped his bag on the floor and settled into one of the armchairs.

"So, what do you do here?" he asked.

"Oh, I come down to help him with his books."

"Has Charles taken to writing too then?"

"No. I mean fiscal books. I'm trying to get his finances under control. He's been losing a hell of a lot by not keeping records."

"From what I've seen of him, he's still got plenty," said Mark. "But why the shorts?"

"That's the other reason. Charles has installed a multi gym upstairs. We both use it."
"A what?"
"Come up. I'll show you."

Mark had never seen anything like it - and I'm not referring only to the machine.
"You set the weights like this and then you go through as many exercises as you can. There's this one. It's very good for the legs," Jon explained. Mark had never seen legs so beautiful. They were long, covered with a delightful fuzz of hair and very powerful looking.
"There's a good one for the chest and arms," said Jon, peeling off the T-shirt. "My chest expansion has gone up a hell of a lot since I started using it." He lay back on the bench and grasped the handles. Weights behind him slid silently up and down. He let go and stood up. "Want a go?" he asked.
"Not just now. I wouldn't have thought you needed to do much exercise."
"Everybody does. The great thing about this machine is that it exercises every part of the body."
"Every part?"

Jon laughed. "Well, perhaps not every part," he said. "Shall we go downstairs again? Are you sure you don't want to have a go?"

Mark would have liked to have a go very much indeed - but not on the multi gym. He followed Jon downstairs, trying (but not very hard) to avoid looking at the young man's delightfully rounded backside and massive thighs. Jon was much more beautiful in the flesh than he had seemed in Dennis' photographs. Mark would certainly have had a go if it wasn't for Charles. The problem with Charles was that one never actually knew and Charles never said. A nineteen-year-old student given the run of the house and apparently in charge of Charles' finances added up to one thing. Jonathan was Charles' boyfriend and Charles was such a nice person that it would be unthinkable to seduce his boyfriend in his absence. If it was Howard now that would be different. 'Hi Howard. I've been playing you at your own game. I've just fucked your friend Jonathan.'

Mr. Spencer's coming for you tomorrow isn't he?" asked Jon.
"Yes. Tomorrow is D day. Tomorrow we get Stuart back."
"Do you know where he is then?"

"Simon does."

"I met Simon Spencer here. He's great, isn't he?"

"I think so, yes." Mark's ass still ached slightly. "You get on pretty well with Charles I imagine," he added.

"We sure do. We're real buddies. If it wasn't for him I think that college would drive me nuts. I can come down here and work-out or do the books or just watch TV. It's a bit lonely when he's not here. That's why I'm glad you're here. I wish to hell I could stay down here tonight."

"Why can't you?"

"You're supposed to put in an application at least two days before saying where you're going to be."

"No!"

"It's true. And they've been known to check."

Mark had often thought Howard was exaggerating when he described the regime at St. Frideswide's. Apparently not.

"But you're all over eighteen. Why do you put up with it?" he asked.

"It's the parents who want it that way. They pay the fees after all."

"It's unbelievable. It must be like living in a prison," said Mark.

"Dead right it is. And the education is not as good as they make out. Their computers are way out of date. There isn't a single computer console in the library with Internet access. The priest who teaches physics stopped learning when they dropped the first atom bomb. Ask him about quantum theory and he thinks you're talking dirty."

"And your parents actually pay fees for that?"

"They do. So do many others. Stuart's for example. It's the discipline, see. Stuart would never pass A levels if he wasn't forced to study."

"But you? You don't look the lazy type."

"My dad just thought a year here would do me good."

"Bloody amazing," said Mark.

For the next hour he listened, unusually enthralled, to Jonathan's comparison of colleges in the United States and St. Frideswide's. It was all a bit confusing. There were credits and grades and semesters and people called sophomores. Most of his attention was concentrated on Jon's long, outspread legs and the slight bulge in the front of his shorts. If Jon's legs were so much better in reality than on photographic paper, how much better would his cock be? As far as Mark could remember, it was more than just substantial. Jon had long fingers. That was a good sign. It was just as well that he had to go back to college.

Jon got a couple of beers out of the fridge. "I suppose I could call Charles and ask if he could fix it," he said.

"Fix what?" Mark licked the foam off his upper lip.

"For me to stay down here tonight."

"Can't you ask them yourself?"

"No. That wouldn't work. I.. er.. got into a spot of bother recently. They'd never agree if I asked."

Mark was on the point of saying that he knew all about it but decided silence would be better.

"I don't think he'll be able to but I can ask," said Jon and he went over to the telephone. Charles apparently said that he would see what could be done and asked to speak to Mark.

"Just answer yes or no," he asked. "Is this your idea? Have you got your beady eyes on the lad?"

"Definitely not," said Mark, deliberately staring out of the window. "I wouldn't do that."

"Probably as well. The news might get back to Howard and I wouldn't want him upset. In the cupboard in what used to be the spare bedroom but which is now a torture chamber, there's a folding bed. Use that. Has he shown you the awful instrument yet?"

"He has."

"Take my advice. Don't let him tempt you. You'll have aches and pains for days afterwards."

Mark picked up his beer and lowered himself gingerly back into his chair. Aches and pains, he thought, were the inevitable result of extreme enjoyment.

———

Monsignor Patrick Kelly, rector of St. Frideswide's, had several pet hates. Number one on the list was the telephone. Bad news always came over telephone lines. Bishops telephoned to announce that they were in the area and would call in. The accountants telephoned frequently to say they were concerned - to say the least - about the balance sheet. The worst were the parents. The degree students' parents were not so bad but the Beaumont boys... There were times when he wanted to close the Beaumont block but he couldn't. If it wasn't for the fees the Beaumont boys parents paid, the entire college would have to close down. Beaumont parents always agreed their sons needed discipline and then kicked up a fuss when it was applied.

Monsignor Kelly yearned for the old days when you could keep an eighteen-year-old under control with a few well placed cuts into his rump. The old cane still hung, unseen, in a cupboard in his study. Its end was frayed and continual use had resulted in it looking more like an archer's bow but in the days when its use was allowed and condoned, the Beaumont boys had been much less trouble.

Coincidentally, he was musing about Jonathan when the telephone rang. If ever there was a boy who would benefit from a good thrashing, it was Jonathan Calder. Drink and sex in the library - under the very eyes of all those saintly portraits! It was unthinkable but the thought of Calder bending over to touch his toes was very thinkable indeed. And there was young Lynch. When he came back - if he ever came back - he'd look particularly attractive bent over and flinching in anticipation. Lynch's parents were rich too. Spoiled boys needed an occasional beating - done by someone who knew how to do it properly - and there was nobody more skilful or experienced than Monsignor Patrick Kelly...

He picked up the receiver. "Rector speaking," he said . "My dear Lord Beresford.. This is indeed a pleasure... Oh dear. How unfortunate... Well, in normal circumstances I would say no but I am most grateful for your assistance in recovering the lad. He will be back for chapel won't he? Good. Yes, I'll tell Father Ramburton. Goodbye." He pressed another button on the telephone. "Rector speaking. Lord Beresford has just rung. He's stuck in London and an unexpected guest has arrived at Mill Cottage. I've given permission for Calder to stay down there overnight... Yes I know but we don't want to upset Lord Beresford. If we play our cards correctly we might get enough money out of him to do all those renovations you want done... No. Of course he'll be safe. Perhaps you'd let the catering staff know. He'll be back in time for chapel."

He put the phone down and picked up his book again. Chapter seven was particularly enthralling. "Corporal Punishment in ancient Japan." He settled down to his studies.

They had just started to watch the film Jonathan particularly wanted to see when the phone rang. Jonathan answered it.

"Hey Charles! That's great! Thanks a lot. Yeah, I'll make sure I'm there on time. Bye."

"He says it's okay. I have to be back for chapel in the morning," he said.

"To confess your sins?" asked Mark.

"I don't have any," said Jon and they sat together on the sofa to watch the adventures of Private First Class Joe Mendoza and his band of Marine desperadoes.

"My dad says those Marine boot camps really are as hard as they make them out to be," said Jon.

"Just like St. Frideswide's," said Mark. "Can I have another beer?"

"Sure. Hang on, I'll get it." Jon went out to the kitchen. He seemed to be there for an inordinately long time, not that Mark minded. The sight of twelve Marine recruits doing press ups for a sadistic sergeant was quite pleasant.

"We don't have to do press ups at St. Fred's. That's one good thing," said Jon when he returned, and then.. "I was thinking."

"Oh yes?"

"It seems kind of stupid for you to sleep in the multi gym room. I'm in Charles' room in the big bed. There's plenty of room for two and it would save on laundry."

Mark raised a questioning eyebrow. An invitation? He didn't reply immediately. The chances were, he thought, that Jon really was thinking of household expenses.

"Better stick to what Charles said," he replied.

CHAPTER SIXTEEN

"I'd better be going back up" said Howard. He was sitting in the college kitchen, having just consumed the biggest steak he'd seen for years. He picked up his wine glass and downed the last drops of Chablis - a particularly good one. Bernard, the chef, said the rector hadn't the slightest idea of what was in the cellar.

The news that it had been Bernard's brother who had interrupted the session in the library office alarmed Howard at first but Bernard assured him that it would go no further. When Bernard started inviting him into the kitchens for illegal meals, Howard soon got the message. But Bernard was fat, gross and well over fifty. He had no chance whatsoever but Howard wasn't going to tell him that.

"There's no need to go back yet," said Bernard. Anyway they're all having a staff meeting. It'll go on for ages. They always do. Have some more."

He didn't wait for an answer but topped Howard's glass up again.

"That Peter Robinson's a big lad wouldn't you say?" he asked.

"Peter Robinson? I don't think I know him. What year is he in?"

"Second I think. Doing dairy farming. I wouldn't mind sucking the cream out of him."

"Oh, Robinson the rugby-player!" said Howard.

"That's him. You want to see him in his shorts! God! He's got a cock like the handle of a sledge hammer."

"And also a fiancee who loves him very much and writes to him three times a week. No chance," said Howard.

"Maybe not but it's a lovely thought. Do you know who else I have lovely thoughts about?"

"Could it be a person sitting in your kitchen at this very moment?" said Howard with a laugh. He wondered how long he could keep Bernard at bay without losing his meals down there.

"Right first time." Bernard reached over and touched his knee. Howard moved it.

"Why don't you?" Bernard asked. "Nobody would ever find out. I promise."

At that point the telephone on the white tiled wall rang. One of the sous-chefs came in to answer it.

"That was Father Ramburton. One less for dinner and breakfast," he said when he had put back the receiver.

"Not another sanatorium meal!" said Bernard.

"No. The Calder lad. The American. He's spending the night down at Lord Beresford's place in the village."

"I didn't think Lord Beresford was around. I haven't seen him in the paper shop for some days."

"Well, he must be, mustn't he? Ramburton says he'll be in for lunch tomorrow."

Howard's euphoria vanished, to be replaced by livid anger. Of course Charles was there. There was no way Jonathan would get permission to sleep in an empty house. Charles must have been in touch with the rector at least - possibly even the bishop and done quite a bit of arm bending. It must have been Charles. He was probably the only man in the world who could get permission . In the previous term, Leo Ffoulkes-Laing had asked for permission to celebrate his twenty-first birthday at the George with his parents and his friends. His father offered to pay for rooms for them all. Howard had been with Leo when the yellow note arrived. 'Party approved but all St. Frideswide's students to be back in college by midnight.'

He climbed the flight of concrete stairs which led up from the kitchens and made his way to his room. He took off his shoes and lay on his bed to think. Everything clicked together. Jon spent most afternoons at Mill Cottage. Just imagining what had been going on made him feel sick with anger. For hypocrisy, Charles would take some beating. One minute he was talking about the need to rescue someone in moral danger and the next - well it was pretty obvious what had been going on. All that giggling when Charles and Jon had washed Simon's car and the gasping noises from the upstairs bedroom. He felt a fool for having idolised Charles in the past. It was odd though. Charles hadn't even said anything - let alone do anything to him. Perhaps Charles preferred Americans. The two of them were probably drinking to the loss of Jon's virginity at that very moment.

He looked at his watch. It was eight-thirty. There was only one thing to do. This time it was going to be Howard to the rescue. It wasn't difficult to get out of college at night. The problem was that his absence might be noticed but that was unlikely. Howard would go down the fire escape, then down the hill into the village and then... The spare key would be in the hollow rock in the garden. He'd need his little torch to find that. Lord bloody Beresford was going to get the shock of his life that night - and serve him right.

———

A tear ran down Jon's cheek. He reached under the pillow for his handkerchief and wiped it away. He didn't often have the 'miseries' (as he called them). At least there was nobody near enough to say 'You were crying last night. I heard you' and then announce at breakfast that Calder had been crying.

Of course if there had been somebody with him, he wouldn't be feeling like this, he thought. Mark was a real stunner but Mark at that moment was sleeping on the folding bed in the multi gym room and probably dreaming about girlfriends. He must have been wrong about Mark. He'd tried hard enough to attract him - but failed. Everybody else he knew had friends. He'd thought he'd found the ideal buddy in Stuart but what had Stuart done? Ditched him. Then there'd been Howard. He'd seemed a nice enough guy to begin with. Charles was a real nice guy but Charles wasn't a friend in the sense that Jon meant. Brits were funny people. If his father had only left him in the States he'd have been able to find a buddy - a real close buddy. He was sure of that. He'd have to go to a new school of course but that wouldn't have been so bad. Anything stateside would be better than the weird British nineteenth century establishment they'd sent him to - just because his mom had caught him and Billy at it in the cellar and told his dad about it.

All that lecturing! His dad had even admitted that he'd done just about the same when he was fourteen. Then the long and private conversations. He knew from the way his parents stopped talking or changed the subject when he came into the room, that they were talking about him. And then the bombshell. The Pentagon decided that his dad would return to England (or had dad asked the Pentagon for a transfer? That was possible.)

This wasn't the England Jon remembered from his pre-school days when dad was a Major. No 'Playland' kindergarten with kind Mrs. Mayhill to run to when you grazed your knee. No trips out to play on the ramparts of old castles. No Cadena tea rooms where the nice waitress gave him extra cream on his cake and told dad what a lovely looking little boy he was. No. This was the real England where your buddies dropped you at a moment's notice.

He reached down and untied the cord of his pyjamas. That felt better. If a guy had no buddies there was always good old John Thomas. He never let you down. The thought brought the first smile that evening. 'Up' was a better word for John Thomas. Jon wriggled out of his pyjamas and arranged John Thomas in his favourite position lying against his abdomen. What to think about was the next problem. This could be a real good, long session. Not like the ones at St. Fred's when you had to wait for your roommate to go to the showers or the toilet.

"You! Marine! What's your name?"

"Calder J., sergeant."

"Calder eh? Well, when I've finished with you, you'll be hotter. Give me another twenty. Get them shorts off. I wanna see that butt moving. That's better. Do you know why Marines have to do push ups?"

"No, sergeant."

"To exercise their butts. It makes 'em fuck better. You'll see what I mean when it's your turn."

That didn't work. John Thomas was still asleep. Jon rang a finger along the ridge on John Thomas' underside. That always brought on pleasant thoughts.

"I've always liked you better than Stuart. Stuart's been spoiled." That was Howard.

Where were they? Not the library office. Definitely not the library office. Howard's room. That was better. Jon had never been in Howard's room but he could imagine it well enough.

"I've never fucked an American ass before. You ever been fucked Jon?"

"No."

And that didn't work either. It was the window which spoiled it. Howard's room would have a window and you never knew...

Mark now. It would be different with Mark. Better too. Mark was older than Howard. He was a nice guy too - and real good looking. John Thomas twitched in agreement. Mark - the name sounded just right. Mark would be something to write Billy about. No more misery letters about Math lessons and stupid cricket.

'Hi Billy, I now have a real good buddy. His name is Mark and he's at college. He's (How old? Jon would have to guess.) 'He's twenty years old and boy! Is he good looking! We go around just about everywhere together and we tell each other everything. The best times are when I visit with him. We do just about everything. Remember that book you showed me? Well we do that too. No kidding, when I'm kneeling on that bed and Mark's sliding his monster cock in my ass it makes what you and me did in the cellar feel like kids' stuff! Of course we do that as well. You can do that most any place. We go for walks and when we find a lonely place we get our cocks out just like you and me used to do and Mark's got a way of doing it which blows your mind.'

John Thomas was standing upright at last. Jon threw off the covers. That felt better. He sat up for a moment, unbuttoned his pyjama top and threw it aside. Then he lay back, spread his legs apart and put his hand under his balls. That was a nice feeling. He tickled around for a few moments and John Thomas nodded enthusiastically. Then a car hooted in the distance and reality began to override imagination. There was about as much chance of doing it with Mark as there was of Jon being appointed Captain of Cricket.

And yet... Surely Mark must be gay. Nobody would go to the trouble and take the risks Mark was taking to rescue Stuart if he wasn't gay. Perhaps the fault lay with him. He'd grown out of the spotty stage ages ago. Sure, Stuart's uncle had told him he was good looking but the guy had probably been lying.

He peered at his watch. It was only ten o'clock. Not late by any means. The chances were that Mark wasn't asleep. He could, perhaps, go in there and say something about not being able to sleep - or, even better, he could go in there as he was and claim to have been sleep walking. There had to be a way. Maybe - it was just possible - maybe Mark was waiting for him to make the first move...

And then he heard it. A sound of stone scraping against stone came from the garden beneath the window. He let go of John Thomas and lay quite still. There it was again. The path to the door was lined with large stones. As far as he knew, only Charles and he knew that one was hollow; the ideal hiding place for the spare key. Oh! Simon Spencer knew as well. He remembered

Howard telling him. So Howard knew too. They were all safe enough but there was no doubt about it. Someone, or something was moving the stones. He got out of bed and peered down through the gap between the curtains. There was nobody there.

There was nothing to worry about really, he thought. All the doors and windows were locked. But yet... if there was someone there and he did nothing about it, what would Charles think of him? Charles hadn't actually told him that he was responsible for security but perhaps he ought to do something or tell someone... Of course! Tell someone. That was what had to be done.

John Thomas had subsided completely which was just as well. Jon got off the bed, opened the door and went across the landing. He tapped on the multi gym door.

"You awake, Mark?" he whispered.

"Sure. Come in." Jon opened the door and groped for the light switch.

Mark had set up the folding bed along the wall opposite the multi gym. His clothes lay on the gym bench. Just his head was visible. "Jesus!" he said. "Do you often visit people like that?"

"I think I heard someone in the garden," said Jon.

"I didn't hear anything."

"This room's on the wrong side. You know those stones on the side of the path?"

"Yes."

"Well. Someone is moving them."

"Some animal I expect. A cat or something."

"Jeez! It'd have to be a grizzly bear to shift some of those. You don't actually understand," said Jon. "I shouldn't tell anyone this really. Charles keeps the spare key in one of them and we move it from time to time. What do you think we ought to do? Should we go outside and have a look round?"

"It's not worth it. There's probably nobody there. Let's go back to your room and listen."

That, thought Jon, was a much better idea. Mark struggled with the bed clothes for a moment and then stood up. Jon put his hand up to restrain a giggle. "Do you always visit with folks like that?" he asked. Mark was even better looking than he had dreamed. He tried not to look but in a second he'd taken in the young man's broad chest and huge nipples; his long legs and his long, swaying cock.

They padded silently back to the main bedroom. Jon sat on the edge of the bed. "We can hear just as well lying down," Mark whispered. "Move over a bit."

They lay side by side. A bed cover would have been a good idea after all, thought Jon. Try as he might to prevent it from happening, John Thomas had started to wake up again. Unfortunately, the quilt lay on the floor on Mark's side of the bed.

"Can you reach for the cover? It's on the floor on your side," said Jon.

"Sssh!" Mark whispered. A hand landed on Jon's knee. He hadn't realised; it had certainly never been mentioned in any biology lectures - that there was a direct neural link from a person's knee to their sex organs. The effect of that touch was electric. In a second John Thomas had switched his attention from the door handle to the ceiling and a strange tingling sensation ran up and down Jon's spine.

"You could..." he gasped.

"We won't hear anything if you talk," Mark explained - and the hand remained where it was. Jon wished he could breathe more quietly and that his heart wouldn't thump so loudly. He was sure Mark could hear it. Then the hand began to move, sliding slowly up his thigh. Was he...? Surely not, but yet... Mark's finger tips didn't actually touch the skin of his groin but he knew what they were doing. They were playing lightly with his pubic hair. His breathing became even more loud and, to his great relief, Mark began to sound as if he were indulging in some form of strenuous exercise. The fingers burrowed through the hair. He felt them on his skin. Instinctively, he thrust his legs apart and John Thomas was captured! It was an entrapment of the gentlest sort. First two fingers, then all of them curled round the unyielding flesh.

"I don't mind..." said Jon. He was about to say, 'I don't mind what you do,' which actually meant 'Do whatever you like,' but Mark shushed him again and the fingers moved slowly up and down, sliding the skin over the shaft as they moved. Until that moment Howard had held top marks in Jon's estimation for skill at cock manipulation. When Howard did it, you realised how much you missed when you did it to yourself.

Mark made Howard look like an amateur! It was the most wonderful feeling in the world. He lay there praying that it would last as long as possible and, as if he could read his thoughts, Mark stopped occasionally and then started up again. He looked over his left shoulder to see if he could see Mark's but the room was far too dark.

Again, Mark seemed to know what he was thinking. A gentle hand took hold of his wrist, lifted it and let go of it again. There was no doubt as to where it had landed. Hair as bristly as that grew in only one place and something as big and as stiff as that could only be one thing. It was magnificent. He curled his fingers round it. Mark sighed. He squeezed it - or tried to - and Mark sighed again.   Then he followed Mark's lead, trying to keep in absolute synchronisation with Mark. When Mark stopped to play with his balls for a few seconds, Jon played with Mark's. They were much bigger than his and Mark's had occasional straggly hairs on the surface. Jon was fairly sure he hadn't any. "Let go for a bit," Mark whispered, suddenly. He took his hand off Jon and Jon did likewise. He felt Mark make a sudden movement, sufficiently violent to make the bed creak. Something soft touched his belly. Lips! Mark was kissing his navel. Then the skin under his navel. Then his hair. He tensed up as Mark's lips touched the top of his cock and then relaxed again as Mark's mouth slid down the shaft, engulfing him in wet warmth; the most wonderful sensation he'd ever experienced. When Howard had done it, he'd been standing up, supporting himself against the book-shelves. That had been good but nothing like as good as this...

The light blinded him. For a moment he thought it was some sort of psychic phenomenon but the voices were real enough.
"What the fuck...?"
"What the hell...?"

Howard! There was no doubt about the voice. No doubt either that Mark had been the second person to speak. John Thomas dripped saliva.
"Oh shit!" said Jon and he nearly burst into tears.
"What's going on?" said Howard. "Where's Charles?"
"In London. As for what's going on, I'd have thought that was pretty obvious," said Mark. He didn't sound in the least upset and that made Jon feel a bit better.
"I thought Charles..."
"You thought Charles what?" said Mark.
"I thought Charles was... Well I thought Charles was having it off with Jon."
"How could he if he's in London? Anyway, I'd have thought that you, of all people, knew Charles better than that."

The bed creaked yet again as Howard sat down. "There were the noises," he said.
"What noises?" This time it was Jon's turn to speak.

"When I came down here the other day. After you'd shut the door you went upstairs and there were noises. You know... like when somebody's..."

"The multi gym," said Jon. It's an exercise machine. I'll show you." He went to get off the bed.

"Stay where you are. We'll both show him in the morning," said Mark.

"Don't concern yourselves. I'm not staying. I know where I'm not wanted," said Howard.

"Jo - on," Mark drawled.

"Uh huh?"

"Go down and make a pot of tea, will you?"

"But I don't drink tea."

"Then make two teas and whatever you drink."

"But..."

"Jon..."

"Yes Mark?"

"Two teas please. We've got one or two things to straighten out."

"Oh. I get it. Sure."

He never did find out what was said. Propriety seemed to demand that he should put on his dressing gown to go downstairs. Whilst the kettle came to the boil they shouted at each other. They were talking in lower tones by the time he came to pour the tea and by the time he climbed the stairs again with the tray, they seemed to be mumbling. He put down the tray to open the door. Neither of them was speaking. When he opened the door he could see why. They lay next to each other on the bed. Both had their arms round the other's shoulders and both grinned as he came in. Howard's shirt, he noticed, had come out of his belt and had ridden up, exposing a good four inches of flesh. A very good four inches. His hand shook slightly as he held the teapot above the first mug.

"Great!" said Mark. "Champagne would be better though."

"There is some. I know where it is," said Jon.

"Tea's good enough for now. Howard's staying the night."

"What about college?"

"No problem," said Howard. "I can always say I woke up with a toothache and went straight to the dentist."

"You're as likely as not to have your cavity filled by the morning," said Mark.

"Pity there's none of that stuff."

"Ah but there is. I decided quite recently never to go anywhere without it. It's in my bag in the other room. I'll go and get it."

"Let's all go," said Howard, putting down his mug of tea. "Jon can show me this wonder machine at the same time."

Showing Howard how to use the multi gym was slightly unnerving and it was obvious that he wasn't concentrating as fully as he should. Jonathan had to put his feet in the stirrups. Howard lay there, staring up at Jon's middle and grinning. Mark was in the corner of the room fumbling in his bag. He found what he was looking for and came to stand next to Jonathan who put the machine onto its middle setting.
"Try that," he said. "Just straighten your legs and then relax them again."

The weights slid up and down in their guides and, in a few minutes, Howard was puffing. Much more loudly, thought Jon proudly, than he had at a much higher setting and Howard was over a year older than he was. Howard was more powerfully built too.

Howard let go of the handle. The brakes came into play immediately, holding the weights fast and then letting them sink slowly to the rest position.
"Harder than it looks," Howard gasped. Mark grinned and put a hand on his jeans.
"This too by the feel of it," he said.
"Dirty old sod!" said Howard with a smile and then, "Go on then. You might as well."

Jon watched with mounting excitement as Mark's fingers unclipped Howard's belt. Howard took his feet out of the stirrups and began to pant even more loudly as his jeans came off, followed by his shorts. Howard took his shirt off and threw it to the side of the room. He lay back, naked. The sight of him in that state made Jon feel nervous for a moment or two. The last time Howard had been in that state had been a disaster. Then common sense prevailed. They weren't in college now. They were in a private house. They could do anything they liked.

He was aware of John Thomas swelling into action stations again - and even more aware that both Howard and Mark were looking at it.
"You could have a lot of fun on a machine like this," said Howard.
"I do. It's amazing. You come up here for a half an hour and two hours have gone by before you know it," said Jon.
Mark smiled. "I think that Howard is thinking of something else," he said.

"Oh! I never thought of that. Yeah. I guess you could."
"Suppose you show us what it can do," said Mark. "If Howard can get up that is."

Jon grinned. "Looks to me like Howard's got up already," he said, looking down at Howard's cock. It was fully erect and nodding slightly.
"You're not doing so badly yourself in that department," said Mark. "No wonder Howard feels so possessive towards you. I'd feel the same."
"It's you that's possessive, not me!" said Howard. He clambered off the bench.
"Of course, you're supposed to wear shorts or trousers," said Jon. He lay on the bench and something like seven inches of all-American cock pointed defiantly at the ceiling from its hairy base.
"So... what would you like to see?" he asked. Both Howard and Mark smiled.
"That depends on what there is to see," said Howard.
"Well, there's shoulder and neck exercises, arm exercises, torso and trunk..."
"Keep going. You're getting there," said Mark.
"There's the leg exercises. There are loads of them. There's the one I showed you, or there's this one." He got off the bench to set the controls and then, with some difficulty, lay on his front and placed the soles of his feet against a bar.
"This is good for the legs and the gluts," he said. He straightened his legs, pushing the bar backwards.
"Where are your gluts?" Howard asked.
"The muscles in your butt. I've got this on seventy-five pounds. That's about right for mine."

Mark thought of something else which would be just right but said nothing. He had rarely seen a bottom as beautiful as Jon's. He'd always considered the male backside the most beautiful expression of geometry. He'd spent hours at the computer calculating degrees of arc and radii trying to arrive at the perfect shape. Howard had a particularly beautiful bottom. Jon's was breathtaking. Nature was more aesthetic than science.

It broadened out naturally from his slim waist and then swelled into two perfectly curved and symmetrical cheeks, separated from one another by what appeared to be a fine dark line drawn on the tense flesh. As Jon pushed the bar back and then let it return, deep dimples formed in the sides and then filled in again.

It was at that moment that Mark made a resolution; a resolution that he would not share with Howard - not until the time came. It might take some time, he thought, but it would be well worth waiting for.

"There is another one but it's real hard," said Jon, turning over onto his front again. "You have to put your feet right through the stirrups, like this. Do you see the knob on the right hand side, Mark?"

"This one?"

"That's it. Turn it to fifty pounds. That's what I'm on at the moment."

Mark turned the control. Jon's legs rose from the bench.

"That's it!" he gasped. "Now go for it!" He gripped the handles on the side of the bench and, using every ounce of strength he had, forced his legs back down onto the bench. Sweat poured from his brow as the counterweight moved slowly upwards in its frame.

"Undo my ankles" he gasped. "I can only do one of those."

Howard did that for him. Mark seemed deep in thought.

Jon got off the machine and wiped his forehead with his hand. "It's a devil, that one," he said. "The problem is that it's real good for you."

"Pretty good for the other person too," said Mark. "You've given me an idea."

"And what might that be?" Howard enquired.

"I'll show you. Get up on the bench."

"There's no way I could lift a weight like that with my legs. Jon's been practising."

"I'm not asking you to try. Up you get."

"You're not playing some nasty sort of practical joke?"

"Promise."

Howard climbed onto the bench and lay on his back holding onto the side grips.

"Now, we put your feet in the stirrups, like this. Can you do the other one, Jon?"

Jon realised what Mark had in mind. He smiled and secured Howard's right ankle.

"And now perhaps you'd set the weights. Get his legs in the air."

"Not too much," said Howard.

Jon put his hand on the control. Howard's legs began to rise at ten pounds.

At twenty pounds his feet were pointing towards the door.
"Just a shade more," said Mark.

Twenty-five pounds; twenty-eight pounds; thirty pounds. Very, very slowly,
he increased the load and then screwed down the knob to anchor it.
"Just right," said Mark. "You okay, Howard?"
"Sure. It's not so bad as I thought. I wouldn't want to fight against it though. "
"You never did," said Mark with a smile. "Can you raise the bench, Jon."

Howard laughed. "I wondered when you'd ask that." he said.
"Sure. It'll go as high as you like," said Jon. "Like this." He put his foot on a
pedal and pumped it up and down. Slowly, the bench moved upwards in little
jerks.
"That's about it," said Mark. "Now come and look at this."

Jon didn't want to look at first. It was a bit like looking into somebody else's
locker at college; a thing you never did. Everyone had a right to some privacy
and it seemed wrong.
"Nicest sight in the world," said Mark, stroking the smooth skin of Howard's
inner thigh. Jon was more interested in Mark's cock. It had started to dribble
slightly. A drop fell onto the parquet floor. Jon rubbed it with the sole of his
foot. He watched as Mark tore open the packet and then, with a skill such as
Jon had never before seen, he rolled the rubber over his cock.
"Are you going to... fuck him?" Jon asked.
"Of course he is," said Howard.
"What about me?" Just looking at Mark's cock had sent Jon into a private
ecstasy he never told anybody about. John Thomas knew about it. He rose
even further.
"Do you know snooker?" Mark asked.
"No. What is it?"
"I think they call it pool in the States," said Howard. "Balls on a table. You play
it with a cue."
"Oh that. Sure I know that."
"Well, I've got the balls and the cue. Come round here and give me a game."

Jon did as he was told. Not, it has to be said, with a great deal of
enthusiasm. He didn't like Howard's outspokenness. Mark, he thought, was
quite different. Mark kept his tongue under control. If Howard hadn't burst in
when he had, he might have been able to persuade Mark to use it in some

place special and then... His anus itched at the prospect. It would have to happen sooner or later, he thought. In the meantime it was Howard who was going to have the pleasure. He wondered how many times Howard had had it in the past.

One touch of Howard's silky - smooth cock was enough to dispel his envy. It would be interesting, he thought, to watch Howard's reactions. When it happened to him he wouldn't be in a fit state to take note of such things.

He slid Howard's foreskin slowly up and down. Howard closed his eyes. Mark's greasy fingers came into his view, under Howard's balls. Jon let go of Howard's cock for a moment and lifted them up out of the way. He wanted to see as much as possible.
"Oh yeah!" Howard panted. Jon couldn't actually see what Mark's fingers were doing but whatever it was, it was turning Howard on. He returned his attention to Howard's cock. It was a nice cock, he thought. It wasn't as big or as nice as Mark's and he'd seen and handled it a good few times before. Nevertheless, it was a nice one. The head was a nice pink colour and reminded him of some flowers his mother had grown when they lived in Seattle. He remembered the way he'd smelt them. He put his nose as near as possible to Howard's cock head. It was a different scent entirely but it was a nice smell; the sort of odour that stayed in your nostrils for some time.
"Suck it!" Howard panted. He wriggled slightly. Jon looked up at Mark. Mark grinned and nodded. Jon touched the tip of Howard's cock with his tongue. It tasted real good; a strong, sort of salty flavour. He lowered his head so that his lips touched it - almost as if he was kissing it. Then he took the whole of it in his mouth.

Another smell became apparent. Mark's bristly hair brushed against his cheek.
Howard groaned out loud and he wriggled violently; so much so that his cock slipped out of Jon's mouth and slapped against his other cheek.
"Oh yeah! Yeah!" Howard gasped and Jon was astonished to catch a glimpse of the weight bobbing up and down. It look one hell of a lot of energy to move it on a thirty pound setting.

He took Howard's cock in his fingers and popped it into his mouth again. He could feel the pulse against his tongue and his cheeks. He moved his head sideways towards Howard's navel and away from Mark's thrusting groin. All of

Mark's cock was deep inside Howard now, he thought, and it was certainly doing things to him. Howard heaved upwards pounding the back of Jon's throat. Both he and Mark were panting. One day, it would be him, Jonathan Calder, who would be panting. It had to be Mark. Mark would be the first person; the very first person to fuck Jonathan Calder. The thought made him feel light headed. As to where it would happen or when he had no idea. He wanted to look up at Mark's face to see if he could make some sort of eye contact but that was impossible. Mark's hand would be on his thighs; not Howard's. Mark's cock would slide into him; not Howard and all that lovely creamy spunk would spurt into him; the very essence of the most handsome young man he'd ever seen would be in him.

Two things happened so closely together that it was as if Jon's mouth had filled with his own semen. His mouth was swamped with warm, rather acrid, sticky fluid. He was aware of a sort of gurgling noise which emanated from his throat and a warm wet sensation on his thighs and his abdomen. Howard shot again. That time Jon managed to swallow. Howard seemed to lose all muscle tension. The sound of Mark's thighs slapping against him became louder. Howard made a little whimpering noise. Mark stopped. Jon took his mouth away and looked up. Perspiration was streaming all over Mark's body. He grinned down at Jon and then at Howard.
"By Christ! That's some machine. First time I've ever used mechanical aids. I'm converted," he said.

Jon looked down. He particularly wanted to see Mark's cock when it came out. He didn't have to wait long and, to his great relief, it wasn't plastered with what he thought it might be. It was half-hard, shiny with grease but it looked just as appetising as ever.

Howard got to his feet rather unsteadily when they released him. To Jon's great joy, Mark put a still sticky hand on his shoulder.
"You were good," he said.
"Very good," said Howard. "I choose my partners with great care."
"We could get up early tomorrow and have another go. I mean... I wouldn't mind," said Jon.
"We certainly will not," said Mark. "I've got a busy day and you're supposed to be in chapel at eight-thirty... Some other time, eh?"
"Sure. Any time," said Jon. "I wonder what the chapel lesson will be tomorrow morning."

Peter Gilbert

"Why should you think of that?"
"It might be something about St. Mark."
"If it is, you'll have to sing 'Oh come all ye faithful," said Howard. "How about us all sharing the same bed for the rest of the night?"

He hadn't wanted to say that but it suddenly seemed the proper thing to say. All rancour had vanished. It wasn't just Howard and Mark any more. It was Howard and Mark - and Jonathan.

CHAPTER SEVENTEEN

"Mmm. Keep doing that," Stuart gasped. Harry, who, up to that moment had shown no signs of stopping, raised his head.
"Eh?" he said.

Stuart lifted his face out of the pillow. "Keep doing it," he repeated and Harry laughed.
"I've got other things to do, you know," he said. "Not as nice as this I admit. The boss will be wondering where we are."
"Let him wonder," said Stuart. Harry laughed. "God! You're going to be so good," he said. He said that every time.

Life at Tom's wasn't so bad once you got used to it; a phrase Stuart had picked up from Dennis. He'd been really scared during the long drive down. They had made him take a tablet which made him feel drowsy but he was still conscious. He struggled and swore as they bundled him into the car but it made no difference. Tom had said nothing; he just sat in the back of the car smoking his foul cigar. Harry had tried to reassure him. There was, said Harry, nothing to worry about but Stuart had had enough experience of the people who went to the Fare and Fowl to know better.

He'd been wrong. Well... almost wrong. By the time he woke up on the following morning, Tom had gone again. Roberto, the Italian cook, prepared a real luxury breakfast. Mrs. Andrews, the housekeeper, said there was no need for him to make his own bed. She would see to that. All Stuart had to do, it seemed, was to spend two hours in the pool every morning and an hour on the sun-bed in the afternoon. Tom, he gathered, was a bit of a health freak.

So the days went by. Harry woke him in the mornings. Breakfast, a brief visit to the garage to talk to Harry. Then the swim, followed by lunch. Another visit to Harry and then they'd both come back to the house together and chat whilst Stuart lay under a battery of ultra violet lights.

It was on his fourth day that it happened. Not that he minded. Harry was such a kind hearted soul that it would have been churlish to refuse.

Apparently Tom had laid down that the sunbathing should be done naked. Stuart had to wear goggles but even the chain he prized so much had to come off before he lay down and Harry lowered the canopy and switched on the lamps.

On that particular afternoon, Stuart kept thinking about the past.
"Are you sure my dad knows where I am, Harry?" he asked.
"I told you. The boss is in touch with him."
"I wish he'd write."
"Stu. I've told you time and time again. He can't. It would blow the whole thing. You're in the papers every day. It's the best publicity stunt ever thought up. Everybody feels sorry for your mum and dad. They're flocking into Cut-Price shops. When the boss has milked that for all it's worth, we rig it so you escape and there's even more publicity. 'Cut-Price hero breaks free.' It's doing wonders for the firm already. Don't worry. Everything will work out right."

It didn't sound very convincing. Stuart decided to ask Tom when he got back. He was apparently abroad on business. The telephone rang in the hall downstairs. He heard Mrs. Andrews answer it. "Harry. For you. The garage," she called.
"Sod it!" said Harry. He got up from his chair. "I shan't be too long. Remember to turn over after half an hour. I'll set the timer," he said and, after he had done so, Stuart was left alone to think.

It just didn't figure, he mused. He remembered the conversation between his dad and another man a few days before he went to St. Frideswide's..
"It's a good place Jack. Me and the missis saw everything. That rector there - he's the boss - the others are all monks but he's a Signor or something. He showed us everything. The lot. They hold their noses down to the grindstone all right. I mean to say, Stuart's a bright lad. Very bright. He's just a bit on the idle side that's all. They reckon he can make three or four A levels there. He's going to Cambridge. I've set my heart on it."
"Yeah but those places breed pooftahs," the other man said. "Hardly a Sunday goes by without there's something in the papers about it. Stands to reason.

Loads of young men all cooped up together. And the monks encourage it. I mean - what normal bloke goes into a monastery eh? There was quite a lot about it in the Pictorial a few weeks back."

"So what?" said Mr. Lynch. "It won't do 'im any 'arm. Maybe do 'im a bit of good. Some of the students there are straight out of the top drawer. Might be a good way to make some useful contacts. Bloody sight easier to lie back and let someone play with your balls than knock one round a golf course like I have to do."

Had his father really planned to have him kidnapped for a publicity stunt? It didn't add up. How could his father have known that he was at the Fare and Fowl?

He wondered how Jon and Howard had fared. Howard, he thought, might have been expelled but not Jon. Howard was too decent a bloke to let that happen. Howard would have taken all the blame. Howard was nice in every possible way. There was that smile of his. A person would do anything for someone who smiled at you like that - and enjoy doing it too.

He put his hand down to his middle. If it hadn't been for that workman, Howard would have been the first and not Dennis. The memory of that evening made him shudder. It had hurt so much. Somehow, he was convinced that it wouldn't have been so bad with Howard. He had been on the point of putting it in too. If that man had been just a shade slower climbing his ladder, Howard would have been right inside him. That would have been much worse. A nicer feeling almost certainly but much worse from the point of view of the workman.

It was an odd business. Doing it with Uncle Dennis had been awful. Yet some of the lads at the Fare and Fowl did it time and time again. One of them said he'd done it four times in one night. He couldn't convince Stuart though. Stuart made it plain right from the first day that he wasn't going to let anyone do that and Harry said it was fair enough. Nobody had to do anything they didn't want to do.

Perhaps he'd been wrong. Perhaps he should have tried it. "Don't knock it till you've tried it," had been his dad's motto, applicable to anything from paella to public schools. He wondered what it really felt like when someone you liked did it to you. Someone like Howard. Not in an office though. With Howard it would have to be in a sort of woodland clearing like the one in the painting over his dad's desk and he would be bending over the mossy bank, not sitting on it like the Greek Goddess or whoever she was meant to be in the picture. A mossy bank would be a damn sight more comfortable than a library table anyway. And Howard would be standing there slightly behind him but within sight, putting some of that stuff on his cock...

"Hello, hello. What have you been up to?" said Harry. Stuart hadn't even been aware of the door opening. He took his hand away. Interrupted sex seemed to be his fate.

"Practising gear changing, were you?" said Harry, laughing

"What?"

Harry walked over to the sun bed, switched off the lamps and lifted the canopy. "Let me show you what I mean," he said, perching on the edge of the sun-bed.

Stuart had grown accustomed to being touched by strange hands in a number of strange ways. Most of the customers at the Fare and Fowl treated his cock as if it were made of fragile porcelain. There were those, it's true, who licked and sucked it until it was sore but they were a minority. Never before had anyone handled it as Harry did.

"Neutral," he announced cupping his hand over the swollen head. "Now we go into first. Put your foot on the clutch. Stuart inclined his toes forward. "Good. Now we'll go straight into third. Clutch again. Very responsive gearbox, this. Now we've got a long straight stretch ahead. We'll slip it into fourth. Clutch. Here we go. We could even go into overdrive. Would you like that?"

Stuart had a good idea what he meant and nodded.

"The only thing is, Stuart, the boss must never ever find out. Never ever. Understand?"

"Sure. Isn't Tom like that then?"

"Never you mind what he's like. Just keep your mouth shut. Now then, where were we?"

"On a long straight road and we know where it leads to."

Harry's hand began to slide up and down. For a mechanic, he had surprisingly soft hands. One of the Fare and Fowl clients was an engineer and his hands felt like rough leather.

"And where does the road lead?" asked Harry, slowing down slightly.

"To a very nice place."

"Nice people there?"

"Very nice." Stuart conjured up Howard and Jonathan. They were both naked and stood in the wooded glade. Both had huge erections and were smiling.

Harry's hand speeded up again. Stuart put his hands behind his head and closed his eyes. He tried, in vain, to animate his mental picture but, somehow, the circumstances weren't right. It had been the same at the Fare and Fowl. Time and time again he'd have come much more quickly and certainly much better if only the punters stopped talking. The only time they were silent was when his cock was in their mouths. Harry's imaginary car journey was tedious in the extreme but it was working. He felt his temperature rising and his breathing becoming more and more rapid.

"Lovely action in this gearbox," said Harry. "Been looked after well. Can't have had many owners."

Perhaps not, thought Stuart grimly, but there had been a good many drivers.

"Ball bearings. They're the secret," said Harry, putting his free hand down between Stuart's thighs. "Nice ones," he added playing with them gently. Stuart parted his legs wider. a fingernail scratched the skin behind his balls. Instinctively, he lifted his behind. Harry took his finger away. "Better get a cloth," he said. He stood up, grabbed the hand towel from the rail by the wash-basin and returned.

"Now let's see what you can do to the gallon," he said. His fingers went round Stuart's cock again and worked up and down at a lightly faster rate. Stuart groaned lightly and lifted himself up again.

"Nicely upholstered too," said Harry, sliding a hand under his bottom. "A really nice little sports model, you are and no mistake. Let's go for the final straight." His hand flew up and down. Stuart groaned again. His leg slid off the sun-bed and his foot touched the cold floor.

"I'm... I'm..." he gasped and then he came. Quick as flash, Harry smothered it in the towel. Stuart sank back. The towel felt warm and damp as successive jets were absorbed.

"God! You're going to be good," said Harry. "Better have a shower when you've finished."

"Sure," said Stuart.

"And not a word. Understand?"

"Sure."

After that, it happened every day though never again on the sun-bed. More often than not he went to Harry's little flat above the garage. He'd tell Mrs.Andrews that he was going to help Harry - which indeed he did. Cleaning a car wasn't much fun but it was something to do and they never actually finished. Harry would make one of his remarks and then grin. "A nice bit of upholstery," he'd say and then transfer his hand from the driver's seat to Stuart's backside. "I think we'd better give it some extra attention, don't you?" - and that was the signal to put the cloths down and to follow Harry up the flight of wooden steps which led to the flat.

By the time Tom returned, Harry had done almost everything. Harry had used Stuart's 'gear lever' and lubricated it with saliva. He'd had Stuart's 'ball race' in his mouth too. Best of all were the long afternoons when he 'cleaned out the exhaust port'. Stuart would lay on the bed wriggling wildly; so much so that Harry had often to tell him to keep still. Harry would hold his buttocks apart. Stuart felt the man's bristly cheeks against his own softer and more sensitive skin. Then, when Harry's tongue started to explore, all discomfort vanished and the old, familiar euphoria took over. Stuart's cock, rock hard, rubbed against the rough bedspread. Images of Howard and of Jonathan raced through his mind. Sometimes it was Howard doing it to him. Sometimes it was Jonathan. Never Harry.

And then it would happen. He'd lie there as it pumped out of him and, every time, Harry would say "God! You're going to be good."

Stuart had no doubt what he meant. He was just surprised that Harry hadn't done it - or tried to do it. He still hadn't made up his mind whether he would let him or not. He knew he could refuse. Just a threat to tell Tom would be enough. Harry was obviously scared that Tom might find out.

They had to be a bit more careful when Tom was at home but only slightly more so. Tom didn't seem that concerned about Stuart helping his chauffeur. Stuart's dad wouldn't have liked it all.
"Don't want you talking to the lower orders, son They're different from us," he'd said when Stuart, then only a very small boy, had been found in the greenhouse helping the gardener's boy water the lilies. The gardener's boy was certainly different. If he was in a good mood and there was nobody else around he could be persuaded to get his 'willy' out and pump it until white stuff came out. For over

a year Stuart thought it an ability limited to the working classes.

But, generally speaking, Tom stayed in the house. Sometimes Harry would have to drive him somewhere but not often. Stuart wondered why the man kept a chauffeur at all, let alone two cars.

One summer's afternoon he and Harry were in the flat as usual. Harry was at the sink scrubbing his hands as he always did before they started. Stuart stripped off to his boxers and stood gazing out of the little circular window at the huge expanse of grass in front of the house. A pair of rabbits hopped over to the old beech tree and stood on their hind legs. It was a nice place, he thought; the view was certainly better than the drainpipes and back yards one could see from his window at the 'Fare and Fowl'. The people were nicer too.
"Right!" said Harry, drying his hands. "Let's take the covers off, shall we?"

Stuart lay on the bed and raised his bottom to let Harry slide the shorts down.
"Bloody marvellous!" said Harry. Stuart opened his legs and lay there wondering if Tom might allow him to have an airgun to pot rabbits. Roberto would probably be thankful for the odd rabbit.
"Never seen balls like yours," said Harry, fingering them appreciatively. Stuart wondered how many Harry had seen. Not as many as he had, surely. His mind went back to the showers at St. Fred's and the many conversations he'd had with Jon after they had both realised they shared the same interests. There were ten shower heads, separated from each other by plastic curtains. Both Jon and Stuart chose a number between one and ten and, after having showered themselves, they sat on the bench waiting until someone went under the appropriate shower. Jon always seemed luckier than Stuart. Some of his choices were outstanding. Stuart smiled. Anthony Richards certainly was. They didn't usually hang around until the prize emerged but in Anthony's case it was worth waiting. Showering obviously did things to Anthony - or perhaps he did it to himself. He emerged with a hard-on and made little attempt to cover it up. Unfortunately, that was as far as it went with Anthony. That was as far as it went with them all.

This lack of co-operation did nothing to brake Jon's and Stuart's imaginations. Afterwards they sat in whatever empty room they could find and, after barricading the door, sat indulging in the most delightful fantasies.
"Jesus Christ! Did you see his balls?"
"Of course I did. Anyway, Anthony's mine. You got Simon Cole."

"Ugh!" said Stuart, recalling the curtain being pulled back to reveal Simon's obese body glistening with water.

"He sucks," said Jon. Stuart laughed. "I wouldn't let him suck mine," he said. "Would you let Anthony suck yours?"

"If he wanted to. I'd sure like to suck his."

"Yeah," Stuart replied, feeling his cock lift inside his trousers. "That'd be great."

"Not sure I'd want you watching though," said Jon.

"Yes you would. I'd let you watch me doing it."

"With Simon Cole?"

"No, idiot. What about Michael Soames - Stephens? He's nice."

"That's not fair. You're not allowed to talk about people you haven't won."

"Okay. Let's forget him and concentrate on Anthony. Where would you do it?"

"That's a problem in this place. I guess I'd have to invite him home for the vacation."

"All the way to America?"

"It'd be worth it. Just to get that great slab of meat in my mouth.."

"More like an eclair. Filled with cream..."

"Yeah! That's it."

"Show me. I'll do you at the same time."

"Better hurry. Father Simeon uses this room for tutorials."

Time was always the problem at St. Fred's. If only they had had time, it would have been so much better. Having Jon's cock in his mouth had been great but the feel of denim on his face spoiled it.

And then, no less a person than Howard Ainsworth had invited them both to join the newly formed Library Committee. It wasn't all work, he said. There were lots of privileges. Members of his Library Committee were allowed in the librarian's office. They could make tea or coffee whenever they felt like it and, because the library was going to stay open for longer, they could go to meals at special times.

They soon decided that, in Jon's words, Howard was a 'real great guy'. He wasn't aloof as most degree students were. He showed them what they had to do, patiently explaining everything. He was also amazingly good looking and very soon replaced Anthony Richards in their imaginary sessions until the evening when he and Howard were alone in the office. It started off with a conversation about Jon. Howard said he'd caught a glimpse of Jon in the showers below.

"Me too?" Stuart asked.

"You too. Come over here. I'll show you what I mean."

Stuart had never paid any attention to that always-open window. Neither, to the best of his knowledge, had anyone else. He stood next to Howard by the window ledge. "Nobody in there at the moment," said Howard. "It's about this time that you and Jon are in there."

"Jon's waiting till I'm ready. He said he would." said Stuart. "There's usually a good few about now. The people who have their showers before the TV... ah! That's Michael Soames-Stephens."

"Is that his name?" said Howard. "Dressing gown by courtesy of... what hotel is that?"

"Belvedere. It isn't pinched. His dad owns the hotel," said Stuart who had seen the garment in question many times before.

They watched as Michael Soames- Stephens selected a shower, tried the temperature of the water on his hand and then stepped back to disrobe.

"Hairy bugger isn't he?" said Howard.

"Not surprising. He's twenty. He's still trying to get grades good enough for him to be doctor."

"Nice ass though," said Howard. For a moment or two Stuart thought he must have mis-heard or, possibly, Howard had some way of speaking other people's thoughts. Jon had always maintained that, in a college of over eight hundred male students, there had to be more with the same sexual inclinations as they had but they'd never found anyone. They had both come to the regrettable conclusion that St. Frideswide's was an exception to the rule. Desperately, Stuart sought for something to say which was sufficiently non committal.

"He's got a good figure, hasn't he?" he said, staring fixedly down into the shower room.

"Not bad at all. Not bad at all. I really like that ass. That's how an ass should be; soft looking and smooth."

"Wait till he turns round again," said Stuart. "He's got a cock that'll make your mouth water. There!"

"Oh yes! And just look at all that hair."

"You don't think he'll look up and see us?" said Stuart, anxiously.

"Not a chance. Nobody ever does. There he goes. I'll bet he'll close the curtain behind him."

Michael did but their conversation continued. Not in whispered tones that Jon and Stuart had been forced to use but openly and that, to Stuart, was infinitely more exciting.

"I'll bet it's quite a sight erect," said Howard.

"Yeah. Like a donkey. He's hairy enough to be a donkey," said Stuart.

"A talking donkey," said Howard. "Not that I'd want him to say a lot. Not at first anyway. I'll bet he'd yell a bit when I got it in. Pound to a penny he's never had anything bigger than a thermometer in his ass. He'd be as tight as a lock."

"He might not fancy that. "

"So what would you do?"

"Suck him I think. I like that."

The prospect was so appealing that Stuart's penis, already stiffened, leapt upward and strained against his jeans. He glanced downwards in Howard's direction. He had nothing to be embarrassed about. Howard's jeans were pressed so far forward that the material was almost touching the wall.

"Do it often?" Howard asked.

"Not often."

"With Jon?"

"Could be."

"He's nice. I like Jon."

"So do I."

He flinched. Something touched it. He looked down. Howard's fingers wrapped round it and squeezed it through the denim. His heart pounded. He put out his right hand and did the same to Howard. It felt enormous - and very hard.

Michael Soames-Stephens re-appeared, dramatically flinging the curtain to one side.

"You'd certainly have a mouthful there," said Howard. They watched it swinging from side to side as its owner plied a towel vigorously across his shoulders.

"Yeah! He'd soon find out that a blow job beats hand work," said Stuart. "I'd..."

"What?"

"It can wait."

It had to. Howard was undoing his belt. He found the button and undid that and then pulled the zip down. Stuart wriggled and had to help. Jeans and boxers slid down to his ankles. Howard's hand wrapped round it and felt warm and tight.

"Take your hand away for a minute. Let's get at yours," said Stuart. His voice was strangely husky.

But there was no need. Howard's other hand had been similarly occupied undoing fastenings on his own clothing. All that was needed was one tug.

Below them, Michael Soames-Stephens continued to dry himself, unaware of four watching eyes. Even if he had looked up, all he would have seen were the heads and respectably clad shoulders of two very good looking young man. He would have had no idea of what their hands were doing. Oblivious of their presence, he embarked on his usual ritual of post shower exercises.

"He always does that," said Stuart, sliding Howard's foreskin up and down and thrilling to the damp warm feel of the helmet-shaped head.

"Good. Keep him nice and supple for me," Howard replied, doing the same to Stuart.

"If he thinks there's nobody watching, he'll lie on his back in a minute and do elbow press-ups. He'll spot us then," said Stuart.

"Not if I turn off the light. Wait there a minute."

Howard shuffled, shackled by jeans, to the light switch by the door. The room was suddenly in darkness. He shuffled back. "That's better," he said and his hand found Stuart's cock again.

It was much better. Darkness intensified feeling. They were both breathing heavily; as heavily, perhaps as the object of their attention who had started to do press-ups on the damp tiled floor below them.

"Oh yes! What an ass!" said Howard. "Just look at it bobbing up and down. A real bobbity little bum. What wouldn't I give to be straddling him at this moment!"

Stuart, whose own fantasy involved being underneath Michael Soames-Stephens at that moment, said nothing.

"You wouldn't need to use much effort. It'd come up and thread itself like the eye of a needle," Howard continued. Stuart's fingers were wrapped round something several thousand times the diameter of thread. He still said nothing. He couldn't.

"I'll bet it feels like ... like...silk," said Howard. For a few seconds he fell silent. Then he gave a long sigh and Stuart felt it running between his fingers, warm and sticky.

"Keep on with me," he said.

"I'm going to," said Howard. "Your friend Michael is a long way away. A bird in the hand and all that."

"And I'm pretty close. Oh yeah! Yeah! Keep doing that!... Any minute... now!"

The stain on the wall under the window stayed there for some days. Then, mysteriously it was joined by another, rather bigger mark which was strangely similar to a map of India. Stuart had his suspicions but said nothing until he and Jon were in the showers one day.

"Don't stand too near the window," said Jon. "If there's anyone in the library office they can see right in here."

———

"Spread your legs a bit, Stu. That's right. You're in a good mood today." Harry lifted a finger to his lips and licked it. "You won't need an oil change," he said. He lowered his head and Stuart shut his eyes. Harry was good at it but Howard had been even better...

"You there, Harry?"

Harry's head jerked up as if he were having some sort of muscular spasm. The sound of a bunch of keys being rattled and then the garage door being opened came up the steep staircase which led to Harry's flat.

"You at home, Harry?" .

"Yeah. What do you want?"

"Have you seen Stuart?"

"Not for some time, no."

"See if you can find him. I've got some visitors coming to see him. Make sure he's bathed and ready."

"In a minute. I'm busy at the moment."

"That boy wants his ass kicked," Tom called. "He can never bloody well be found when he's wanted. Mrs.Andrews said he was with you."

"Don't worry," Harry replied. "I'll pin him down for you."

The door slammed shut. "Silly bastard," Harry muttered. "He's put me off my stroke. Kick your ass indeed! I guess you've gone off the boil as well."

His hand slid under Stuart's sweating buttocks and Tom was soon forgotten..

Just as in the library office, it was all over far too soon. Stuart lay with his heart pounding. Harry stroked his forehead and cheek, and went over to the sink to wipe his mouth with a towel. "We'd better go and find you, I guess," he said. "Better get your skates on if you've got to have a bath."

"I'm clean enough," said Stuart. "What are people coming to see me for? Is at about going home?"

"For Christ's sake, Stu! Do what you're told and don't argue! Go and have a bloody bath!"

That was the first time Harry had ever been sharp with him. Stuart said nothing but got dressed and went over to the house.

There was still time for a bit of enjoyable daydreaming in the bath: his favourite place for such pastimes. He lay in the warm water and found himself thinking about Jon and Howard again. If only they hadn't been disturbed on that dreadful Sunday, life would have been so much nicer. He and Jon could have both been Howard's boys; sharing him. Howard had more than enough to keep both of them happy. He shut his eyes the better to envisage Howard's anatomy. He loved the way Howard's cock erected so that the head peeped timorously out from the enveloping foreskin. It was like a little animal peering curiously out of its burrow. And there were Howard's balls. They were nice too. In fact everything about Howard was nice. He wondered how it would feel to be fucked by Howard. Painful at first probably but if a cock felt anything like the tip of Harry's tongue, it must feel really nice...

There was a knock on the door. It was Harry. "Boss wants you in the sitting room at six," he said.

"What's the time now, Harry? My watch is on the shelf."

"Half past five. He says you're not to get dressed. Come down naked."

"But what if someone sees me?"

"Don't worry yourself. There's only me. Mrs.Anderson's gone out."

Stuart was alarmed. This was a bit like the old times at the Fare and Fowl. To enter a room without any clothes in front of strangers seemed odd to say the least; not to say degrading. Not wishing further to upset Harry, he said nothing but resolved to go down with a towel round him.

At six o'clock exactly, draped in the largest towel he could find, he knocked on the sitting room door.

There were three of them; all wearing dark suits and sitting on the long sofa along the side of the room. Tom sat in his usual corner seat, smoking the inevitable cigar.

"This is him," said Tom. He turned to Stuart. "Who the bloody hell do you think you are; the Sheikh of Arabia?" he asked. "I told Harry to tell you to come down naked."

"I thought..."

"Take it off."

Stuart untied the towel.

"Nice one. Well done!" said one of the men. Judging from his grey hair he was the eldest of the three.

"How old did you say he was?" said another. Stuart could have told him exactly but Tom didn't give him time.

"Eighteen," he said, and blew a gust of cigar smoke in Stuart's direction.

"Nice cock on it. That'll be good with the right lighting," said another. From his voice, Stuart guessed him to be American but the accent was different from Jon's.

"And definitely unbroken?" said another.

"I checked carefully. Certainly never at Chris' place."

"Great!" said the American. "I've got the scenario and the camera angles worked out, boss. Would you care to see them now?" He reached over the arm of the sofa to retrieve a briefcase. He opened it and passed a sheaf of papers over to Tom.

Stuart stood there, wondering if he should sit down or leave the room. Curiosity prompted him to stay. Camera angles? Scenario?

Tom flicked through the papers. "Looks good but we're going to have to revise it," he said. "There's another one coming."

"Another?" said the elder man. "You didn't say anything about that."

"Only confirmed the other day. A cast off. Surplus to the requirements of a certain well known personality. Bob and Pete went up and looked him over and did some checking on the story. Sounds like a good one."

"Risk element?" said the American.

"None at all apparently. No family to speak of. At university. Lives with another gay couple. He'll hardly be missed."

"Not like the only son of the owner of the biggest supermarket chain in the country. Why don't we use him instead of this one? I'd feel happier," said the third man.

"Don't be crass, Mike. What would we do with this one for God's sake? Say 'Run home to mummy and daddy and don't tell them where you've been'? Anyway, the younger ones have more pulling power."

He looked up and seemed suddenly to become aware of Stuart's presence. "You can go to your room, Stuart," he said. "Don't get dressed. We may need you again."

Stuart picked up the towel and left the room. Confused, he stopped for a moment outside the door. Mrs.Anderson was out. As far as he knew, Harry was not in the house. He wrapped himself in the towel, bent down and out his ear to the door.

"It'll be much better with the two of them. Double the length you might say." That was Tom's voice.

"Yes - but boss, it's taken weeks to work out this scenario."

"Okay. Postpone filming for a few days. Ernesto won't mind. He's not finished 'Singing Cage-birds' yet and I'm not completely happy with Stuart's sun-tan. He doesn't look like a lad who's been adrift in an open boat to me."

"What about the other one? He'll be as white as a sheet."

"I've thought of that. He's the dashing young officer who's come to look for Stuart. The navy have sent a ship to try and find him."

"It gets more like real life every minute," said one of the men. "I wouldn't be a bit surprised if they did. There are still posters up and old man Lynch has upped the ante. That'll start a few people talking."

"No they won't. They've all got too much to lose. Chris is the only other person who knows where he is and I've got enough on Chris to send him down for a very long time and enough friends where he'd go to make his life a series of painful accidents. No... we're safe."

"So this navy guy...?"

"Comes ashore in a rubber boat. Gets captured by the tribe. Bit of the usual. Possibly between Stuart and Mark - that his name. Then comes the festival."

"Which one first, boss? I'll need to know that."

"I was thinking about that. The older lad. It'd be nice to get the expression in the younger one's eyes as he watches. Don't want to drag it out unduly but it should be good."

"Yeah! I like it. I really like it!" said the American.

Stuart had heard enough. So.. he was going to star in a blue film! That was a move up from Dennis' photographs. And he was going to do it with a university student. That might be fun, providing he didn't do it too quickly. But what was that about his dad upping his auntie? The thought was laughable. He had only three aunties. Two were married and lived abroad and the other was the personnel manager of his dad's firm. "She's no oil painting, that's for sure, but she's efficient," had been his dad's opinion of Auntie Iris.

He lay on his bed trying to get his thoughts in order. He was going to play someone who'd been cast on the shore and he'd be rescued by a handsome sailor. That bit was good. But 'captured by the tribe'? That didn't sound very alluring. There were hundreds of questions he wanted to ask. At dinner that evening (for which he was allowed to get properly dressed) not one of the men gave the slightest clue. There was some talk about the price of film. Otherwise it was a perfectly ordinary dinner party. There was some banter about the fact that Tom had bought the chickens from a supermarket. The American said he preferred South American chicken. Stuart chipped in to explain that transport costs would make them uneconomical. "Besides which, they don't have our rigid control standards for meat," he said. The American laughed. Tom said he was absolutely right and they changed the subject again.

That night, Stuart went to bed none the wiser.

CHAPTER EIGHTEEN

"And they say that crime doesn't pay!" said Simon as the car swept into the drive. The house was huge and remarkable both for its Spanish style and its green roof. It lay, miles from anywhere, in the New Forest at the end of a lane lined with rhododendron bushes. Twice they had caught sight of deer nibbling at the bark of trees.

The front door opened almost as soon as the car had stopped. A man stepped out onto the porch. He was tall, very dark and the old army pullover he wore failed to disguise a middle aged spread.

"Mr. Spencer?" he asked, as they climbed out of the car. Mark glanced at the dashboard. Simon hadn't forgotten. The key was still in place.

"And this is Mark I presume," said Tom after introducing himself and shaking hands with Simon. "You did tell me how old he was, Simon, but I can't remember. Twenty-one is it?"

"Twenty-two," said Mark. Simon had told him about Tom's elaborate checks during the last few days and warned him to watch out for catch questions.

"Oh yes. Come on in."

The opulent interior of the house matched the outside. Somehow, Mark thought, it looked overdone. It all seemed a desperate attempt to show off.

"This room is warmest," said Tom, opening two huge doors. A fire burned beneath a gigantic copper awning. The chairs were of leather and the table was quite the biggest Mark had ever seen.

"So..." said Tom, sitting in a chair by the fire. "You want to be in films, young man. Is that right?"

"It's always been an ambition," said Mark. "And Simon said this is a quick way of getting to the top."

"So you believe in getting to the top by using your bottom, eh? Interesting idea," said Tom. "Mr. Spencer, er, Simon is quite right. Several of my lads have made the big time. You know what's involved of course?"

"I've got a pretty good idea, yes."
"How versatile are you?"
"How do you mean?"

Tom blew a couple of smoke rings. "Put it this way," he said. "You've had a cock in your ass a good many times. Have you used yours the same way?"
"Once or twice," said Mark, blushing.
"Good! I was afraid you might be passive only. Not that it's necessarily an obstacle but I like a lad who's versatile. Get undressed for me. Let's have a look at you."
"In here?"
"Why not? Room not warm enough for you?"
"Oh yes. It's only..."
"Natural modesty. You'll have to forget that. Come on. Get them off."

If anything, Simon was more embarrassed than Mark. He had seen, smelt and felt Mark naked many times but to see him stripping in someone else's room angered him. He wanted, there and then, to strike Tom. That, however, would do nothing to get Stuart back. He forced a grin. Mark laid the last item of clothing on a chair.

Tom peered at him through a cloud of cigar smoke. "Hmm. Not bad," he said. "Quite good in fact."

Simon could hardly contain his fury. The man was talking about one of the most good looking young men he had ever met.
"Nice strong ass, good legs. A nice fuck I should think, isn't it?"

Simon forced the words out. "Very good," he said.
"Turn round," said Tom. Mark did so.
"Nice cock. I like 'em like that. They're more photogenic," said Tom. "Nice big balls too. Has anyone else been at it apart from Simon?"

Mark was about to say 'No' when he remembered the role he had to play. He sat down.
"Well.. er... Simon doesn't know about this," he said. "There's a professor at university. Professor Carpenter. He's a theologian."
"Thirty-six Burwell Road," said Tom.

Mark looked at him aghast.

"Don't worry. I don't know him but I know you've been to the house. I also know that you were in the Leather Bottle with one of his regulars and you took him home. Good was he?"

"I didn't do anything," said Mark, blushing despite himself.

"I believe you. I'm told he was as pissed as a newt."

"Who told you that?"

"Never you mind. I know more about you than you think. There's one thing I'd like to clear up."

"What's that?"

Tom reached over to a little cabinet, opened a drawer and took out four large photographs. He handed them to Mark. "How did you get mixed up with Singleton?" He asked.

Looking at himself in those positions was an odd sensation. There he was, splayed over a fallen tree; lying on the bed in Dennis' studio - bedroom with his cock standing upright and spots of semen glittering on his belly. Another one made him shudder; not because of that he was having to do but because of the spider which had crawled up his leg just after the flash had gone off.

"What the hell did you do this for?" asked Simon. Mark would have liked to say 'Because you told me to,' but they both had their parts to play. He tried hard to look embarrassed.

"I met him at a swimming pool in south London," he said. "I was with two friends. He asked me to help him and he wanted to take some pictures. He said they were just for him."

"These would be the two gay boys you live with?"

"That's right. They went off to London for the weekend."

"Mmm. That tallies. Okay, get dressed and leave us to talk business. There's another lad around somewhere. Go and make friends. He's probably in the pool at the back. He's going to be your first co star but don't tell him that. He's a nice lad. Well built. You'll get on like a house on fire. Only don't touch the goods till I tell you, okay?"

Mark was tying his shoe-laces as the man spoke. That was as well. Tom couldn't see the anger in his face.

"Can you tell me how much I'll get paid?" Mark asked, remembering the carefully worked out script Simon had written.

"A lot. How does a hundred pounds a minute sound?"

"Very good. Thanks a lot," said Mark.

"Good. " Now off you go and find young Stuart. Only keep your hands to yourself. Understand?"

Mark left the room without a backward glance..

"I see what you mean," said Tom. "He's lethal, especially to a man in your position. I've heard of this Professor Carpenter before."

"I confess that I hadn't," said Simon truthfully.

"Well, I'll take him gladly," said Tom. "You won't be seeing him again. Not in the flesh anyway."

"I confess that I'm relieved," said Simon. "I shall miss him of course."

"One doesn't miss them for long," said Tom. "Quite a few people have disposed of their used ones with me. A few weeks of loneliness and then you find another one and a new asshole feels a lot better than one which has been screwed time and time again."

"So, what are your plans for Mark?" asked Simon.

"I'll keep him here for a week or so. Then we'll try him and the other lad under lights. Funny thing about youngsters is that they can be as randy as hell with their cocks raring to go and the moment you put 'em in front of a cine camera they lose all their urges. Costs a mint in wasted film. Young Mark might be better. He's had experience."

"I wish I'd known about that photographer. What did you say his name was? I'd like to have a few words with him," said Simon.

"That'd make your situation worse. Forget him. He's not worth bothering about."

"Do you make the films here?" Simon asked.

"No way! Everything that happens under this roof is strictly on the level. I make sure of that. No... When they're ready, they'll be off to America. I've got young Stuart's passport already. It doesn't take long to get one if you know the right people."

"America?"

"South America actually but we never tell them that. The market's good down there and I have very good contacts with the police. They leave us well alone. A few of those films about the young Caucasian getting a job on the ranch and being screwed silly by every gaucho for miles around. Then a few of the local lads getting a British cock up their asses..."

"And what about the other youngster?"

"Much the same."

"And what happens to them when you've finished with them? I wouldn't like to

think of Mark being stranded in a strange country."
"Let's just say that Mark won't be a burden to anyone, shall we? Drink?"
"That would be nice. Thank you."

Tom went to a drinks cabinet which was quite the most tasteless piece of furniture Simon had seen for a long time and poured two scotches.
"Ice? Soda?"
"Just a splash, please."

Tom handed over the glass and sat back in his chair.
"No.. You won't have any further problems with Mark," he said, taking a sip of his drink. Mark won't be around for long."
"How many miles is it from Britain to wherever he's going?" asked Simon.
"I wasn't thinking of geographic distances."
"How do you mean?"
"I can trust you? You know I could blow your fame and fortune away like a candle flame if I wanted to."
"Of course you could."
"Well, your friend Mark..." He took another sip and licked his lips. "Your friend Mark hasn't got an awful long time left in this world. He won't see many more birthdays. That's for sure."
"Murder?" asked Simon.
"Artistic demise. Have you seen 'Chicken Farm'?"
"No."
"Shame. I don't have a copy here of course. It's made a hell of a lot of money. You'd be amazed at the number of punters who pay thousands of dollars to watch a couple of South American beggars having their asses fucked and then their throats cut. Bit like your books I suppose. People like reading about murder. They like it even more when they can see it in real life."
"I suppose so," Simon replied, secretly enraged that a masterpiece like 'Murder Mystery' could be compared with anything so horrible.
"So what's the plot?" he asked. "Do you work that out in advance like I have to, or do you.. er.. .let nature take its course?"
"Oh we work it out very carefully. My lads are still working on 'Sun God Sacrifice'. Basically, young Stuart gets washed up on the shore and gets captured by a tribe of Maya Indians. Mark's going to be a naval officer sent ashore to try and find him. He gets caught too and has it off with Stuart in the cave where they're being held. Then comes the bit where they're both tied to posts and the Indians are chanting. You know the sort of thing I mean.

Firelight, painted faces; all that?"

Simon nodded.
"Then they get sucked off or fucked - maybe both and then - whoosh. Blood all over the lens and spunk all over the punters' pants."

Simon felt physically sick but knew that he had to prolong the conversation. "That tape won't exactly be in every video library," he said.
"Too right it won't. It won't be a tape. It'll be a film. Slightly harder to copy and we can keep control of the master."

Simon glanced at his watch. He had to keep going. He hoped that the tiny microphone sewn into his lapel was working and that the recorder in the car outside was picking up the signal clearly.
"And this 'Chicken Farm' film. How old were the boys in that?" he asked.
"Young. It's easy down there and nobody looks for them. In fact the police would give you a pat on the back for polishing them off. The funny thing was that they both enjoyed it - until the last take of course. We had 'em hanging upside down on a rail just like they do in those places."
"My greatest problem in books is disposing of the bodies." said Simon. "How do you manage that? I kill them off in a paragraph and then spend a chapter trying to dispose of the body!"
"Well," said Tom... "What was that?" He stood up and went to the window.
"What?"
"I thought I heard somebody. There's nobody there. One of the deer I expect. They're a bloody nuisance and you're not allowed to shoot them."
"Interesting thought," said Simon.

Tom sat down again. "What is?" he asked.
"In one country the police are prepared to let you murder a couple of boys. In this one, they'd run you in for shooting a deer."

Stones cascaded on the window. They both jumped up.
"That's my bloody car!" said Simon.
"Sod your car! It's my lawn!"

The car sped across the grass, slinging up clumps of grass and clay. It slewed onto the drive, accelerated and vanished.
"Your bloody Mark!" shouted Tom.

"I must have left the key in the lock," said Simon. "Can I use your phone to call the police?"

"Sod that! I don't want them here. Wait a moment." He ran out of the room and returned a few minutes later. "He's taken Stuart!" he said.

"Christ! They'll both be wrapped round a tree."

"Best thing for them!"

"They can't get far. Not with your security gate."

"Left open," said Tom ruefully. "Harry always goes out at this time to fill the Rolls."

"We've got to get them back!" said Simon.

"Or make sure they don't get too far. What the hell are we going to do?"

"Can you take me into town? I can report the car stolen from there. Say it was parked outside a shop or something."

"Could do. We'll take the B.M.W. I'll go and pack a bag."

"What do you need a bag for?"

"You don't think I'm going to hang around here if there's a chance of those two blabbing their heads off? I'll drop you at the police station and go straight to the airport. The bastards! I'll kill them!"

CHAPTER NINETEEN

"Where are we going?" asked Stuart.

"To a rather seedy hotel in the Midlands," said Mark.

"Why?"

"Because that's what Simon said."

"You are telling the truth aren't you? You really are a friend of Howard's and this car belongs to Simon Spencer and he lets you drive it?"

"Absolutely. Hold on tight!" Mark swung the car into a violent left hand turn.

"So where is Mr. Spencer?"

Mark looked at the car clock. "Just about now he's run into a police station to ask for an address. After that he will let slip who he is and hope they will keep him talking."

"Why?"

"Because Tom will be waiting outside to make sure he's in there, ostensibly to report that this car has been stolen."

"But you said you had permission..."

"I do. Look Stuart. Pack in the questions for the moment. My job is to get you as far as possible as fast as possible. I can't do that if you keep asking questions."

"I'm sorry. It's just that so many people have told me so many lies just recently."

"I know. We're on the level. Trust me."

There was a long pause. Mark reached the motorway and put his foot down.

"What will Mr. Spencer do when he's finished with the police?" asked Stuart.

"Take a fast train to London. He'll meet us there. Watch out for the next exit. I have to take country roads for a bit."

"And what will happen to me?"

"Simon will tell the college you've been found. The summer vac starts soon so there's no need for you to go back this term."

"I doubt if they'll take me back."

"If you want to go back, they will. Simon will sort everything out. The college won't want bad publicity. He'll tell your parents too."

They drove on. Stuart dozed spasmodically. When he woke, he bombarded Mark with more questions and then fell asleep again. Mark drove as carefully as possible, keeping as Simon had advised, to the country roads. He managed to negotiate the traffic on the edge of London. Simon had told him not to stop to ask for directions in case someone recognised Stuart from the many posters. In London he had no alternative but to wake Stuart, give him a road map and use him as a navigator - which he did surprisingly well.

"You're tired," Mark observed.

"I didn't get a lot of sleep last night," said Stuart.

"I can well believe it," said Mark. He could feel his anger rising. "Did he take pictures of you?" he asked.

"Only once. "

"He made me undress in the living room!" said Mark, furiously.

"I had to do that in front of his friends. The garage should be at the end of this road. Yes, look! There it is!"

"Well done! And there's Simon. Thank God for that! He made it."

Simon seemed more relieved to see his car than either Stuart or Mark. He even walked round inspecting it before taking the wheel for the rest of the journey.

"You made good time," he said.

"What about the others?" asked Mark.

"On their way. Charles even got permission to bring Jonathan."

"Do you mean Jonathan Calder?" asked Stuart.

"Yes."

"Oh good! Who's Charles?"

"Lord Charles Beresford. He lives in the village."

"Oh yes. I've heard of him. What famous company I'm moving in!"

"Better company than the last lot," said Mark bitterly.

The car seemed to eat up the miles. Simon was such an accomplished driver that one could relax totally, even when they were travelling really fast. By the time they reached the Lakeside Hotel, it was early in the evening. Jon and Charles were waiting for them in the reception area.

Jon seemed more pleased to see Mark than his long lost friend. Mark got a "Hi, Mark!" and a friendly handshake. The boy seemed strangely distant from Stuart. "I took all the keys for everybody," he said after greeting Stuart as if he had just been to the local shops. "Here's yours, Simon. There are two young guys waiting for you in the bar."

"Waiting somewhat anxiously," Charles added. "Not to mention one's self. Did it go as planned?"

"It all went very well," said Simon. "Mark was superb!"

Jon grinned at Mark "I knew it would be okay," he whispered.

"It wasn't a very pleasant experience, all the same," Mark replied.

"Come over here a minute."

Stuart, already smarting about people who talked about him behind his back, watched as the two of them stood in a corner of the reception area, occasionally looking at him and then averting their eyes. He heard Mark say something about a better idea and was about to go over to challenge them when they came back. Then he decided not to after all.

"Mark and Howard in room sixteen. You and me in room seventeen, Stu," said Jon, handing Mark his key."

Simon laughed. "I begin to wonder how Charles managed before you came along," he said.

Jon grinned happily. "I guess I like organising things," he said. Mark smiled.

It was, as he said, a few minutes later, just like old times to be sitting in the bar of the Lakeside again. Simon had given strict instructions that Stuart was not to be questioned about his adventures in case it upset him. "He's going to have to spend hours tomorrow making statements to the police," he explained. "That'll be bad enough for him. Leave him well alone."

In fact, Stuart seemed little the worse for his experience. Both he and Jon seemed to fit in perfectly. Stuart laughed happily at Charles' story of his alcoholic ancestor. Jon was giving Simon all sorts of advice about his forthcoming tour of the United States. Adam and Ben sat together laughing about something.

"It's quite like the good old times again," said Mark happily.

"I was hoping you'd say that," said Howard. He squeezed Mark's thigh affectionately. "Let's not be too late going to bed," he said.

In fact, they all retired early that night. It was Simon's suggestion. The first policemen arrived whilst they were having dinner. By the time they finished, there were three of them sitting in the hotel foyer looking, despite their business suits and briefcases, very police - like indeed. Stuart was briefly introduced to them.

"I think the best idea," said Simon, is for Lord Charles and I to give you the facts as we know them tonight. All the lads are tired. They'll be in a fitter state to face questions in the morning."

The leading policeman seemed to think this a good idea. The management opened the private lounge. Simon retrieved the tape cassette from the car. Charles brought his notes and the younger members of the party trooped upstairs.

———

Ben lay in bed enjoying his favourite spectator sport; watching Adam undress. He'd seen the performance many times but, like a good film, there always something he hadn't noticed before. This time it was the narrowness of Adam's waist compared with his shoulders. Ben's cock was already hard but he left it alone. Adam slipped out of his boxers and stood by the bed. His cock stood out at its usual steep angle.

"What's a good looking boy like you doing in a place like this?" asked Ben, imitating on the Fare and Fowl's clients.

Adam laughed. Ben had a gift for mimicking voices perfectly.

"The same as my friend Ben," he said.

"What I would really like to do," said Ben, changing to another voice, "is..."

"Yes?"

"I'd like to take you home with me. You'd have to tell my wife that you're the new clerk at the office. She doesn't understand, see?"

Adam slipped into the bed. "Oh, I remember him!" he said. "I hope he does it better with his wife than he did with me. He was fumbling around for so long that he came before he even got it in. It was hardly worth the effort."

"So poor Adam was frustrated?"

"Too right I was. I'm not often in a mood to be screwed but I was that night. I had to wait an hour and a half before I bagged that Norwegian. He was good."

"And what sort of mood are you in tonight?" asked Ben. His heart beat faster.

"Randy as ever with you in bed with me. Silly question. Why do you ask?"

"I was just wondering if I might be a bit better than a Norwegian," said Ben.

"You could try," said Adam. "Hang on. The cream and the rubbers are on my side of the bed. Here they are."

———

"There were times when I wondered if I would ever do this again," said Mark.

"I thought the same," said Howard. He lay across the bed. Mark, naked and with an erection which was almost uncomfortable in its intensity, knelt beside him. There was a volcano - shaped lump in the towel wrapped round Howard's middle. His body smelt delightful. Mark bent forward and nibbled his right nipple.

"Mmmm," Howard murmured. "Tell me what you're going to do to me."

"Why not wait and see?"

"I like it when you tell me first. Go on...wind me up."

"Well, first I'm going to take this towel off. And then I'll look at you for a few seconds, just to think that you're all mine again. Then, I'll have a good suck on your cock. I like a nice big cock especially when it goes with balls like yours."

"'Comes' would be more appropriate."

"Point taken."

"And then?"

"I'll turn you over onto your front, spread those long legs out, get on top of you and screw you."

"Different position eh?" said Howard, laughing. "Getting adventurous, are you?"

Mark smiled as he remembered the night in the gym-room at Charles' house.

"It could be fun," he said.

"Well, you'd better start then, hadn't you?" said Howard. Mark began to untie the towel. "You are so bloody beautiful!" he said as he parted it.

"So are you," Howard replied reaching up and taking Mark's cock in his hand. "I'm going to enjoy this."

"So am I," said Mark and he lowered his mouth onto the plum-like head of

Howard's cock.

"Oh yes! Oh yes!" Howard breathed and began, as he always did, to wriggle slightly.

Mark licked the head, pushing the tip of his tongue against the slit.

"Oh God! That feels so good!" Howard gasped as Mark took as much of it as he could into his mouth. He lifted his behind off the bed. For a moment the towel stuck to his buttocks. Mark pulled it away and slid his hand under. Howard still felt warm and damp from his shower. Mark raised and lowered his head, delighting in the flavour released every time Howard's foreskin retracted.

He knew that he had to keep himself under control; difficult though it was and he knew enough about Howard to know that Howard had a tendency to let himself go. One of them would have to put the brakes on if Howard was to enjoy it as Mark intended. He lifted his head off. Instinctively, Howard put his hand down and clasped his sodden, stiff member. Mark brushed it away.

"Turn over," he whispered. Howard did so.

Even lubricating Howard's ass was almost enough to cause Mark to shoot prematurely. Howard wriggled as Mark's finger went in. The hand which was supposed to be parting Howard's right cheek from the left began to stroke the soft skin instead.

"Control! Control!" Mark whispered to himself.

"Eh?"

"Nothing. Just lie still."

But Howard wasn't in the mood to lie still. That finger was doing things to him. The self-possessed student was rapidly turning into a sex-hungry animal yearning to be possessed by someone else. Mark! The name itself was nice. That finger, boring into his insides, preparing the tissues for something bigger and equally nice, felt heavenly.

Only the sudden coolness told him that it had been taken out. He was aware of the huge bed creaking as Mark shifted around. He heard the top of the tube fall onto the floor and the sound of the packet being torn open. Then Mark's hands were on his shoulders. Something cool and sticky brushed over his left buttock.

"Ready?" Mark whispered into his ear. Howard nodded as best he could and held onto the pillow. It slid between his cheeks. He held on even tighter. He could feel it pressing against him.

Any minute n... "Ow!" It hadn't felt anything like that when he'd been on the multi gym. It had gone in easily then. It wasn't too bad when he was kneeling. This time it really felt as if it was a red hot poker burning its way into him. He yelled again. Mark stopped for a moment. Gradually, the pain subsided. For some reason he didn't have to tell Mark. It started to move forwards again, very slowly; almost hesitantly, stopping occasionally and then starting again.

Finally, all of it was inside him. Mark's chest lay against his shoulders. He suddenly realised that it had stopped hurting. He gave a little wriggle to make sure. Amazing. It was stone-hard but it really felt good. He wriggled again and Mark started.

Being fucked by Mark was an experience like no other. Mark didn't seem to raise and lower his behind as one would expect. It was more like being stirred by a giant wooden spoon than being fucked. Howard let go of the pillow and put his hands behind him, just to feel those muscular ass cheeks clenching and unclenching like twin motors driving the shaft inside him.

He felt himself sweating and shook his head slightly against the pillow. That felt better but he knew it wouldn't be long. Not for him and not for Mark. He wanted it to last for hours and hours. Mark's tongue licked the back of his neck. Howard's cock and balls were being pressed against the bed. He lifted himself - or tried to. Mark grunted. So did he and then, all too soon, he felt it welling upwards. He groaned again as the first jet gushed out of him and then felt Mark's grip on his shoulders tighten. Mark stopped. The delightful warm, swelling sensation inside him made Howard feel quite faint. He lay quite still as successive spurts filled the rubber nipple deep inside him.
"Christ! That was good!" said Mark after a few seconds had gone by.
"Mmm," said Howard, speaking into the pillow. It twitched inside him. Someone, he thought, ought to invent something to make cocks stay hard for twenty-four hours.

It began to slip out. He compressed his cheeks against it but it was no good. He felt it, wet against his skin. Mark let go of his shoulders and rolled over onto his back.

For a long time neither of them said anything. They were both puffing as if they'd been in some sort of race.
"Shouldn't you have a shower?" said Mark, suddenly.
"In a minute," said Howard with his face still buried in the pillow.

"I'd have one now if I was you."

"In a minute," Howard repeated. Common sense was on Mark's side. He could feel it wet and cooling rapidly on his thighs. On the other hand, it meant clambering off the bed and walking all of twelve feet into the bathroom.

"Have it now, Howard. I need to get in there as well."

"Go now then."

"No. I'll wait for you."

The old anger began to boil again. Why did Mark always have to spoil things? He got out of bed and did his usual tight-assed walk into the bathroom.

He felt better after a shower. "Ready for you," he said as he climbed in between the sheets on his side. "I don't think I've seen a bed as big as this in all my born days," he added.

"It's the room Simon usually has," said Mark.

"So why isn't he using it now?"

"Don't ask me. I suppose it's because he's not sleeping with Ben or Adam."

"Why isn't he sleeping with Ben or Adam? He did last time."

"Because he and Charles feel that Adam and Ben have been through a lot of nasty experiences and need to be together again. Anyway, hang on. I'm dying to get in the bathroom. What's the time?"

"Quarter to twelve."

"Just fifteen minutes before midnight. Keep talking to me. I'll leave the door open."

For some time they exchanged shouted remarks about future plans. Neither of them had done anything to plan for the long college vacation.

Mark returned. "That's better," he said.

"I wonder how Stuart and Jon feel now that they're safe," said Howard, basking in the warmth that emanated from his friend's naked body.

"All right. It doesn't seem to have done either of them any harm. Did Jon say anything on the journey up?"

"No. Not about that anyway. How was Stuart? I'd have been terrified if I had to go through what he's been through. That Tom person. Simon told me. Ugh!"

"I don't think it's affected him at all. He's so incredibly vain and conceited that he quite liked having his photo taken and of course he had no idea why he was at Tom's."

"He's not conceited really. It's just that his old man is rich. I expect he gets it from him," said Howard.

"Balls! He told me all about the family fortune the moment I met him and he spent most of the journey up here looking at himself in the rear-view mirror."

"Who should know him better? Me or you? I was at school with him. You've only just met him."

"I know a conceited person when I meet one. Take it from me. Your friend Stuart has a very high opinion of himself. He's extremely good looking I admit but he's still big-headed."

"That's right! Pass judgement on the rest of the world. Typical. A few hours in a car and Mark the ace psychologist has got him summed up for all time. God! You are so fucking arrogant!" Howard lifted himself, intending to swipe at Mark with a pillow. Instead of flinching, Mark started to laugh.

"What's so funny?"

"Us. We are. We're fighting again."

Howard sank back. "So we are," he said.

"It's amazing. We always fight after sex. The only time we didn't was when Jon was there."

"That's right," said Howard. "We were laughing then. Remember?"

"Maybe we both need somebody else. Maybe you were right from the start," said Mark.

It was a revolutionary thought; a pleasant one too, thought Howard, mulling it over. A church clock in the distance struck midnight.

"Happy birthday," said Mark, leaning over him to kiss him.

"You remembered my birthday?" said Howard incredulously. "I haven't told anybody."

"Of course I remembered. How does if feel to be out of your teens at last?"

"Pretty good but I think my twenties are going to be even better."

Howard put his arms round his friend's broad shoulders. "Thanks," he whispered - and at that moment there was a knock on the door.

"Christ!" said Howard. "Who the hell is that?"

"Only one way to find out."

"You go."

"No. You."

"Who is it?" Howard called. There was no answer but another, more timid knock.

"The police I guess," he said. "They've decided they can't wait till the morning after all." Once again, he climbed out of bed. "Coming!" he shouted. He picked up the towel from the floor, wrapped himself in it and walked over to open the door.

"We couldn't sleep so we came to talk to you," said Stuart. Both he and Jonathan stood there. Jon was in pyjamas. Stuart just wore his boxer shorts.

"Oh... you'd better come in."

"It's Jon and Stuart. They couldn't sleep," said Howard.

"I heard," Mark replied.

"Gee! That's some bed you got!" said Jon. "You could get a whole family in that!"

Mark smiled. "Or four people," he said. He lifted the sheet invitingly. "Pyjamas off and in you get," he said.

"Could this possibly have been planned?" asked Howard as he climbed back into bed.

"I can't imagine what you mean," Mark replied and Jon giggled.

Stuart didn't need to be invited. Howard moved over to make room for him. "I shall get to the bottom of this tomorrow," he said.

"Before that I should hope," Mark replied.

———

"That was great!" said Ben. "Ready for the out?"

"Not yet. Leave it in." said Adam. "I'm beginning to develop a taste for a good cock in my ass."

"Was I as good as the Norwegian?"

"Better," said Adam. Do you think Mark and Howard will get together again?"

"Not a doubt about it," said Ben. "They're both as randy as March hares."

"Jon and Stuart seem a nice couple of lads," said Adam.

"I thought so too. They've both got a lot of the right stuff in them."

If Stuart and Jonathan could have heard, they would certainly have agreed.

THE HARDLINE
MAN 2 MAN
Credit Card Line
0171 915 6100
CRUISELINE
MAIL BOX
FANTASIES
CONFESSIONS
0839 400 370
calls cost 50p per minute
WEB COMMUNICATIONS, PO BOX 2041 RH20 1YB

more sexy novels from

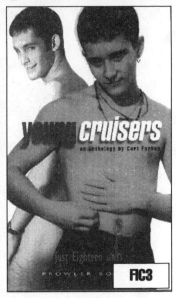

Corporal In Charge   FIC4   £5.99

Twenty short stories of hot and sleazy sex. Fritscher details each story down to the last drop of cum. From teenage wank sessions to college locker room fun to hard sex in the army, this book covers every fantasy.

Young Cruisers   FIC3   £5.99

The third novel to cum out of the Just Eighteen series is a tantalising selection of short stories on sleazy first time adventures. Black and Blue is a passionate story of how a young guy gets fucked for the first time by his fantasy man, a stud with a giant cock. Been There, Done That takes us into the world of hustlers where Ty unsatisfied with his tricks goes out and gets his fair share of hot spunky action.

PROWLER BOOKS

Slaves FIC2 £5.99
Slaves is the tale of Jack's sexual encounters which begin as he joins the mile high club. Cumming off the plane he falls headlong into one horny sexploit after another. Under cover as a journalist writing about the slave trade, Jack gets more than his fair share of native cock.

HARD by Jim Hardacre FIC5 £5.99
An all-new collection of 19 tales of shocking, SLEAZY, stories of dirty young men. Jim Hardacre has written for numerous publications including Hunk, Prowl, Spunky and EuroGuy. This is his first collection of red-hot short stories.

£5.99 each from good bookstores or via mail-order from MaleXpress 0800 45 45 66

JE7

Young And In Love   JE7   £15.99

A beautifully shot voyeuristic & erotic film of young love.
Two young'n'cheeky English couples go on a hot'n'sleazy
holiday to Amsterdam. Let well endowed PJ and slim
Mark turn you on as their passionate clinches reach a
steamy climax. See Sean and big Brian's smooth, naked
bodies as they writhe in ecstasy. Good storyline & five
sexy boys who obviously enjoy one another as much as
you will.   75 MINS   BBFC CERT 18

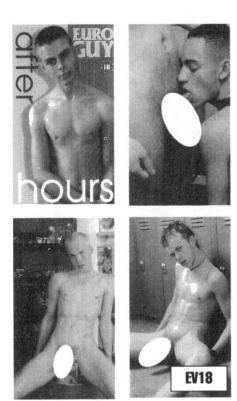

EuroGuy After Hours EV18 £15.99

Here's your chance to find out what really goes on in a
shop after closing as five sexy boytoys let you in on their
horny exploits. Slim smooth Dave shows what you really
do with a penis pump. Discover cheeky Viper's intentions
as he gets caught by blond Matthew for stealing. Cute,
hung and ready for anything these guys are the best we
have seen in ages. 60 MINS BBFC CERT 18

**Prowler videos available from all good video stores
or direct by mail-order**
send orders to: **male**×**press**
3 Broadbent Close London N6 5GG
or call our 24hr-credit-card hotline
(quote the product's code): **0800 45 45 66**

Prowler Press publish Europe's hottest gay magazines; *Spunky, EuroGuy, Prowl & Real Men* as well a
travel books, erotic novels and video titles.
They also distribute gay toys, fetish, leather and rubber, sports & scenewear.

MaleXpress are Europe's leading gay mail-order company. Drop us a line, or call for your free sexy
catalogue: 0800 45 45 66 (international +44 181 340 8644). Fax +44 181 347 7667.
Or write to MaleXpress, 3 Broadbent Close, London N6 5GG

In the US call ***MaleXpress US*** toll-free 1-888-EUROGAY.
Or write to 759 Bloomfield Avenue, Suite 342, West Caldwell, Jersey, NJ 07006 US.

Prowler web-site is where you can see the hottest new pictures from up-coming magazines and
videos. PLUS you can order direct. Find us at ***www.prowler.co.uk***

PROWLER SOHO is Europe's largest gay superstore situated in the heart of London's Soho. Designer
clothing, mags, erotica, videos, books, rubber and sex toys. Plus lots, lots more. 3-7 Brewer Street,
London W1. Behind 'The Village', opposite 'The Yard'.

prowler